The Alaerton Alumni Mysteries:

REUNION

By

Charlotte Helion

THE BEACHCOMBERS BOOKERY
The Alaerton Alumni Mysteries:
REUNION
First Published in Canada 2019
Copyright © Charlotte H. Broadfoot
writing under the name Charlotte Helion

ISBN: 978-1-9992373-1-8 (paperback)
ISBN: 978-1-9992373-0-1 (e-book)

Typeset is Times New Roman

Our books may be purchased through the Kindlestore at https://www.amazon.com

This book is dedicated to
The Pack at My Back -
Jesse, Bliss, Travis, Sandy, Frankie, Cimba,
and Dickens
Loyal, Hilarious, Willing and Sensitive: 24-7
I think of one or other or all, every day.
They were and are, to use and paraphrase
Pierre Tielhard de Chardin:
Spiritual Beings living [with] a Human['s]
experience

'Come on guys, let's go.'

Acknowledgements

In the development of this work over a considerable period, I have appreciated the ongoing encouragement of Rennie, 'no-hands' Queen of the Toronto CNE '*Flyer*'; the good-humoured support of tea-grannies George and Millen, doyens of the Stratford Scene; and Joanne, who bought the first anthology book that I was ever published in, presenting it to me as a Christmas surprise (best ever) BEFORE I had even been sent an author's copy. I would also be remiss in not thanking both my late parents for somehow in my early years, through osmosis probably, embedding the necessary traits for completing any endeavour: perseverance, patience, and especially in the case of my Dad, James Sydney, creative critical thinking. He never lost his sense of adventure. I guess I *AM* my father's daughter.

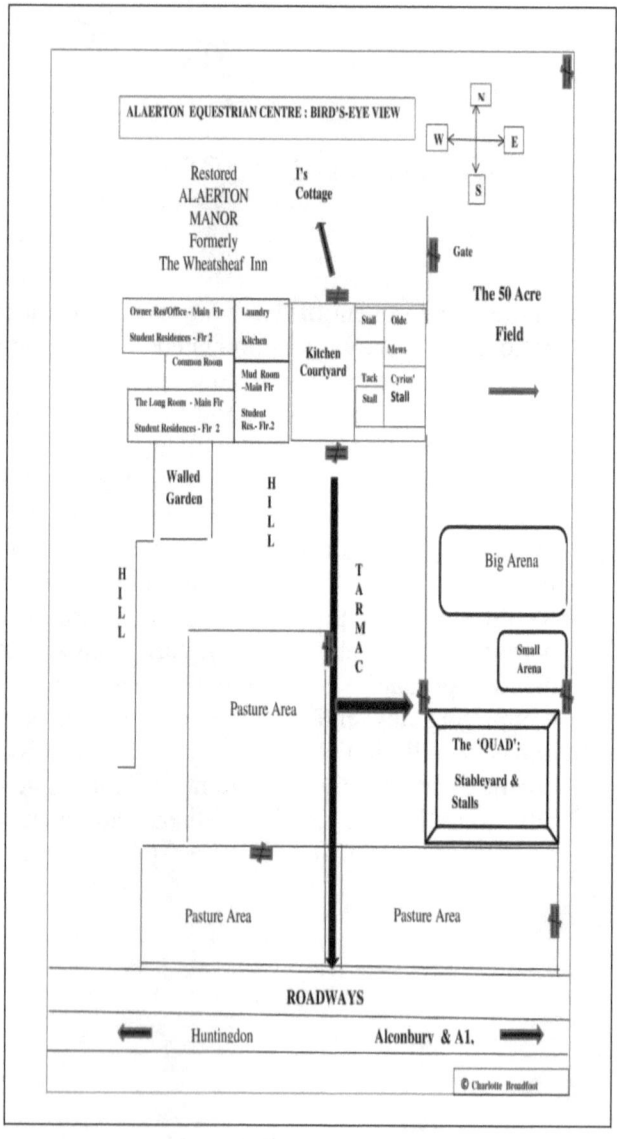

Prologue

Pouring the hot coffee carefully into an oversized mug, Cerby grabbed a manual *frother,* absently pumping the mechanism up and down in an almost sensual motion until the half-and-half cream inside climaxed into bubbling foam. Half pouring, half spooning the whipped result on top of the deep roasted Columbian java, the milky cloud floated like a tropical mangrove island on a dark sea of finely ground beans. Out of habit she ran a toothpick artfully through the concoction, creating a decadent design, an attractive visual to go with the enticing aroma. Taking a sip, her acrobatic tongue licked off most of the resulting clingy white mustache, flicking off the residue with a well angled shot.

Tentatively, she picked up the envelope lying on the white marble-topped kitchen island where she'd tossed it the day before. Mug in the other hand and an Oreo clasped between her teeth, Cerby sock-footed it through the sunlit *open plan* main floor toward the oriental rug-delineated living room area, plunking herself down on a poufy sage coloured leather sofa. Immediately she was besieged by wet French kisses and paw-nches to the gut as Frankie and Cimba hurled themselves at her face and body for some petting attention.

"Off me, you Furballs. *WATCH* the coff-ee! NOW! Damn it!"

Struggling up into a sitting position, fighting against the combined weight and momentum of the Rat Terrier and the Shih-Poo, Cerby laughed hilariously despite the confusion of bodies and hot spray.

"Okay, settle now. SETTLE down! That's better. Geez, can't grab a moment's peace with you two around." (Not that she was complaining; they were without question the finest permanent roomies a gal could have - Best *Fiends* Forever.)

Cerby managed to gain her feet, wiped herself off briskly, and fending off the *terrible two-some* retreated to the fireside mantle on which she placed the offending mug, well out of reach of her energized pets. Eyes drawn to the glittering, embossed lettering of her own name on the front of the envelope, she used both hands now to hold and rip open one end, being careful not to tear the part sporting a current British stamp. She'd give that to Marcie later to add to her collection.

Reading the calligraphed invitation over twice, she tapped it against her cheek, then chewed a corner of it, thoughtfully gazing out a large bay window to the multitude of Rose of Sharons just beginning to bud in the backyard. The fine gilt-edged stationary beckoned:

Miss Cerdwyn Llewelyn

**You are cordially invited to
Alaerton Equestrian Centre's
25th Anniversary Celebrations**

Details printed on the back, she had to admit, looked enticing. She wondered if all the 'Cavaliers' would be coming. She'd have to put out a feeler - it wouldn't be quite the same if she were the only one, but she owed the proprietor BIG TIME, regardless!

Her heart gave a nervous thump. Who else might show up for this shindig? She hardly dared speculate, but the image of her first real love materialized suddenly like Banquo's ghost. Brusquely she wiped a fallen wisp of red-gold hair from her forehead. She flipped the card over, turning her full attention to the instructions on the back of the stark invitation. She could feel a cosmic pull, inexorably, into the past:

Commencement June 19th, 20___
You may choose one of One/ Two/ Three-week packages
(Forms enclosed)
Fun, Food, Midsummer Fête and Fundraiser
In-house Accommodation provided on First come,
First serve basis,
Alternative Reservations available at The St. George
(in Huntingdon)
Please RSVP no later than June 1st, to:
Mrs. Rowena Hill
Alaerton Equestrian Centre
Alconbury Hill
Huntingdonshire PE 28 OZO, UK

Cerby's eyes misted. It'd been almost a decade since she'd spent a year at the Alaerton Equestrian Centre. Just seventeen then, an only child and angry teen who'd survived the sudden death of her parents' months before, but at great emotional cost. A lot had happened at that time and since, to shape and mature her into the woman she now was. She mused on the decade that had slipped by so unobtrusively. *How did I let that happen?*

In her defence, after returning home from Britain to take up the reins of her modest inheritance, she bravely resumed life in Vermont: finishing university, then entering the job market. She'd had a certain talent for administration and took maternity leave or sabbatical short-term executive assistant assignments. It suited her lifestyle. She could pick and choose *when* and *where* and *how long*, but she had to admit those first years she was driven to work back-to-back assignments, trying to forget her family tragedy.

Immediately after her England sojourn and for the first year or so afterward, Cerby had kept up religiously with her new British friends, but life happens, and the correspondence grew mutually sporadic with time and distance though the intense affection remained. None of them had been Facebook devotees. Prompted now by the invitation, embarrassed by her lack of commitment, she wondered: *What were they all doing these days,* and *Could one pick up again where we all left off?* It was a bit scary to contemplate a return to a past fraught with a certain level of pain and self-discovery…but ten years on? Her lips pursed in a sour expression.

*It might just be a wise idea to put some distance between me and, well...**this** side of The Pond; de-tox a relationship or two - ONE, at least! If the Atlantic isn't big enough to do that, what could?*

Yes! Her eyes sparkled at the thought of a trip. *It's been a while after all, since I've had any kind of vacation really.*

She looked down at the munchkins playing around her feet and spoke aloud to them. "Hmm. We're not going to like being separated, are *WE*, but I'm pretty sure our friend Marcie next door will step into the breach. *Thing One* and *Thing Two*, (trying to convince them as well as herself), she's stayed here overnight with you before and I bet Marcie wouldn't mind at all moving in for a bit longer this time. Besides, (crouching down to twiddle Frankie's ears and give Cimba's rump a fond tap) *'absence does make the heart grow fonder'* eh?"

"Crikey!" The gaiety suddenly cut short by the ominous realization; "Blast, only a couple of weeks to prepare. Better make some phone calls." Why was it though, that in times of crisis, the disembodied voice of her beloved father - in life a Professor of Celtic Arts and History (proudly Welsh) - so often had the last word:

Devil yn ei gymryd, dwi'n dod

'Devil take it, here I come!'

Chapter One

Saturday

Seventy-five yards away, the argument had clearly escalated. A petite female's fingers jabbed so hard into the man's chest, the action forced him to take a step backwards in response. The woman turned a surly back on her male partner after this vicious frontal attack. *His* posture seemed to indicate an equal animosity, and taking this slight woman by one arm, he shook her almost off balance. Abruptly letting her go, shoving his face angrily in hers, he waved his hand in a graphicly non-verbal '*I'm done with you,*' and pushed her away from him. Turning resolutely on his heel, he stalked off. The woman stood there looking after him, tension visible in the arms locked down at her sides, fists balled. Then *she* stomped off in the opposite direction.

Monte stood back, trying to refocus his *DSLR* camera having accidentally caught the developing melodrama in the sweep of his panoramic shot. Knocking the Tilly hat back off his wide forehead, he cursed his pudgy fingers, not for the first time: *Crap. They're like bloody sausages!*

He fumbled with the shutter timing option. "Stand still," he commanded, eyes focused once more on his subject. The previous digital attempt hadn't turned out too well - Cerby had moved. Now he had her once again in the crosshairs of the camera's screen. The fisheye- lens' focal point in an artistic wide shot of the landscape, was a young woman of average build in her late twenties. The breeze ruffled her short curly 'bob.' Sunlight brought out the blonde in the 'strawberry'. He was trying to frame her using the white fences, verdant pastures, and the muted colours of the old stone Manor on the hill in the background.

Wonder what that was all about? Cerby's concentration was still on the micro-drama she'd just witnessed also. It evoked a similar scene from her own recent past, emotional but without the hint of physical violence in the one just viewed. Suddenly the pettiness of *her own* argument couldn't be denied. She sighed longingly ...

"Earth calling Cerby. You were off in La-La land. Is that a tear welling, or just gas?"

"Oh, shut up, Mitch!" Cerby turned to Monte; "You done now, Mr. Leibowitz?"

"We can't even joke, now? Come- on C. Jolly up will you!" The short slender blonde man at the brunt end of the young woman's ire, heaved himself upright from a draped position over the hood of the sportscar they had rented for the duration of the trip.

"I'm plenty *jolly* Mitch, thank you!"

"'Bout as jolly as that ass over there."

"What did you say?" Cerby whirled about, now fully engaged, pinning him with narrowed eyes, the green flecks in the light blue eyes suddenly prominent. "You should talk, you ...*you*...blinking fart factory!"

Mitch fell against his boyfriend Monte, braying with hilarity. "I didn't say 'gas' that time Cerb. I said '*ass*' - as in that one *over there* in fact, *Old Trout*!" And to be sure, moseying its way towards them across the lush clover pasture *was* a miniature donkey.

Five minutes previous, the trio of friends had stopped the car at the bottom of the Alaerton Equestrian Centre property, so Cerby could get out and reacquaint her bearings. She'd already pointed out to her companions the corrals at the front of the property, the roofs of the structures indicating the barns and the arenas, and the Manor residence at the summit.

"You must have *dyslexia of the **hearing*** too!" Mitch punctuated with 'air quotes,' poking fun at the origin of her Christian name.

Cerby tilted her head and looked the epitome of bored. The reference - to a nickname born of a dyslexic incident in infancy confusing the 'd' in Cerdwyn with a 'b' - had resulted in the misnomer that stuck among family and friends ever after. In truth however, she preferred Cerby to Cerdy.

"Well *pilgrim*, are we gonna stand here all day?" Mitch's average height, *Tony Hillfigure* outfit and skinny frame couldn't quite do justice to the mock John Wayne stance he'd assumed. Waggling an accusatory finger at Cerby; "'Cause Cerb, we didn't pour the Mini Monte here into a plane for seven ..."

"Seven and *a half,* 'gainst a head-wind," the slightly more diminutive and paunchier Monte grunted, putting the Nikon FX camera carefully away into its camera bag.

"...stuffy hours across *The Pond,* just so you could back out now. You're the one that insisted we come with you," Mitch continued in his annoying *I told you so* tone; "so here we are. Or rather, here you are, because as soon as you're haply ensconced at the *Wheatsheaf,* we're taking the car back to Alconbury.

When you've settled down... er...*in*, we'll meet at the *Highwayman* for a dram of something, what?"

Cerby looked past Mitch's left shoulder, to the eye-candy landscape. A few minutes earlier, she'd rested chin on arms folded uncomfortably atop white oak corral fencing. Ruminatively, she checked now for splinters. "Sorry, *my bad*. It's just kind of strange coming back here, even for only a week."

Touched, Monte reached out a short chubby arm and gave the top of her head a brotherly-like tussle. Bi-racial as well as bi-sexual, late father Parisian, mother one elegant Creole from Louisiana, Monte was ever the peacemaker. *Rattling a skeleton or two would be good for her soul,* he thought. Knowing her history here as he did, he empathized fully, but looking at her country coordinated outfit: boot cut jean, colour blocked denim shirt, and designer jean jacket - a part of her obviously still belonged at Alaerton. This trip he was sure, would lay some ghosts to rest, one way or another. Accordingly, his full dark eyebrows telegraphed Morse code to Mitch - *cease and desist* - which true to Mitch's nature, was summarily deflected.

"Well, you were young...ah... '*-er*' then weren't you, Cerb?" Mitch ran a hesitant hand through his prematurely thinning, wispy hair.

Monte tried a withering glance this time.

Mitch hurried on, ignoring this also: "It's always hard to *go home again* isn't it, though more I guess when things turn out, well, indecisive."

Monte 's mouth set in a firm line.

"But looking at it from another angle," (Mitch gaged Monte for support with *this* attempt and finding a *speck* there, his voice brightened appropriately), "you really loved your time here at the school, didn't you? That's got to be a plus?"

"Sometimes that's worse in a way though." Cerby gazed into Monte 's more sensitive deep brown Teddy bear eyes, snubbing Mitch. "I don't want to ruin anything; that period of my life was hard, but very special too."

There ensued a long pregnant pause. Monte looked at Mitch, Mitch looked at Cerby, and Cerby looked back at both. Each knew about keeping some memories sacred. However, the effect of the heightened atmosphere so paralleled a scene out of *any* Latin soap opera (without the corresponding dramatic musical score) that Cerby's *funny was* tickled to the bone, her emotions finally breaking in a storm of laughter. Her companions joining in simultaneously, tensions evaporated immediately as they each tried to outdo the other in imitations of sexy foreign ham-actors: "*Pablo. Es Bianca morto?*"

"*Si, Si Senorita!*"

"*Que?* "

"*Lo que ha ocurrido aquí?*" Monte had a smattering of Spanish, whilst the others only pretended they had.

Crumpled with laughter, Cerby resumed eventually. "You *are* totally right though, guys; no time like the present, eh?" She bent down and roughly picked a bunch of the long fragrant grass, pushing it through the slats of the fence on the curious donkey who snatched at it indelicately.

"Some manners," she chided the animal. Straightening up with determination, she turned, arms crossed for emphasis, to face Mitch specifically: "but *YOU* my little *Mock* Turtle, might want to drop the English slang before the locals decide to hang, draw,

and quarter you - or *I* do!"
"Certainly...*Old Trout!*"

"Hel-lo! You look familiar. The American Girl. Wait a mo; I know. Tip of my tongue. Sherise? (Blank look.) Charlene? (Lips compressing.) Wait, not that funny name? Means 'blessed,' 'poetry' - something like that."

"Cerdwyn actually, as you are very well aware, and *you* I know. You haven't changed a bit Saf. Still into blood sports?" Cerby leaned down and gave her seated haughty interlocutor an impulsive hug.

Lady Saffira Hatton-Blythwood stiffened petulantly. The corruption, 'Saf' or 'Saffi' never jibed with the Blenheim Public School persona that still dripped off her in a multitude of finely wrought gold necklaces and namesake bangles. She grimaced theatrically as she tossed her long ashe-blonde (expensively coifed) tresses. "Fancy *you* remembering *moi* first thing. They let you out of the Colonies then, did they?"

"Only for good behaviour." Cerby was struggling to maintain *hers,* given the *aristo-cat-ic* reception. "And I'm only here for the week, so let's not waste time playing at 'Queen of the Castle'." She refused as expected, to compliment Saffi's beautifully tanned olive skin and expertly tailored monochromatic Burberry pantsuit, instead searching the room for the other half of the *dynamic duo.* "What about you gals?"

Saffi reached out and grabbed hold of the arm of a passing plumpish elfin-like redhead in gingham shirt and short-shorts, propelling her almost into Cerdwyn. "Came *up* from down Sussex way with Stevey. Stevey, look who's here: 'Whatsits'."

Stephanie Bankshaw, always a bit short-sighted despite a set of specs perpetually perched atop her short henna-streaked spikes, suddenly lit up and she lunged forward. Her emerald, green eyes sparkled: "Cerby Llewelyn, it's you; it's really you. I didn't think you were actually coming, I mean, all the way from Vermont! Good Lord! Well good for you! The old gang back together again. Awesome. We'll have such fun, right Saf?"

Saffi demurred, pulling absently on a simple drop diamond and sapphire earring. *G*awd. *How does she do that*, secretly admired Cerby. *Watching Saffi rise from a chair was like looking at a beautiful gazelle unfolding its long legs in preparation for flight.*

Instead, Saffi, intent on her own agenda, began to drag her protesting pal away. Half-turning Stevey managed: "We haven't unpacked yet, but we'll see you at supper at least, right? We're all in our old rooms, rememb..." Saffi pulled her along, non-too gently, but over her shoulder tossed Cerby one of her languorous signature 'Noblesse Oblige' nods.

"La di Dahhh" chortled Cerby in response, summarily dismissing any references to class distinction. "*To the Manor born...*" she called after Saffi, mincing and bowing to *milady* to emphasize it hadn't worked ten years ago on her and wouldn't now either.

Saffi flipped her hair and huffed: "So juvenile Cerb. Is that what they teach you out there in the 'Wilds'? Hurry up Stevey or we'll never get settled in."

Just then, Cerdwyn caught site of Bron, her best friend and boon companion from 'the old days.' She stopped in mid-stride, repeating softly under her breath her father's favourite oath:

cf tuathal déithe

*(*loosely translated by him*: O, Ye Contrary Gods)*.

'Ten years gone. We're all tickling thirty; but where I've added the odd pound, Bron's just plain despicable,' she exhaled.

The young woman in question could never be mistaken for other than a descendent of the ancient dark-haired Welsh hill people - '*ye olde ones*' as her father used to refer to them. Bron Wyldwyn just missed being starkly beautiful, but any self-respecting Arch-Druid would have sacrificed her to the stag god Cernunnos without a qualm and expected *Spring* to follow *Winter* because of her.

Cool serenity and Celtic fire warred eternally in Bron, but the hotter elements were rarely visible on her strong facial features, submerged almost perpetually under an outwardly calm exterior. This fascinating dichotomy had drawn Cerdwyn to her side then (when she had needed it), as now. Suddenly she felt a terrible pang for her late father and their shared love of Celtic myths. The moment passed...

"Hey Bron. Bron! It's *ME*; over here!" trumpeted Cerby as she unceremoniously parted a group of *Reunionistas* (as Monte had dubbed them) and rushed to Bron's side.

Bron's head came up in unhurried recognition, and her more reserved, "Cerby, lovely to see you. Didn't

13

really expect to see you here," shocked Cerby into toning down her own enthusiasm too.

A bit puzzled by this lukewarm reception she nevertheless forced the European double cheek kiss on her old friend and pulling back asked a bit hesitantly: "I *did* e you. Are we bunking together again in our old room?"

Bron, for the first time with a glimmer of a smile in her eyes: "Of course… and it's still that God-awful salmon pink!"

Sitting down to *dinner* reminded Cerby of dining at Hogwarts. There were four ancient oak trestle tables with benches to match that could sit eight on either side in the *Long Room*. Little had changed at Alaerton Manor, formerly the Wheatsheaf Inn in ages past, since Cerby had last set foot on the premises. Indeed, not since *John Byng, Fifth Viscount Torrington* toured the county in 1789, ending up at the *Wheatsheaf* upon encountering inclement weather.

The present 21st century visitors could read a framed tea-stained parchment of his travelogue hanging on the wall:

> '*This delay seemed to throw us out of our time of dinner; which was to be prepared for us at 3 o'clock at Alconbury, where we did not arrive till half past that time; and then dinner not ready! The dinner was better than I expected in this filthy inn, which to*

the miseries of a cold ale house, joins the charges of a London Tavern: for 2 small Tench stew'd in a black sauce; we're charged 7 shillings.

The road from Huntingdon is pleasant (at least, the morning sun made it appear so), passing thro' the two Stuekelys; and before the night lodgers had got away from the Wheatsheaf on Alconbury Hill, I sat there at my breakfast. Alconbury Hill Inn, the Wheatsheaf, as standing single, high, and free from noise, is most agreeable; but as to furniture, waiting etc., it is little better than an alehouse and in winter must be a cold abode. My stay here was very pleasant. The garden was fill'd with flowers, and the morning was gay These are the delights of touring. I hence took a walk, endeavouring to make my dogs hunt, for above a mile to the bottom of the hill below Monkswood; below which, to my right, stood Sawtry Abbey, where are now some cottages and many foundations of old buildings.'

Two centuries on, in the waning teenage days of Cerdwyn, Saffi, Stevey and Bron, who were all Horsemaster students together at the Alaerton Equestrian Centre, there'd been plenty of humorous grumblings along the same lines of Viscount Byng regarding the 'amenities' of the place.

Years had passed since then and Cerdwyn, now a young woman in her own right, found herself standing in the rustic frame of the wide solid oak Dutch door, looking out over the garden and musing.

15

Other former students chatting amongst themselves were seated in various postures on the benches, except for Stevey who suddenly appearing beside her, poked her with one hand, while she attempted to stuff a canapé or two in her mouth with the other.

"You always did love the garden here Cerb. Pity, it's been so let go."

Stevey's appreciation of the desolation was brief, however. There was a titter behind them. Stevey swung around to follow one of the current crop of equitation students trying to balance on one hand a large 'Welcome Back' platter sporting watercress, salmon, ham, and deviled egg crustless sandwiches. Cerby watched Stevey chase down the tray with a happy smile: *Now that one **never** changes!*

She stepped off the low rough-hewn stone threshold into the long grass and breathed in the sweet smell of the past. 'What a shame,' the thought vocalized as Cerby glanced around the familiar enclosure. As English gardens go, it was certainly dilapidated. Bounded on three sides by a crumbling yellow brick wall, the area she was presently occupying was the same manor's kitchen garden Torrington had referred to, centuries before. It had been better tended when she was last here herself, with some semblance of borders and even some espaliered fruit trees. Now it was all quite patchy with weeds interspersed amongst the remaining perennials.

She strolled down the worn garden path scanning the beds for familiar plantings, but her intent, as she rounded the side of the house on a mossy incline, was to find the ancient Briar Rose descendent whose ancestors had been growing up that side of the Inn in the time of Cromwell. For a moment she felt a pang of intense sadness; *Oh no, it's gone!* quickly followed by intense relief as she pulled away some clingy grape vines to see a chunky old stem bravely 'shooting' forth it's fragile buds for yet another summer.

Cerby never denied the romantic streak fanned by her late father. Her mother Isla, more pragmatic, would shake her head at the two of them engrossed in determining the romantic truth behind a myth or event. Griff her 'Da' would laugh gently at her mother: 'Why look at Winston Churchill. He was a romantic if ever there was one - actually stated as a young man that he was destined to do remarkable things, and he did!'

So, it came as no surprise that Cerdwyn had felt the intangible ambience of the old Manor house *'that was'* from the very first. It called to her of love and war, births and deaths, lawlessness and justice denied. Whenever she had pulled one of the wild white roses to her for a stolen whiff of its fragrance, she couldn't help but conjure the original owners.

Before the Wheatsheaf was an Inn it had long belonged to a family with Royalist tendencies in the 16th century. The family, by the name of Alaerton, had later been wiped out in the English Civil War and the land became the property of the Roundheads. The elegance of its U-shaped winged architecture and former life was systematically stripped away through the years, and gradually the *Wheatsheaf Inn and Coach Stop* was born, a far cry from its former glory.

All this Cerby had learned (on her days off as a *working pupil*), at the local library/museum in the town of Huntingdon, the birthplace of Cromwell himself. She had needed something to focus on at the time, and perhaps being a Colonial as well made her much more appreciative of the history of the place than the 'locals.' Her friends had only grumbled about the Inn's inadequate facilities - old fashioned water closets and lack of central heating. But to Cerby: '*There be ghosts here*,' never tiring of chiding her friends gleefully. How exciting was *that*!

With a final tentative weeding around the base of the Heraldic Rose, and a long look over the wall and down the hill at the surrounding rolling and verdant landscape, Cerby headed back inside. There would be plenty of time to reminisce, but just now she needed a change of outfit. Mitch and Monte would be waiting in the village for afternoon drinks with her. That'd be the least she could do for finagling them to come on this trip in the first place. She already felt guilty enough for not having much time to spend with them and considering that Monte (sole scion of the wealthy Bonesquet wine producing family) had arranged for their three airline business class tickets, she wasn't sure how she'd be able to pay back Mitch's partner's kindness.

She scooted up the kitchen back stairs to avoid any of those 'Old Girls' spilling out of every orifice to sit, eat and chat on the wide main oak staircase. She didn't want to be detained; there would be plenty of time to talk to and reacquaint with some of them later.

Upstairs it was like a college dorm. Plenty of laughter! Youthful and mature female voices blended, calling from room to room; bustlings to the single bathroom down the hall; heavy tromping up and down to the garret - it made Cerby bubble up with good humour.

"Bron, think fast!" she cackled, as she threw a pair of riding breeches at her friend, bowed over her own open suitcase on one of the twin beds.

"Cer-by! You never grow up do you? So...*You*...Take that!" Bron retaliated by hitting Cerby full in the face with a rolled-up turtleneck.

Cerby held out the offending weapon and studied the small, embroidered horse on its left breast. "Oooooooooo. *I say*. Ralph Lauren! We *have* come up in the world. D'you remember those cheap retro polyester-stretch bubble shirts we used to buy at Marks and Sparks or the Vintage on the High Street in Huntingdon? We thought they were the height of fashion. We'd swap to go to the 'disco' or the pub. Wow, back in the day, eh?" They both sat down on their beds and looked intently across the small divide at each other. Bron smiled companionably at the memories.

Cerby spoke first, excited to get their friendship back on track. She hid the emotional catch in her throat with a fake cough. "So; what's the plan Bron, before supper? Are we heading out pubbing? Maybe into Huntingdon later?"

Cerby's expectations were dashed however, as Bron returned to her unpacking. "I rather think I'll just meet up with the others tonight at supper. It's been a long drive down from my brother Dylan's in Northamps where I was for a couple of days. I'm a bit tired actually."

After their recent playful exchange, Cerby didn't understand the sudden chill in the air. *If it WAS a brushoff? Well, after all, she'd come all the way from Vermont; she was tired too but not too tired to go out and have a drink with her former 'best' friend and*

19

introduce her to her current BFF's Monte and Mitch!

She was hurt but tried to sound nonchalant as she put away her travelling clothes, donning more appropriate ones. "Ok then, I'll catch you up at supper." (Privately, she thought Bron's temporary aloofness might vanish by then.)

She was also a bit taken aback by her easy fall into quasi-British lingo. Always susceptible to speech patterns, as a girl she'd often aped her Scottish mother and the lilting Welsh tongue of her father unconsciously. *Lord, I've only been in residence a couple of hours. Goodness knows what kind of hybrid accent I'll go back with this time, even after only a week...*

"Bron; promised my friends who flew over with me that we'd have a *shandy* around *teatime*, so I'll be back after that. Try to corral Stevey and Saf for supper, and we'll all sit together, just..."

"...like old times," Bron finished the sentence softly.

There was something in Bron's tone that made Cerby look up with a hopeful half-smile as she thrust her trunk under the bed, but the spark that might have been there had been replaced by Bron's blank 'Madonna' expression, so Cerby still couldn't tell whether Bron was looking forward to meeting later that evening or not. Puzzled anew, with a final 'oomph' and push however, her own over-stuffed suitcase was stowed under the bed. She stood up, swiping a cosmetics bag off a chest of drawers. "Well, better put on my *day face,*" she said, masking her annoyance, and hustled down to the *WC* before someone else locked her out.

Cerby felt suitably 'tweedy' and genteel for her trip into the nearby village of Alconbury. She'd donned a brown and cream herringbone equestrian-style jacket with oyster lining and leather-patched elbows, over cream slacks and a nice sturdy pair of fringed brown flats. Elated to be back at Alaerton, she skipped down the wide worn stairs of the entrance staircase and nearly bumped into a tall, chignoned woman at the bottom.

"*SO* sorry," began Cerby apologetically, but was interrupted in turn.

"No, my fault entirely m'dear."

"Mrs. Hill! ROWENA… (forgetting herself). Mrs. Hill; how *ARE* you? It's Cerdwyn; Cerdwyn Llewelyn," she shouted with joy. "Mrs. H, you know…" and laughing, she began to whistle Monty Python's 'Life of Brian' theme song: *Look on the Brighter Side of Life.*

"Could I *EVER* forget such a musical rendition," Mrs. Hill wagged a playfully stern finger in her face; "and usually at the most inappropriate times."

Both women laughed. Long forgotten was the stilted behaviour on first acquaintance: the harried, widowed owner of a riding school and the emotionally lost young colonial working pupil. Mrs. Hill had reached out first, slowly and subtly taking the withdrawn and resistant Cerby under her maternal wing. A mutually respectful friendship had developed over time. They hugged warmly now.

21

Mrs. Hill turned Cerby's face gently from side to side. "Yes," she said with approval, innate honesty (and horse sense): "Good teeth. Soft eyes. An unruly mane. A touch big boned; you haven't changed Cerby. So lovely you could come along to Alaerton's 25th Founding Anniversary - it wouldn't have been the same at all without you!"

"Happy to be here, Mrs. H," Cerby gushed sincerely; "Although I'm actually in a bit of a rush right now. Could we have tea together do you think, perhaps in the garden like we used to? Maybe one day this week?"

"I'd look forward to it, Dear, although you've probably noticed already the garden isn't quite as, well, manicured as it was."

"No problem, Mrs. H. Looks the same to me. So; it's a deal then! Well, got to run. I'm expected at the *Highwayman*. Some friends of mine are waiting."

"Would you like me to call a cab for you, Cerby? I can ask Jasper to do that if you'd like? I just saw him out in the kitchen, (at Cerby's cocking of the head); Jasper is our resident farm hand. He's been with us for the past several weeks. We lost Mr. Smalley to retirement I'm afraid."

"Oh, that *is* too bad - about Mr. Smalley I mean. I know he was an immense help to you when your husband died and well after that too. Thanks for the offer though, Mrs. H. Think, as it's a sunny day, I'll just walk to the village."

"Of course, Dear. I was about to show you the way, but I forget; you know it quite well." Mrs. Hill's fine, high cheekboned visage, crumbled a bit and she smiled rather sadly. There was a bit too much hopeful expectation in Cerby's face.

Oblivious, Cerby gave her another affectionate buzz on the cheek, moving an escaped strand of gray hair in place behind Mrs. Hill's ear. "See you later then, and that's a promise!"

She brushed quickly by some of the reunion alumni and hailed a few faces on the run whom she quasi-remembered. Letting herself out through the garden door, she made her way down through long strands of sweet grass and English heather to the hedge rows that bordered the property.

Probably Mrs. H wouldn't recall that Cerby never had a sense of direction, (especially after ten years absence), but standing at the road side, looking first one way and then the other - some of the original landmarks were no longer there - she finally caught sight of a distinctive old Mulberry tree almost hidden by the curve of the hedge row that had grown taller since her being in residence.

Ah, that way Jeeves...

So; striking off in the direction of the village, she began to *walk with a purpose* in the manner the *A.I.* 's had drummed into their pupils when she was a student.

The sun was out but it was not hot for June (this was England after all). She was glad of her jacket. All she needed to ape Viscount Byng was a mastiff or Scottish wolfhound at her side. Rounding the bend, she was still on the grade; spread out below to her delight was the same landscape she had been used to long ago, with extraordinarily little 'townie' encroachment to ruin the rural aspects. Even the rubbly remains of Sawtry Abbey could still be seen in a rough outline amongst the grasses.

Although not native to the area, in the fields abutting the hedge rows were Scottish cattle as well as a few Herefords. Some pastures were bound by stone fences, also a bit of an anomaly although very picturesque. It reminded her of New England. She looked about, then sat on one, shutting her eyes and basking her face in the sun while the appropriate phrase: *Make hay while the sun shines* played in her head. A cool breeze whimsically rearranged her natural curls.

Cheeks flushed from the exercise and squinting now, she breathed it all in. Time stood still. There was Alconbury spread out below her, the highway junction of the A1 and A14 running under the overpass, and further along closer to the village, the old stone bridge which held specific memories for her. She wouldn't go *there* yet - too soon - but coming to the overpass she drew in her breath.

Here years before, she had *had* the frightening experience of doing 'road work 'on Knobby Knees, an aptly named four-year-old 17.5-hand high Roan gelding. Like a lot of young very tall horses he had to learn how to use his long gangly 'giraffe' legs properly. The walking exercise was supposed to aid and abet such development. Cerby shook her head as the memories flooded back. When the A.I. in charge of a select group of expensive young horses had first asked her to take Knobby out, she felt only pride at being picked for the challenge. Hmmm. The episode played in her mind like a chapter out of a book…

> *Knobby had run through quite a few early morning exercisers, but Cerdwyn hadn't thought deeply enough about that or her first*

24

impression of Cecily, the A.I., who hesitantly offered Cerby the job. Cerby felt instinctively that Cec didn't think she could actually 'handle' Knobby; he was, after all, a 'lot of horse' even for a very experienced rider.

The youthful Cerby had needed approval at the time and wasn't averse to the advantage that Road Workers had, of being exempt from early morning mucking-out duties before 'brekkie'.

'Should be a breeze,' she'd tried to convince herself and Cec that first day. Swallowing a growing, niggling fear however, she groomed the pre-adolescent for his 'walkies.' She should have known as her friends had surmised (by the way Knobby managed to almost completely chew through each one of his reins on tack up) that this was going to be no ordinary 'walk in the park'.

Present day Cerdwyn put a shading hand up to her forehead and let her eyes rove down the country lane. In fact, she recalled, Cec had gone out with her initially, on the buddy system. They took this very same back road in towards Alconbury. Back then…

… traffic on the hedgerow road itself was not an issue as it was still a sleepy little rural area, so there was little enough of that at the best of times to contend with; thankfully, as Knobby was hardly 'bomb proofed.' But as Cerby was to discover on the first sortie, Knobby was also afraid of absolutely everything else, shying away from paper bags, pop bottles on the verge, birds,

rustling trees - you name it: 'Knobbbbbby...Stop it!! Pul—eeese!'

*The consequence of not moving more than 20 feet at a time without a pull up, resulted in horse and rider falling quite a distance behind Cec and her mount. To some degree this was advantageous. With heart in mouth, Cerby didn't want to have to pretend to a bravery she no longer felt in front of Cec. She deemed herself a right chump - just wanted to **live** through the road work experience, heroics be dammed!*

The worst part of this exercise was taking Knobby over the overpass. The cement side-barriers and metal rails along the bridge rose barely a meter above on either side. This only came up to the level of Knobby's stomach. On top of that safety issue, Knobby had the uncomfortable habit of dancing sideways over to the rails (which in Dressage would have been a reasonably difficult manoeuvre known as a 'side-pass') - the animal obviously trying to reconcile his own terror at the moving cars below by getting a 'closer' look at them. An equally terror-stricken Cerby sat three feet higher than the top of the guard rail, astride the squirming tonnage. She had an unparalleled view of the busy A1 Motorway directly below.

It was a curse to have her imagination. She conjured horror-filled images of Knobby shying/bolting/rearing and one or both falling over the parapet to land on the highway below only to be further mashed by some 'bloody geet lorry.'

*Testing the fates further, the unresponsive Knobby, not content with ball-rooming it over to one side, sashayed (despite Cerby's frantic attempts at reining-in) in a 'half- pass' over to the other, to inspect **that** portion of the A1. Despite Knobby demonstrating real dressage talent, Cerby sweated bullets cajoling and coaxing him back to the middle of the road. Finally, and with much prayerful thankfulness, they successfully reached the other end of the bridge 'too far.'*

A journey of ten miles starts with one step
                                                        –Confucius

*To Cerby, **one** step with Knobby **felt** like a hundred miles.*

Even now ten years on, (Cerby unconsciously raking her locks with one hand), presumably any gray hairs tucked in amongst her curls were directly attributable to Knobby.

OH. And not forgetting that of course, by the time she'd gotten over to the far side of the bridge, finally breathing a sigh of relief, Cec was coming back the other way urging: 'Alright there Cerdwyn? We'd best get back to the yard. The others will be mucking out by now. We'll be late for breakfast.'
Cerby went a whiter shade of pale at the mere thought of the return journey. She had never felt

27

less like eating in her life (and that was saying something!)

The second crossing was as frightful as the first but at least there was no levade *or* capriole *on the bridge; (fortunately the youthful Knobby's repertoire appeared somewhat limited). Not surprisingly, Cerby found after the terror of the overpass, Knobby's continuous shying on the way home was a minor nuisance in comparison. Like an airline passenger who has survived major turbulence 35,000 feet up, Cerby nearly kissed the ground when she slid off Knobby's back once they were back in the stable yard. Knobby however, like the youngster he was, had barely broken a sweat. When Cec came by, carrying her saddle forward on her arms, asking: 'Same time tomorrow then?' Cerby nearly croaked when she heard herself immediately reply without thinking: 'Sure.'*

Alas, under the circumstances, Cerdwyn's and Knobby's partnership was not to last. After about five terror-stricken 'hacks,' (Knobby never did master his knees or his obsession with the overpass) she'd conceded defeat and advised Cec one morning: 'That's it—I'm done!'

'Now who're we going to get then,' was Cec's heated and annoyed response. 'No one else will ride the bloody beast.' It occurred to Cerby simultaneously that the A.I. herself had never offered, and she was far and away the more competent rider. Cerby, having begun to doubt her ridership, felt righteously vindicated in the moment. After that, she'd always given Knobby an extra pat as she passed his whinnying head

hanging over his stall door during early morning muck out. She'd been one of a select few who had taken him for 'walkies'- and lived to tell the tale.

The present intruded. Cerby sighed. What *coming of age* adventures she *had* had here. Poor old Knobby could very likely be dead now. Horses had terrible lives generally; *'always saying goodbye,'* and so short for the most part. She hoped he had had a good life—and learned to love the overpass.

Cerby stopped outside the Highwayman pub on seeing *Mister* Wentworth, who'd been the school physician when she was a student at Alaerton at the same time as he'd GP'd in Alconbury. She waved but he 'd not seen her apparently. He seemed in rather a hurry. She looked after him as he strode away down the opposite side of the High Street. She hadn't realized until now what a strong military-bearing he had; now in his early 60's he could easily have been mistaken for a retired officer, (which he might well be, as school gossip once had it that he'd army medical experience before his civilian career.) Cerby would make sure they connected at some point. It had probably been just a rumour all those years ago that he'd had a thing for Mrs. Hill, but there was no mistaking his kindness and sage advice to her as an alienated teenager. That was the problem with this place - memories every which way you turned ...

She pulled open the heavy doors of the pub. The *Highwayman* hadn't changed much either when she found herself in the bar - all dark wood stain and oak beams with dusty leaded windows and a slightly smoky atmosphere. (Even if there was now a civilized bylaw and ban on smoking, the locals didn't seem to worry about it apparently). She coughed phlemily and at the same time, a couple of hands shot up from a booth situated at the back of the room by a window. She smiled and immediately felt happier, grateful Monte and Mitch had accompanied her on this journey, although the bright sweaters draped over their mutual shoulders and tied around their necks in preppy style, screamed 'tourist.'

"Watch your step young lady," said the stocky barman in passing with a tray, glasses and a bottle balanced in hand. Cerby just in time remembered the raised portion of the *snuggery*, preventing a rather inelegant entrance.

He did say 'young' lady, didn't he?

"Hi Guys. Seems you've started without me. Looks like you're enjoying whatever it is, though." She surveyed the mutilated remains of the repast spread out before them.

"We have, and we are. Just had to try a steak and kidney pie. They're always eating it on *Corie*. Not my cup of tea though really; pastry's too thick. Monte 's got something called '*A Blimpie.*' What 'd you like from the bar Cerb? (Afterthought) Want anything to eat for yourself? Monte will get it, won't you Toff-ee?"

Thinking of supper in a couple of hours, Cerby declined but raised her eyebrows in mock concern at Monte. Monte grimaced, shooting a look of forbearance at Mitch and one of long suffering at Cerby. "YES, I suppose it's better than being called 'Wanker' in public, so don't feel so bad '*Old Trout'.*" Monte shuffled off to get Cerby 's *Shandy & Chips,* another relic from the past.

"You know Cerb, I'm finding this place rather fascinating," began Mitch in Monte 's absence. "I remember you told me some of the history, but I've read up some more on the back of this serviette…" He held up what was a touristy paper placemat, marked with local sites and advertising on the front as well as a brief history of Alconbury in the side bar. "It even mentions your Inn here, and look here, this bit about an ostler practising the time-honoured *Stand and Deliver* route to financial success."

"Here, let me see that." Cerb turned the sheet around so she could read it right side up. "Yes, I remember hearing and reading something about this years ago." She made a mental note to plumb Mrs. Hill more about it.

"Geez Monte, you're no waiter!" as some ale slopped on to the sheet. "Better set everything down here," indicating an uncluttered spot on the table. Monte, wearing a slightly frazzled look on his chubby face was happy to oblige.

"So Guys: how do you like it here, your accommodations etc. so far?"

"Well, it is pretty much just a village, isn't it?" Mitch preferred *big city* lights. "But it's okay. We've got a large room with an ensuite (this for Cerby's benefit, her insistence on clean bathroom facilities legendary) which I was surprised to find at this type of hotel. It's reasonable though for

England in June. We've already been up and down the main street; it's not *too* long."

"That 's *High Street,"* put in Cerby.

"'High Street' then," corrected Mitch with a snort.

"It's really lovely, Cerb." Monte interrupted.

Monte was such a positive fellow. Cerby loved that about him. He was short and roly-poly but full of heart. He'd never leave Mitch whatever the cause. Both had lost friends and partners to Aids in the years past; that was how they had met, at a grief counselling session in Burlington hosted by Mitch in his social worker capacity. They'd been the solid couple and *Besties* that Cerby'd admired ever since.

"I just love the stone houses and the lovely gardens. All those romantic house names, just like yours, Cerb."

Cerby felt a twinge of remorse for leaving her *'Rose Cottage'* and rambunctious pets Frankie and Cimba behind, even if only for little more than a week. And then she remembered she would be doing battle again when she returned with the Rose of Sharons for which her home was named - that incessantly seeded themselves throughout the property. Her inability to cull the beautiful shrubs, only bringing herself to transplant, had resulted in a forest of these specimens front and back of the rose-bricked home. Friends laughed at her soft-hearted approach to gardening, but her property looked like one big bouquet in mid-to-late summer with white, pink, and purple blooms.

"There's one called 'Rooks Roost' and another one, 'Whislton's Aery.' It's given me an idea for a new article, perhaps a book even." Monte was referring to his successful free-lance hobby/career as a published travel and culinary author. One might have thought that such a side-line would have interfered with his duties as CEO of Maine's well known Bonesquet Fruit and Berry Winery, but rather, it was often complimentary to those obligations.

Mitch burst in excitedly: "It's a great idea, especially for the North American market - they 'd eat it up."

Monte pursed his thick lips and sent Mitch a silent searing message. "Perhaps a coffee table book - à la Abrams Publishing - on the cottages or maybe narrow it down to just those lychgate thingies. I see luxuriant climbing Roses; grey wood; old stone, mullioned windows…Can't fail."

Well, with Monte's expertise in these matters, it probably wouldn't. "Good. It's settled then!" Cerby enthused. Tapping Monte's arm: 'Brought your usual?"

"Need you even ask?" Mitch laughed. (Monte always travelled with more than the average compliment of camera lens, scopes, tripods etc.)

Cerby raised her glass, happy that her friends would be well occupied during their stay. She felt a little less guilty. "Guys, I'm so glad this trip hasn't been a total loss for you after all! "

"Hardly that *old bean*!"

"Cerby, we wouldn't have missed it, would we Mitch?"

They all clinked their glasses—***HARD,*** in general accord. Cerby sighed. She had gone *almost* a whole hour without spilling/staining/soiling her light-coloured attire; a record in fact!

After heading to the loo to try to prevent said stains from setting, Cerby left Mitch and Monte eager to pursue a list of possible photographic images suitable for the intended publishing theme they had discussed. She detoured on her walk back over the long village green to the river front and slowed as she approached the 15th century stone bridge that arched over the languid and picturesque Alconbury Brook. She marvelled again at the beauty of the four arches. *If only its builder could know it was still standing and in use 500 years later.*

She walked up the incline of the bridge, caressing the rough stone and railing with one hand until she reached the median, where turning into the sun and shading her eyes, Cerby looked out over the weeping willows and rushes that crowded the edges of the stream. The brook seemed smaller than she remembered, but further down the way, it widened into a pond, narrowing again almost to nothing at the 'ford' as it curved like a snake at the base of Alconbury Hill.

She leaned tentatively over the stone wall of the bridge, clasping her hands prayerfully out before her. Carefully balancing her torso as far out as she dared, she could look straight down into the brook's sluggish depths. The occasional *chub*-like fish could be seen darting about in the shallows, but no anglers were visible along the worn paths by the stream's margins. It was noticeably quiet except for the bubbling symphony where the stream passed over pebbly sandbars. All of this was conducive to introspection, and Cerby let herself go –at last.

Was it the right decision, after all? It's not like we kept in touch all these years. A clean break it was - best thing really. I was so young after all, and traumatized. He had a career to build. Bad timing, that's for sure.

The sequence of events that had made it all so untenable sprang to mind. *Would never have worked; no, never, I guess... But could it have?* Memories have a way of crowding in unbidden, and so for some minutes they came and warred with each other in her head, until she shook them loose again. *What's the point,* she reprimanded herself uncertainly.

Oh, oh! The village clock chimed. *I'd better get a move on if I'm gonna get any supper.* Cerby's stomach dictated a hasty retreat. She hadn't eaten more than a small bag of chips at the Pub and if Mrs. Momfrey, Alaerton's heritage live-in cook, was still adhering to strict dining schedules, she knew if she missed this meal, she wouldn't be eating at all the rest of the evening.

Now, which way back ...

A trip to the WC, quick splash to the face and less than the two minutes of washing your hands that was considered hygienic nowadays, Cerby soon found herself sitting in the *Long Room* between Bron and Stevey across from Saffi and another

35

woman whose presence pricked Cerby's spidey-sense for some reason. There was no time to explore the inexplicable discomfort further, or even introduce herself, as the woman had looked directly at Cerby with a long thoughtful stare, then, jostling Saffi in the process and without apology, got up hurriedly and left the room.

Stevey bristled herself: "Plonker! Where's the fire? How extraordinary. Some people have no manners whatsoever, do they?"

A rustic head table had been hastily arranged at one end of the room. It was now the scene of much activity and commotion that immediately drew everybody's attention as a few 'honoured' guests sat down and shuffled in their seats. Gradually however, the scraping of chair legs on the stone flags settled down, and Mrs. Hill stood up, lovely in a flowery pink dress.

"Well, what a fine company we make," she said, sweeping her arm about the room. "Old pupils, new pupils, our inestimable *A.I...* The 'I' was held up, although he should be here in a day or so. (Cerby's heart fluttered). I'm so happy you all are here to help celebrate the 25th Founding Anniversary of Alaerton Equestrian Centre. I can promise you we've arranged full weeks of riding and entertaining events; you won't regret the trip!

"Now, we've promised to keep this short, and I've already talked enough so I'll just re-introduce the rest of the head table, who I'm sure many of you will recognize. *Mister* Wentworth, could you please stand up."

To Mrs. Hill's right, the solidly built older gentleman with close-cropped silver hair and thick mustache gamely rose to his feet but with a brief salute sat down again with a nod and a thump. Cerby realized with a bit of a start, that whenever he glanced at Mrs. Hill, the good doctor's stern visage relaxed into nothing short of infatuation. And switching her gaze to Mrs. Hill, who was fully aware of the attention, she noticed the faint blush spreading across the lady's cheeks.

"Next, our long-suffering cook of over twenty years. Mrs. Momfrey, take a bow please. (That *worthy* stood, grinned, and waved a large ladle at the onlookers - a good-humoured groan rose from the audience in response.)

"Oh, and perhaps you'll all remember to be kind enough to remove your boots in the mud room as you come and go so that our house-help here, Mayfair, doesn't end up doing more work than she ought."

As a sulky straggly-haired woman rose reluctantly, looking totally bored with the proceedings, Cerby realized she'd seen her before. *Ah, yes; the domestic dispute.*

"Now here's a new face for some of you, but you'll certainly be seeing a lot of her - Kalyn Hartenson - your A.I. for the next week. Kally, you have the floor."

A tall, well-proportioned Nordic woman in a rumpled white blouse stood up, wearing black dry-mucked riding boots, obviously fresh from the barn. Her severe ice-blonde ponytail bobbed about as she paced the front of the room. She delivered her speech with a slight Scandinavian accent.

``I 'ope you all enjoy your ev'ning tonight but tomorrov," she warned; "you vill be up early at 6:30

37

of the clock and out in the stable yard as zoon as you can."

This intelligence greeted by the audience with audible whinging.

"You were advised on book-kink," she continued sternly, "this would be a week reminiscent of your courses 'ere. Therevore you vill be dressed and mucking out by 7 am."

Met with a chorus of 'Ooohh, steady on...' and nervous giggles.

"Breakfast will be served to 8:30 am. You vill please be prop'ly attired and tacked up for riding in large arena at 9:30 or 10:30 respectively, dependink on your assigned group. *Elevenses* vill be served here in the *Long Room*. Stable work to continue afterwards until 1:00 pm at which time *dinner* vill be served 'ere then of cours' alzo. At 2:30 every day, there vill be a practis' for the Musak Ride you are performing for local branch of National RSPCA foondraising ef'ort in konjunktion vith the Alconbury Midsum'er Village Fête, this Fraeday komink."

A lot of puzzled faces peered back at her and each other with uncertainty.

"Ja!"

Collective gasp! Followed by muffled comments: *'Seriously.' 'She must be joking?'*

Kally added: "O, and ther vill be a faux Horsemaster's test alzo."

Another shocked intake of breath around the room.

"Doc-*tor* Wentworth and the 'I' vill alternate in giving clinics and refresher seminars jusst aft'r tea at 4:30 pm daily and supper vill be at 7. Please read schedule after brakfast tomorrov to find oot your mount for the tenure of your stay. Late hayink duty at 8 pm vill - as ever - be posted on the chalk board by mud room door."

Kally paused for breath in front of a rather stunned audience. A slow smile mellowed the Teutonic bearing and address: "You vill see; it vill all kom back to you. Jusst lak falling off a horse, Ja!"

"Nah!" grumbled Cerby, who had only ridden sporadically in the last few years. "Look at this bod, will you?" She flexed her arms and exaggerated the flab by pulling down on the underarm skin. "No thighs of iron here either!" She punched the offending flesh.

Bron laughed. "I`d say you`re in surprisingly good shape Cerby. Perhaps the '*lady doth protest too much?* '"

"Well, you should talk Bron. You look like you could give Kally a run for her money. Do you still do all your exercises on horseback?"

Bron did not look Cerby in the eye when she responded slyly: "Yes, you could say that…"

Chapter Two

Sunday

A loud knock on the bedroom door, and a voluble someone standing at the threshold: "Come on! Everbody! Kit on an' down to the barn. Hurry up yourself please."

Bron and Cerby were occupying a tiny bedroom on the second floor of Alaerton Manor's original hewn- stone back entry. They could hear Kally move on to the adjacent bedroom and then up a step to the residential wing; Mayfair followed suit in the garret. Cerby groaned and turned on her side, but Bron was already sitting up on her bed rummaging through her early morning working apparel (typically jeans and a sweatshirt). Cerby stretched languorously, until she suddenly realized there 'd be a stampede for the bathroom. Bron apparently had the same notion at the same time. Cerby threw back the covers and jumped out of the bed. They both raced towards the door, getting stuck in the doorframe, laughing like two teenagers caught in boarding school antics.

Cerby stepped back and swept a bow towards Bron. "After you milady." Bron didn't wait to hear it twice, racing down the corridor - pushing Saffi and Stevey aside, whose recovery and subsequent efforts still left them locked out of the WC at the 'finish'. As Cerby came up behind, chuckling at

Saffi's ineffectual pounding on the bathroom door, cursing Bron roundly for beating her to it, Stevey smiled in greeting.

"Bit hungry; aren't you as well Cerb? And (as she shivered slightly) it's a little damp out there today. It's The Fens' misty air. Would have liked to have had some breakfast first ..."

Cerdwyn wryly agreed. "I was *ALWAYS* hungry doing early morning muck out but at least it meant you could stuff down even Mrs. Momfrey's cold toast and tepid tea without complaint. I hope things have improved slightly since we were here last!!"

Saffi snorted. "Well, you *WOULD* be a *working pupil*", a put down that both acknowledged the privileges accorded to *Residential Students* at the time (eggs benedict and COFFEE as opposed to scrambled eggs and tea for the 'plebs') and reminded Stevey and Cerdwyn that they had been on the other side of the blanket as far as the *Rezzies* were concerned. They met each other's eyes for a moment and guffawed. Saffi momentarily left out, elbowed both her friends in annoyance.

"What, for goodness sakes? You two are just plain barmy!"

Which caused Stevey and Cerdwyn to laugh even harder, annoying Saffi exponentially. Bron stepped out of the WC just at that moment and unintentionally broke up the hilarity as Saffi, claiming *noblesse oblige,* shoved the others aside not too gently and gained entry to the WC next.

Cerby caught the surprise in Bron and Stevey's faces, but said amid remnants of the previous laughter bubbling up to the surface again: "You

41

have to admire her *slight of foot,"* just as the door crashed closed and the bolt slid in.

Eventually, all toilettes having been seen to in record time, the women plunged down the stairs like noisy elephants, ending up outside in the Kitchen Courtyard with the rest of the sleepy-eyed, kerchiefed, denimed and rubber booted *army* –all shuffling and waiting for Kally, (standing empirically off to one side) to vocalize the assignments. Soon, everyone but Cerdwyn knew the stall number and horse that would be under their care for the duration of their stay. The majority of the group marched off down the tarmac to the stable square or 'Quad' as it was commonly known, to pick up the tools of the trade: pitchforks, water pails, and wheel barrels for mucking out - with the exception of one Reunionista...

Kally motioned kindly to a puzzled Cerdwyn. "Mrs. Hill is waiting for you around za corner of the stables 'ere in the Olde Mews." She pointed to the side alley across the cobbled courtyard that led to the back of the original centuries-old stone stable.

Cerdwyn's first thought as she tramped in that direction, was that she was lucky to get out of mucking out. And then she saw Mrs. Hill, puffing on a cigarette and gazing out over the level *50 Acre Field* that Cerdwyn remembered humorously from their re-enactment exercise of the 'Charge of the Light Brigade' a decade ago. She smiled at the scene in her mind's eye —*the proverbial horses running off in all directions.*

"Mrs. H, what is...?"

Mrs. Hill turned slowly and without speaking,

gestured eloquently behind her to a large rough fieldstone stall that looked over this pretty view.

Cerby's head swiveled and suddenly she seemed to be moving in slow motion, her voice following suit. 'Cyr-...NO! Can't be? Cyri—us? O My DOG! Cyrius!" And then, practically unhinging the lower stall door in her haste, her arms were holding tight around the old white Andalusian's neck, her face buried in his softly flowing mane, hiding her tears of joy! After precious moments, Cerdwyn turned her tear-stained face to Mrs. Hill. "I can't believe it Mrs. H. Thank you, thank you! I never thought he'd be... I was always afraid to ask about..."

Mrs. Hill coughed and took an extra-long drag on her cigarette. She came over to stand by the open stall door, where the stallion now moved over for a loving pat on the muzzle. "Yes, he *is* 21, but in extraordinary shape. He's still used for riding you know. It gives him exercise and of course he 'teaches' the rider, not the other way around —just like he taught you," she smiled. "He is our mascot in many ways; it wouldn't be Alaerton Equestrian Centre without him."

Cerdwyn looked into the liquid knowing eye of her old friend: "Cyrius, do you remember me, Boy?"

Up his head went on hearing her voice, followed by a long speculative stare. Then he laid that huge head gently on her shoulder. She blubbered anew and kissed his cheek, all the while stroking him as if he'd disappear. Mrs. Hill's voice came to her as from far, far away: *'thought you would like to be in charge of him for the duration of your stay.'*

Cerdwyn nodded enthusiastically with bright eyes, sweeping Mrs. Hill into a bear hug. The older woman tottered unsteadily. "Oh, so sorry Mrs. H. I'll be back in a jiff," she called over her shoulder, and ran all the way down the tarmac road with elation, only too happy now to get the mucking out tools she had eschewed from the Quad only a few minutes before.

There was stunned disbelief at breakfast amongst the small group of friends when apprised of Cerdwyn's reunion with Cyrius - Saffi showing the same touch of jealousy she had years before when Cyrius had been assigned to Cerby. Then, he'd been the acknowledged best horse in the school, and Saffi without doubt had been the better rider (having come from a *Hunting* family and more or less born on horseback.) Mrs. Hill however, immediately sensing the connection between the stallion and Cerdwyn, (given Cerdwyn's recent tragic loss), had no doubts and her decision was law. During the *Year of the Horse* in Cerdwyn's life, the two were inseparable. When she finally had to leave to return to Vermont, it nearly broke her heart again to leave Cyrius behind. But everyone in *the present*, including a grudging Saffi, were happy for Cerdwyn at this new turn of events.

Breakfast turned out to be better than remembered. Alaerton fare for everyone now (regardless of *caste*) included waffles, bacon, eggs, and breakfast sausages, although toast remained a bit of a challenge for Mrs. Momfrey. Presumably however, the equitation centre's affiliation with the local Tourist Association had resulted in a corresponding number of changes. Fortunately for the *Reunionistas,* the culinary esthetic had risen in relation to those expectations.

"See!" Stevey squealed in delight. "I told you. There's cereals, fruits and yogurt." The food on the sideboards in the *Long Room* was actually tempting for a change. Cerdwyn couldn't complain this time around, but she'd make sure she didn't eat so much she would be uncomfortable for the 9:30 'Morning Ride'. That was one lesson she'd learned the hard way as a student.

Breakfast being finished by about 8:30, everyone filtered into the Common Room to lounge and digest for quarter of an hour before returning to their rooms to don breeches and riding apparel. Once they reached the stables and their mounts, they were to do a normal groom before saddling up. Even someone like Cerdwyn who had only ridden intermittently over the intervening years, could still do it in her sleep.

She mentally recited the instructions of yore:

> *Take the small hard curry brush to work out the dirt over the neck, withers, sides, and rump. Then the larger softer curry brush to sweep it away and brush gently down the legs—all around, checking for bot flies to remove with the special knife provided. Rub a chamois or soft cloth all over the body bringing out the natural oil shine. Next, brush*

45

out the mane and tail, inspect all 4 feet, investigating hooves for dirt packs and stones, picking them out with a hoof pick. Clean and refresh the horse's face by running a damp clean face cloth over the forehead, around the eyes, and muzzle—transferring at last to the rear end, to wipe around and under the dock. *Finally, apply some hoof oil to keep their 'nails' from cracking.*

Tacking Up of course came next, the appropriate saddle casually perched on the top of the lower Dutch door, reins thrown over the back of it. Cyrius having been fully groomed, Cerby removed his halter first. (Why he had one on in the stall was a bit of a mystery, as most horses were turned in without one, but there was no time to dwell on it.) Opening his mouth wide enough to accept the simple Snaffle bit, she was careful not to knock his teeth or tongue. Pulling up the headband over his ears and adjusting over the forehead had to be done carefully as well, making sure no mane hair was caught uncomfortably underneath. For safety and comfort's sake, Cerby had been taught to judge proper tightness and fit by sliding two fingers width between the neck band and jaw —she did this now.

Once the 'controlling mechanism' was on, next came his personal saddle blanket or under pad, and then the saddle itself with stirrups pulled high so as not to bang the horse on the walk to the arena. The girth was attached and buckled but allowed to hang loose.

Cyrius had turned his head every now and again to judge her progress during this entire process, standing quite still for the most part, allowing her to tack him up with little fuss.

Cerby couldn't wait to be on his back again. He was yet a beautiful specimen: his back strong and compact; well-rounded musculature where he should have been in the chest and rump; clear eyed and ears pricked forward with intent. In so many ways, it was hard to believe the number of years that had elapsed. She felt older than he did apparently as in evidence, once she had led him out of his stall and round the small stable into the open cobbled courtyard opposite the back door of the Inn, his head had come up; his feet picked up; his tail swished in anticipation. The excitement was mutual.

He must be channeling Northern Dancer, Cerby mused, 'the Dancer' being one of her equestrian icons. Eyes bright, they walked together the long stretch towards the Quad and the arena!

On arrival, kicking up with his prancing steps the sawdust floor-bed laid down, she led him to the centre of the arena where others had gathered, commencing the final tightening adjustment of the girth strap. (A gentle knee to the stomach forced the animal to breathe out. 'Bloating' was the favourite trick of many a savvy horse, with a dangerously loose saddle the result.) Finally, Cerby always liked to pull down the stirrups with a snap prior to mounting. It seemed to say to both horse and rider: '*here we are, ready for business.*'

The school had two covered arenas at the Northeast corner of the Quad: a smaller one for individual schooling of horse and or rider, and a larger one for group sessions. The latter's proportions were generally bigger than North American standards. In Alaerton's heyday twenty years ago, equitation shows of some note had taken place there, and even an Olympic rider or two had graced the premises for promotional jump-offs in those early days.

Now the arena looked rather worn in spots. The floor did not look like it had been 'sanded' or groomed on a regular basis, the sawdust mix appearing thin in the tracks along the walls especially. The paint on the bleachers at the ends and sides were peeling. Old, reclaimed boards of various states were being used along the walls of the horse arena as 'kick plates' instead of the uniformity of thick plywood sheets normally used. They were painted white though, which helped camouflage a multitude of sins. To an untrained eye, the wooden interior of the building appeared serviceable, but Cerby's heart sank at the current condition in comparison with her memories.

Still, mounting Cyrius and feeling the energy surge through both their bodies was a pleasant shock to Cerdwyn. When there is a trusting bond between horse and rider, it's like morphing into a Centaur - one brain, one beast - something magical and ethereal. She felt blessed to own the experience once again!

Automatically she 'assumed the position,' centred on his back in the correct posture: legs 'long;' heels down; slightly curled hands - the reins clasped between the 2nd and 4th fingers - held just above the pommel of the saddle; and eyes pointed in the direction to follow. How fluid the whole transformation was! One never forgot, and a horse can always be counted on to sense the level of confidence in its rider.

Kally stood in the centre of the arena. Her voice was permanently hoarse from perpetually shouting at students. The damp air blowing in from the Fen country in Cambridgeshire, lying not far to the North and East, didn't help either. However, the 'blonde bombshell' (as students old and new had nicknamed her) took command of the various levels of horsemanship before her in a way that cowed all the horsewomen instantly.

"Face me. Stan' square please!" she barked. Then she walked to the side of each horse and rider and handed up cardboard numbers from 1 to 26 as if they were competing in an equestrian event. She had the riders help each other tie these on their backs, so that if she did not recognize the face, she could at least call out the number and instruct the appropriate party. Also, the women knew that only 16 were required for the Musical Ride. A cull would occur shortly.

"This process - a bit like 'America's Top Model,'" Cerby whispered to Stevey on her left.

"Yes, we'll all have to strut our stuff if we want to be chosen for the fête event."

Cerby glancing at her competition to the rear, noticed at the entrance end of the arena a baseball-capped man dressed in a farmer's denim overall, carrying a hand rake. He glowered in the students' direction, presumably wanting to get on with a work schedule which the Reunion had no doubt turned on its head. Eventually he stalked out through the sliding barn doors, which were subsequently closed by Kally. The excited chatter continuing earned a glare from the A.I. as she strode back to centre ring. Everybody stopped talking.

At first, Cerdwyn on Cyrius had troubles just trying to get him to stand still in the line. He knew he was 'at work' and wanted to get started. When he began to nervously paw the ground with determination, she turned him to walk in small circles, always bringing him back to stand square and face forward to reset his attention. Kally took note and nodded approvingly. Cerby felt she was back in Kally's good books.

In the few minutes before the lesson commenced, Cerby studied the giant training letters posted in measured lengths around the arena. Although the arrangement of these was standard for equestrian classes and shows, she had never had the ability to memorize them, probably a result of her slight dyslexia. She would just have to imprint a rough visual but keep her eyes peeled.

ALAERTON EQUESTRIAN CENTRE· LARGE ARENA

DRESSAGE & MUSICAL RIDE LETTERING & LAYOUT

Eventually the group was ordered to '*Walk on*,' forming a *Single file, Indian Style* parade along the sides of the arena. After distancing each rider and horse from the one in front and behind, Kally wanted to gage the group at the trot. Although none were less than *intermediate level* riders (which in British Horse Society terms meant a higher level of skill than was accorded to the same term internationally) some like Cerby hadn't ridden too regularly over the years. However, with Kally shouting instructions: 'Sit up'! 'Heels Down'! 'Do not bounce; thiss iss not a *Sitting Trot*' etc., soon there was some semblance of the riders they had been in their prime.

Kally got them used to crossing at various 'stations' around the arena, doing circles from
E-X-B-F-K or *B-X-E-H-M* to longitudinals from *A* to *C*, and diagonals from *H* to *F* and *K* to *M*. Finally, Kally had them *walk on* in two lines: one side-by-side group using the *F* to *M* and *O* to *N* as their guide and the other using the *Q* to *J* and *K* to *H* line, meeting and turning in at *C* to halt at last, four abreast, at *X*.

At a trot or a canter, Cerby was in heaven with Cyrius' *Flying Changes* but a concentrated hour of this was just enough for everyone (including their steeds). At the end of the lesson, Kally asked the women all to line up in the centre again in two rows and called out to certain of the numbered riders to take a pace forward. These would be the 'chosen few' for the Musical Ride, along with a couple of spares.

"Hurrah Gals!" Cerby was ecstatic to find that she and all her friends were amongst those picked. She

51

would have been ashamed if Cyrius had not taken his rightful place in the celebrations because of her. On *dismount*, most of the riders were cursing atrophied muscles and sore glutes but not Cerdwyn, who hugged Cyrius with glee: 'Don't worry Cyrius! I'm going to make the most of my time together with you - no matter how much physio's required afterwards.'

"Thank God for *Elevenses,*" Saffi pouted sarcastically, pouring herself a lukewarm cup of tea in the Long Room. The horses had been cooled down and put away in their respective stalls. Light sandwiches had been placed on the tables, but this time she wasn't too proud to scoff up a few.

"No watercress I'm afraid Saf," Cerby apologized innocently to Saffi, whose mouth was too full to respond...fortunately for Cerby.

Stevey of course, had already corralled her share and was munching contentedly. "How're you feeling Cerb after your first ride?" She unintentionally spit a few crumbs in Cerby's direction. "Don't know about you but I'm a bit sore, and I've ridden more than you've done, sounds like, in the last few years."

Cerby, her mouth full also - *amazing how hungry barn work and riding could make a person* - let out an imitation groan, belied by her smile. She swallowed hard and laughed: "Don't you worry about me Stevey. I saw you on Malachi and you seemed to have your hands full yourself. I'm sore, but Cyrius is the Cadillac he always was, so don't worry. Come that Musical Ride, we won't be crashing into you; just you do likewise!"

As she toasted with her teacup in mock emphasis, Cerdwyn caught the eye briefly of the same swarthy-faced woman who had caught her attention the evening before. The niggling doubt at the back of her mind surfaced, but she just couldn't put her finger on it. Bron sitting at the end of their table, ate her snack with a slightly distracted air. Cerdwyn tried to draw her into the conversation.

"Bron, when I left Alaerton your parents were willing to bribe you with an Irish Hunter if you went home to Wales and settled down. What came of all that? I had a few letters and then I presumed you'd gone to Ireland to manage that small stable you'd mentioned instead."

The unspoken history was that Bron's beloved younger brother Barri had committed suicide shortly before she had arrived at Alaerton. The equitation centre and Cerby had been her main refuge for the year after the event. Because of Cerby's family tragedy also, their friendship at Alaerton was almost instantaneous. So in sync were they, that Bron had been devastated once again when Cerby finally left at the end of her student year: the resulting consequence being a barely maintained perfunctory correspondence. It was plain now that both regretted losing touch. There was no point with added maturity, to skirt the painful issues of the past.

"Yes," Bron nodded her head slowly in guilty hindsight: "I blamed my parents terribly for Barri's suicide, which was childish and immature."

Cerby nodded in remembrance, adding throatily; "At least you *had* parents."

Bron reached out impulsively and squeezed Cerby's hand sympathetically as she continued: "They weren't responsible for his drug habit, though more unforgiving I thought, but I was close to Barri and I had to lash out at someone I suppose. It was too bad of me, as they not only lost him but me too for a while. I did draw nigh to my older brother Dylan, but he was at Uni so I couldn't spend a lot of time with him when I really needed to. I took that offer of *supervising groomsman* in Ireland not long after you left Cerby - I must have mentioned it to you in a letter - and I *was* there for quite a few years actually, working my way up towards farm manager. Had some relationships over time too, but p'rhaps it was what happened to my brother... I just couldn't seem to commit to anything really. I moved about a bit in the horsey world. Then later I came back into this vicinity, (looking curiously at Cerby); I've come back here, full circle."

Why was it Cerby got the distinct impression Bron was withholding something from her. She couldn't dwell on that thought however, because Saffi in a bid for some attention, took up the '*talking stick*' and began recounting her own history.

"I don't know where the years have gone," she said, flipping her hair back with the elegant, manicured nails that even barn work couldn't chip. "I left shortly before you all —remember I had brought my own horse Asterisk to board here back then. I went on to finish reading English at Cambridge."

"Naturally," murmured Cerby. An honours BA in English and History from the University of Burlington in Vermont paled against her friend's hoity-toity Oxford/Cambridge credits. Her business admin courses? Too trite to mention.

Saffi scowled theatrically. "Yes Cerby, I *DID* complete my scholarly pursuits, and wonder of wonders, graduated! And I also ran through the usual beaus..." poking Stevey in the ribs.

"The '*Long and the short and the tall*'", Stevey began to sing; "*Bless 'em all, Bless 'em all...* "

"Shut up Stevey! I wasn't that bad. Where was I? Ah yes. Well, I did end up eventually marrying - about 5 years ago it was."

"Holy Cow, you got married?" whistled Cerby. "Why wasn't I informed of all this?"

Saffi paused again, stirring the tea in her cup unnecessarily. "Probably because it was doomed from the start. As I was saying, I married Lorne Brakesby, the son of one of my parents' friends. A huge mistake. Crashed after only a couple of years. Good settlement of course, not that I needed it really. Thank God, no children." Her voice quietly trailing off belied Saffi 's real feelings on that score. Silence reigned for a moment.

"What have you been doing then, the last few years Saf," asked Cerby, quickly trying to redirect the conversation which threatened to become maudlin.

"Well, my Mother got cancer about four years ago, and my father died of a heart attack two years later..."

Stevey had kept in touch with Saf and was therefore aware of these events, but Cerby and Bron who hadn't, now expressed their genuine sympathy: 'Oh Saf! Why did you never write?'

"…so, I had to run the estate didn't I - as the only child." She stoically avoided their sympathy. "I've been pretty successful in keeping it going if I do say, but it took up every ounce of energy. As I wasn't a 'son' father never bothered to teach me much about managing the estate; (figured 'a husband' would I suppose). I had to learn everything from scratch and on the fly. There was just no time to correspond. I'm sorry, that all sounds so terribly lame."

"Are you kidding, Saf. We're all guilty, obviously. Tempus fugit, eh? But we have to promise that now we've found each other, never to let that happen ever again." Cerby looked them all intently in the eye, and each nodded affirmatively.

"Anyway, no false modesty there Saf," grinned Cerby, attempting to lighten the mood. "Or have I said that already?"

Ignoring the barb, sounding uncharacteristically vulnerable, Saffi added; "Would've been nice though to have had some help in the early days. It hasn't been easy." Then, recovering her poise: "And of course, I take my trips to Italy, Spain, and Provence when I need a break."

"Well, I've always been envious of Saffi, and that's a fact," Stevey admitted; "though she's been exceedingly kind in letting me exercise her horses often enough to keep 'my hand in'. Hey! I guess I'm the only one of us with kids then." Looking at her comrades, she waved a sandwich authoritatively in their faces; "Clock's ticking you know!"

Saffi countered: "Oh yes, how is it you've forgotten to mention the terrible 'twinks,' *Thank you* very much!"

"Who **YOU'VE** babysat on more than one occasion!" Stevey shot back.

"And lived to tell the tale," confirmed Saffi, laughing now.

Cerby's jaw dropped. 'Well, who are they and where are they when you're here?"

"Finn and Fiona - twins. Actually," Stevey affectionately tapped Saffi on the shoulder; "this one has been there for me a lot when I've needed a little support, one way or another, and my Mom too who has the dubious custodial honour for the week. Being a single Mom I dare say is equally as hard as running an estate. Peter," she stammered, embarrassed; "my Ex, wasn't the home type in the end. Left the country when the kids were only two years old. Hasn't been in contact since."

Murmurs of *'What a rotter!'* and, *'Hard luck, Stevey.'*

"So how have you managed all these years then Stevey?" Cerdwyn asked, concern dripping from every word.

"You recall Cerb, I was always *computer friendly* from the beginning. I started to do work at home when the kids were just little tykes. Through the years, and they're just coming on seven now, I started a small business enterprise and began to do consulting locally.

"Crikey!" Cerby blurted: "We have a *Stevey Jobs* in our midst —who knew?" Somehow Stevey being an IT guru didn't jive. *Running a pastry shop maybe*, which thought was unconsciously voiced aloud. Cerby flushing, apologized profusely.

Stevey laughed: "I'm not offended Cerb. You're absolutely right. My second choice of a career *would* have been running an eatery of some kind. I love to cook."

"And eat!" chimed in Saffi.

"Well, so act-u-ally do you Saf!" Cerby pointed to the few remaining crumbs on her friend's plate.

Saffira's finely made-up lashes batted several times, her chin stuck out determinedly. "Well don't be so surprised everyone. Yes, I do know my way around a boiled egg. I spent most of my childhood sitting around the *AGA* at home absorbing the culinary acumen of our wonderful Parisian cook, Madame Burlieu. She taught me a lot, and some of those trips to France and Italy were 'cooking sprees' - courses to augment what I'd already learned." She glanced haughtily at Cerby. "I'm not entirely frivolous you know."

"Cripes Saf. My bib's off to you, I mean it." Cerdwyn gave her an affectionate slap on the back. Saffi shrugged it off but accepted the apology.

"And what about you *Cerdwyn of Vermont:* the adventurous one of the pack?" Stevey took a big bite out of a dessert-square Brownie, smacking her lips in anticipation of more revelations.

"Well, thanks Stevey, but I wouldn't say *that* exactly... " hemmed Cerdwyn. "Seems to me you've all had quite interesting lives up to now."

"Yes," rejoined Stevey, "but not many of us got to be involved in a murder, (Cerdwyn held up her index and middle fingers.) Or *two*?" The others stopped eating, looking askance.

Cerby shook her head. "I'll fill you in on all that some other time. Believe me though, life has been fairly quiet otherwise. As you know, my parents died in that winter driving accident some months before I came to Alaerton, which was at the suggestion of the executor of my father's will, a family friend who knew Mrs. H. I was here for that year and then I left. I never did take further equine studies once back in the States as I had intended or get into the horse business in any way. Funny how things work out, eh? Oh, I leased horses occasionally and rode my friends' mounts, but all strictly casual.

"That's left a few years in between for me to go through my inheritance (laughing at the concerned faces.) Just joking! Still comfortable enough to enjoy the odd jaunt, *comme ci*. I still live in New Westminster too - just your normal small American town. Close enough to the Canadian Border to throw a stone at, and near enough to Stowe for the winter sports. I mainly work out of Burlington, which has a decent airport if you ever want to come to visit...I mean, WHEN you come to visit."

"I seem to recall," Stevey's forehead puckered in concentration: "pictures you showed us once Cerby. Might be typical for you but I thought the stone homes, white churches and covered bridge were gorgeous."

"Yes, if you like Sleepy Hollow," Cerby laughed. "No, it really *IS* a lovely place, and I wouldn't want to live anywhere else. It was difficult to live in my parents' house after they were gone - too painful. But I couldn't leave the town either, so I bought my own place there and moved everything in.

"But, to continue, I found I liked to work occasionally for a living, and the social aspects of course, and *especially* if I wanted to retire in the style to which I wish I had been born (flashing a toothy grin at Saffi). So; I've worked up to taking executive office admin contract jobs mostly there in town and within commutable distances, as that allows me to pick and choose when I want to work and what I want to do. Somehow the odd 'incident' has occurred, but not sought after, believe me!

"My love life on the other hand has been absolutely dismal and unexciting. I'm always a near 'Miss' in that department. Sure, I've got any number of romantic skiing, boating, fly fishing stories I could regale you with, but that will have to be over a bottle of wine on a 'truth or dare' night if we ever get to it."

"Oh yes, let's do! Like we used to!" squealed Stevey excitedly. Bron looked uncertain, and Saffi just snorted.

Cerby put down her teacup with a resounding crack: "By golly, so we will. We'll have to pick a day; some time soon since I'm only here for the week. By the way, I almost forgot..." She rummaged in her breech pocket. "Did anyone lose this earring? I found it on the tarmac just outside the old Mews in the KC. Looks kind of pricey."

The women gave it a cursory glance, each in turn glancing at pearls and amethyst in an antique setting, but no one claimed or recognized the tarnished jewelry.

"No? Right. I'll just put a notice up on the bulletin board and put it in the *Lost and Found* bin then." (Mrs. Momfrey had always kept a slotted box in the pantry for just such a purpose.)

Mayfair drifted by in her capacity of general house-help, stopping abruptly and leaning over into their midst. Somewhat uncharacteristically she offered the group tea refills.

"Pass your cup then, Miss."

She poured Stevey's beverage, awkwardly bending well over Cerby's shoulder - obviously taken with the earring Cerby had on view. The clock chimed, reminding them all that their horses deserved a 'flake' before being ridden again in the afternoon's Musical Ride. Cerby straightened up at the prompt and de-benched. In doing so, she knocked the tea pot in Mayfair's hands, which spilled a bit on to the server's smock. Cerby apologized immediately, but Mayfair shuffled quickly away without a backward glance.

"An odd one, that," Stevey pronounced, watching the hasty retreat. No one disagreed.

Dinner would normally have been served around one o'clock but as almost all the riders had *had* their fill of food during the *Elevenses*, and as *all* were expecting a workout come the Musical Ride lesson mid-afternoon, it was collectively decided to advise Mrs. Momfrey to forgo a big lunch. Instead, riders lounged in the Common Room until the appointed hour in animated chatter with new and old acquaintances.

When the 'chosen few' were once again on horseback, Cerby strained to memorize for the second time the training 'alphabet' set up for the lesson. Being even a bit dyslexic, her right brain didn't always chat with her left, and so she was particularly happy with the size of the letters that were easily seen from any point in the arena.

Kally looked over her handpicked troop. From the earlier rides she had determined sixteen riders who (still) had the experience and the coordination to carry the project off. She was confident that either way, whether it was a success or a fiasco, it would be entertaining for the audience. She would preface in the announcement before the event anyway, that riders *had* only had one week to prepare, and if a success, promote that their earlier training at the school had been the prime factor for the 'fast-forward' in the circumstances.

Cerby on Cyrius was totally chuffed that she had been among those selected. It was a no-brainer that her friends Saffi, Bron and Stevey would naturally be part of the elite core: two owned horses and the third had leased.

However. The first Musical Ride practise that afternoon *was* something of a disaster. Although mostly everyone held on to their 'seats,' it was like a soapbox derby in the beginning. Riding in two's and branching off from the centre line at the bottom of the arena was performed without incident, but after that had been practised a few times, Kally's instructions to do the diagonals from *H* to *F* on the left lead and then from *M* to *K* on the right lead in pairs, resulted in several 'crashes.'

Cerby and Cyrius were run into by the stranger whose name had still not been determined. Cerby had flashed her an angry look and angrier:" Watch out, blast you! That's the second time you've done that. If you can't control Andover, stand in the centre with Kally and keep out of the way!"

The woman responded with a mirthless grin in passing, and later, crossed so close in front of Cerby doing a small circle at *E-X-P-A-K* as to nearly force Cyrius into the boards. *What the hell?* Cerby muttered to herself, concentrating on the pace and her letters. Fortunately, there were no further incidents for the rest of the lesson.

The riders were sweaty and ready for a wash and refreshments after putting away their horses. They had walked their charges first to cool them down and then stabled them, not forgetting to take some dry straw from the bedding and wipe down any excess dried sweat from the horses' backs. Before leaving the Quad, they made sure the tack was cleaned and put away. Their steeds were left contentedly munching on their dinner (alphalfa cubes, a bit of sweet feed, and carrots) and slurping fresh pails of water.

The four friends walked more or less astride, with Cerby on the outside leading Cyrius back to his stable by the KC a.k.a. Kitchen Courtyard. As they made their way up the winding tarmac driveway, the lanky American who Cerby had had her run-ins with during the ride, stalked past at a faster pace.

"What's her name anyway?" Cerby, still steamed by the arena incidents, inclined her head in the woman's direction, the figure quickly disappearing ahead of them.

"Shasta something," Stevey volunteered.

Bron amended: "Shasta Denning."

Something about that first name had twigged Cerby. She stopped suddenly, midway to the KC and the others did too. "Yes, that's her. How could I forget that little prick!" The others shocked and puzzled at the vehemence of the outburst, came to an abrupt halt. Cyrius, stamping his feet, pranced to the side.

"Don't you remember that snotty-nosed kid whose father was a film, slash, TV scriptwriter for Disney? About six months after I arrived here, he was working up in the North of England somewhere and dumped her off at Alaerton for a couple of weeks. She thought she was a Vanderbilt or something."

Blank looks all around.

Cerby continued." You must remember this. One day I found her in our room Bron. She said she knew I had some North American skin cream that she used too and couldn't find it over here in *BOOTS*. My hands were always chapped. I didn't use many products, but that was an especial favorite of mine; I had several containers. She knew the brand and wanted to buy the lot off me, but I was staying for six months longer so I said: 'No! That's the last of my year's supply.' I also didn't like the way she had busted into our room, without our *say so*. When her two weeks were up, she left alright, and so did my skin cream; the whole supply!"

Bron piped up, the light dawning in her face. "I do recall now. You were furious! You had to get into your suitcase for something, and almost immediately saw the stuff was gone. I helped you look all around the room, the bathrooms, everywhere. Then you stopped and said as if you knew without a doubt: *'I know where it is...'*"

"What a bloody nerve...and to come back here and all!" cried Stevey. "Are you going to confront her Cerb?"

Saffi chorused: "Cheeky Monkey!"

Cerby grimaced. "It *was* a long time ago, granted, and we *were* still in our teens. I'll have to think on it'." But Cerby was uncomfortable. She was fairly sure this Shasta had recognized *HER* long before, and oddly, Shasta seemed to be the one holding a grudge.

Tea served at 4 pm was once again a mass of carbohydrates. Besides the huge *Brown Betty* pots of steeping tea set around the table, there were tiered trays of tarts with little filling, as well as oatmeal cookies and date squares that were in fact, filling. The riders' first aid session with Doctor Wentworth was to proceed in half an hour so the repast was hastily demolished. Without changing their riding clothes, now beginning to smell strongly of horse and hay, they filed into the Common Room which would serve as the lecture room and scattered among the comfy old, distressed leather chairs and sofas.

The good doctor had certainly aged in the ten years since Cerby had been studying for her Horsemaster's exam: salt and pepper close-cropped hair offset by fuzzy Einstein-like eyebrows. Cerby had gone to him 'back in the day' for successful treatment of painful tendonitis and birth control pills, appreciating his straightforward approach as the school's Medical Retainer. On his part, knowing something of her history from Mrs. Hill, Dr. Wentworth had been prepared despite his bachelor status, to be 'uncle-ish' if the need ever arose.

Before launching into 'Basic First Aid for the Rider,' Wentworth reminded his audience that when the 'I' gave a lecture the next day - same time, same place - it would be on veterinary medicine. Placing hands on hips, head thrust forward in lecture mode, he looked sternly around the room.

"You can't expect to be sitting on a half-ton and more of raw power and not expect that you might get seriously hurt, although goodness knows most of you riders think you're totally indestructible." He shook his head in mock resignation, but nevertheless began to re-educate them all on the basic tenets of rider safety. Cerby's mind began to drift.

She'd only been at Alaerton a month or so. She'd been given an assignment; trusted to walk solo across the 50 Acre Field, cross the county road at the far gate to another pasture, and march back to the Quad with a couple of feisty colts in tow. A crotchety old farmer had been leaning up against the fence watching her transit with the horses, proffering up his stone-

*cold visage in response to her friendly smile.
His animosity was palpable. Like a portent he
had cried out to her: 'My brother broke 'is fool
neck in an 'unting accident. You just watch it
don't 'ap to you my girl!' It had unsettled her,
coming out of the blue as it did, though she had
shrugged him off as being the local curmudgeon
cum village idiot. It did reinforce however that
safety should never be too far behind in her
thoughts.*

She came back to herself and paid strict attention
to what the doctor described as 'Masterly Inactivity'
or *the art of doing nothing* i.e., if you didn't know
what to do in the case of broken bones, possible
neck injury etc. then, *Do No Harm*! The doctor held
up a cell phone. "This is the single most important
item to carry in your first aid kit," holding it high
above his head and turning around so everyone
could see. "Call Emergency at 112 or 999 if you
witness a serious accident and wait for instructions.
I don't want to hear of anyone going out on a 'hack'
without one, and always, **always** use the buddy
system so that if one is injured the other can call for
help. It's only common sense," he added gruffly.

"So: to business!" He began handing out triangles
of cloth to accompany a cursory lecture on
bandaging for stabilizing injuries and embedded
objects. There was much giggling and some mild
profanities as the women tried not to create
'mummies' out of their patients.

Mrs. Hill poked her nose into the room, and the
Doctor dropped everything to be by her side. They
chatted in lowered voices. Once or twice Cerby

heard the word 'idler' and 'Jasper' from Mrs. H and the more severe 'useless layabout' and 'I'll have a word, alright' from Wentworth. Then Mrs. Hill withdrew, obviously in a bit of a flap, leaving Doctor Wentworth exhibiting some consternation before he resumed his position by the desk at the front of the room. Cerby saw him glance at the closed door with a steely determination she'd not witnessed in him before.

Her attention however was diverted to her first aid duties. As Cerby had no partner, Bron had offered to be hers. Cerby couldn't tie her shoelaces, let alone create horse-bandages that stayed in place, but Bron with her more advanced veterinary experience capably instructed Cerby in the basics. Cerby enjoyed the repartee during the session, feeling like Bron and herself were making some headway in recapturing their youthful friendship. At the end of the session, Cerby punned: 'Is that a wrap?' rewarded by a mock-censorious smile from Bron.

That evening, back in the dorm wing: "Whew! It's been a long day hasn't it Bron?" Cerby allowed herself to fall languidly backwards on to her twin bed. Light coming in through the double-hung windows above was already feebler and slanting. It would be dark soon.

Bron however, was once again in a concentrated way going through her dresser drawers, only this time putting clothing away *into* the suitcase open on the bed.

What the...Is she taking that stuff to the laundromat or doesn't she like rooming with me anymore?

Because Cerby's radar was picking up signs of an

underlying skittishness in Bron, she decided not to tackle her friend outright but rather just to *try* and engage her in conversation.

"So, we'll finally get to see Ewan again tonight, Bron!" Cerby could hardly keep the enthusiasm out of her voice. "Can't wait, can you? Can you believe it's been a decade since he and I used to tryst on the so-called *Bridge of Sighs* in Alconbury? Not that I was complaining then. Certainly not now either."

No response from Bron, who was fastidiously arranging her socks. Cerby felt it was like pulling teeth to get a reaction. *Darn it*! She had a fuse too, and despite her earlier intentions to move slowly, now *she* was getting fed up with Bron's reticent ways. Having decided to voice her true feelings, she gathered up a bath robe.

"You know Bron, you might at least *appear* to be a little more interested in this reunion. It *has* been years, and we certainly all liked each other *once*!" In a huff she departed through the doorway, missing the turn of Bron's head and the concern on her face.

At supper, Cerby could hardly contain herself on the hard benches of the *Long Room*, squirming so much that Saffi pinched her thigh in annoyance. 'Ouch!' She jerked back, glaring at Saffi.

Cerby had made a special effort to put on a little make up and brush through her virtually untameable curly hair. '*Damn English climate! A wig couldn't stay straight in this humidity.*'

Although she wore her second-best camel breeches (having drawn the short straw to do late haying that night) she had also selected a form fitting, crisp open-necked white blouse with three-quarter cuffed sleeves that very much complimented her colour and features.

"A bit '*ton*-y' this evening, aren't you Cerb? Sleepy horses won't notice," sniffed Saffi under her breath. She and Stevey exchanged a meaningful glance, making no attempt to stifle the ensuing laughter. They knew why Cerby was on pins and needles and let fly a few appropriate romantic barbs summoning up Jane Eyre and Rochester, Heathcliff and Catherine. Cerby ignored them but couldn't help but wonder why Bron was nowhere in sight to add her *two cents*. She was more annoyed at Bron's absence than the tongue-in-cheek jibes from her other two friends, having saved a spot beside her for Bron, wanting to make up for her own churlishness earlier.

Mrs. Hill appeared by the stone fireplace before supper was to be served, trusting that everyone had had a great day (this being accompanied by fake moans or cheers from individuals in the audience). Then she turned to her left and waved a hand to the exit door, announcing the arrival of the 'I' - British Horse Society Instructor and Alaerton's de facto manager, Ewan Ogilvy. Striding confidently to her side, Ewan gave Mrs. Hill an affectionate peck on the cheek before turning to the audience.

Cerby panicking, was of two minds: shrink back behind the others in order to tentatively inspect Ewan over Stevey's head OR, *accidentally* fall off the bench to attract his attention. She behaved like a young filly, actually quivering with excitement.

He still looked the same: just on six feet, lanky build, flinty eyes like a stormy sky. Even the hunter green *Outback Short Duster* oilskin he wore looked familiar, (or perhaps it was 2nd or 3rd generation.) The barest indication of gray beginning to show around his sideburns only added distinction to his dark chestnut hair. The familiar mouth crinkled as he smiled in acknowledgment of the group before him.

After welcoming them all back to Alaerton, the 'I' started to talk seriously about his lecture tomorrow and what would be expected in the pseudo-Horsemaster's test on the day of the fête. Concern being etched on the faces of the *Reunionistas*, he assured them there would be a preliminary run-through first, and that he was available for consultation any time during the day if anyone had questions. He reminded them all it was for a worthy cause: promoting Alaerton and fundraising for the RSPCA. 'Just do your best.' He explained that he had been away on a tour of equitation centres in Scotland the last few weeks but informed the listeners he could now be found in his current digs, the stone cottage at the back of the property, if necessary.

This was news to Cerby. *Why hadn't anyone mentioned that he lived on site?* She perched well off the edge of her seat, poking into the aisle ostentatiously so that he couldn't help but notice her. Her eyes sparkled with anticipation.

Won't he be surprised!

She mentally fast-forwarded a cinematic reel of her reunion with Ewan:

Glancing around the room, suddenly connecting with smoldering eyes, he'll abandon conversations in mid-speech. Bounding down the length of the Long Room, knocking over tables in his wake but oblivious of the crowd, I'll be swept up in his arms and twirled. (Um, yes, maybe not twirled, just ate.) *Locking lips sensually, he'll murmur softly: 'It's been so long Cerby, so terribly long....'*

Instead, when Ewan was finishing up his monologue, he swept the room with his eyes, smiled casually at several people he seemed to know already, nodded briefly on seeing her, and continued talking for a few minutes more on the importance of using appropriate tack for the Musical Ride, again emphasizing the importance of the fête to Alaerton's future. Then he calmly walked off the floor in the direction he came in, with Cerby now half off her seat in amazement at the lack of acknowledgment. Was this the man who had proposed all those years ago? She began to burn a blotchy red as Stevey and Saffi looked at her with concern.

"That **WAS t**he same Ewan you wrote to us about, after we'd all scattered to the four winds, wasn't it?" Stevey suspended a celery stick in mid-air, puzzled.

Saffi couldn't help but add solicitously; "You know, I don't think he recognized you Cerby, um, after ten years. Perhaps you should try to catch him up. Maybe he 's just gone all myopic."

Cerby was way ahead of that directive. Pushing back the heavy bench seating, she walked swiftly back to the other exit in the room that led to the hall entrance and corridor linking to the mudroom and Kitchen Courtyard.

She stepped into the hallway thinking Ewan might have been waylaid by Mrs. Hill. Surely, he'd have to come her way to exit out the KC in the direction of the *'I's Cottage, (*as the domestic structure had always been referred to, whoever was in residence.) Her smile quickly faded. She'd been stopped in her tracks on seeing in the dim light of the mudroom, Bron reaching up to stroke Ewan's face and the two locked in a long, loving, and what looked like – very familiar embrace.

Cerby felt rooted to the spot, mouth open, unable to move with the impact of the scene. The lovers were not immediately aware of her presence. She didn't know whether to stay or go.

Bron made the decision for her by being the first to turn in her direction. She pulled on Ewan's sleeve, and he also became aware of Cerby's presence. They both tentatively started toward her, Bron 's concern written openly (for once) across her face and Ewan gently steering Bron behind him.

Really? Although WE are not amused, reports of my temper have been greatly exaggerated...

Cerby was used to saving face in romantic situations; rejection in relationships was certainly nothing new and by now she sourly reflected, she'd had more than her share. She pulled her wits about her and smiled wanly as her leaden feet moved forward and her hands stretched out in front of her (seemingly of their own accord) in a semblance of greeting.

"Ewan, how nice to see you," she managed to croak out, as he hugged her warmly if a bit awkwardly also: "...and Bron? Well, this is ...something. I mean, um, to all be back together again?"

Suddenly Bron's mysterious behaviour - the holding back - all made sense. Cerby felt unreasonably betrayed, by both, but she wasn't about to let her true feelings show. She'd had a great deal of practise in subordinating them to her will, and she especially wouldn't explode like they were expecting. Anger management therapy in her twenties had helped control mild emotional outbursts; still, no one wanted to be on the end of her rapier wit.

Funny how you can be thinking two things in the same instance. A decade's passage of time and distance could not now be denied. The foolishness of her previous schoolgirl daydream smacked her in the jaw like a right upper cut. However, just like a boxer rising in the ring she put on a brave face, preparing for *round two* by agreeing (as always, without thinking) to Ewan's slightly forced invitation to a dinner party - with the two of them at *'their'* cottage *'one night soon.'* Bron tried to mitigate Ewan's insensitivity, adding solicitously that perhaps Cerby's American friends might consider coming as well.

The underlying shock of Bron and Ewan's relationship still lay thinly veiled under the faux smile on Cerby's face. "Yes of course, they'd love that," she quickly confirmed on behalf of Mitch and

Monte. (She wouldn't be able to face that trauma alone, that was certain.)

Somehow, in an emotional fog, Cerby managed to extricate herself with a few other small pleasantries. Mercifully, she found her way back to the dining room where she rather fell into her seat.

"Well, any *joy* Cerby?"

Stevey and Saffi slowly pried the story out of her, just as surprised to hear about Bron and Ewan.

"Zounds! There's a deep one," pronounced a wide-eyed Stevey.

The two women did their level best to divert Cerby's attention during the rest of the supper hour. It was plain however, from her lack of appetite and poking at her food, that an inner dialogue was the only conversation worth having in the event. At last, she roused herself and prepared to exit, with the excuse of having to do the late haying duties in the stable Quad. She dismissed offers of help from Stevey and Saffi who wisely didn't push the issue, and quickly left behind the chatter and clatter of the *Long Room*, making a beeline to Cyrius' stall.

"Poor ole Cyrius." She stroked his forehead and soft muzzle absently. He seemed to feel her distress. *What a downright fool,* she denigrated herself silently; *especially after ten years, for Pete's sake! 'Time and Tide wait for no man.' And no woman either I guess, but why am I always the one caught in the undertow? "*

Feeling sorry for herself, her eyes moistened. She hugged the big horse's neck as if clinging to a life buoy." Well, you'll always be my best guy, won't you Cyrius…for ever and ever. That at least will **never** change!"

Communing with the big animal for a few minutes calmed Cerby, gradually toning down her perspective of the evening's events. Even she had begun to admit to herself that Bron and Ewan fit together like Celtic spoons. They both loved the country life and horses. They would devote their entire lives to equestrian pursuits, something Cerby acknowledged, would never have worked between Ewan and herself. Horses were a passion in *her* life (one of many) but not a *raison d'être*. Life was a smorgasbord she was fond of saying —and meant it!

Silly of me really, letting all the emotions of the original infatuation (*infestation more-like*) carry her away without thinking about the current reality at all. *Amazing.* And she had to admit that *at the time,* she had been too young: totally vulnerable and lonely with the loss of her folks, and eventually abandoned by her friends as well as they all left Alaerton for the wider world.

In stroking and fondling the big horse, on sad reflection she began the process of mentally divorcing herself from, and deconstructing, that old relationship. An image popped into her brain of a carpet bag plastered with travel stickers: '*Who needs one bloke when you can have twenty cats,*' and perhaps a bit cruder, (along the lines of Dante's hellish perspective); '*Abandon hope, all ye who enter 'her'.*

It further helped assuage her feelings to have to carry out the late haying routine, starting with checking Cyrius' water, bedding and hay net before a final kiss on the muzzle. "Sleep tight m'boy," she nuzzled him back affectionately, closing and bolting the bottom half of the Dutch door of his stall. She retraced her steps 'round the building, over the ancient cobbles of the KC, to the gated tarmacked driveway that led down to the Quad.

Only twenty more to do ....

Cerby had to keep her eyes to the ground as she walked to stay on the path. The black tarmac blended into the advanced twilight and there was no lighting along this stretch. As she rounded a slight bend the stable yard complex came into full view. It was set up as a large square, with one story rectangular buildings on all four sides and a black 'macadam' (easily swept) interior courtyard. Closest to her as she came in onto the North-west corner were stalls *1* through *5*, plus the tack and feed rooms. Adjacent in the next building were stalls *6* to *12*, and the next to that, *13* to *20*. The last side of the Quadrangle housed four oversized stalls for any horses *16.5 h* or taller, and a couple of general storage areas for tools and miscellaneous.

She stopped first to pick up a wheelbarrow, then directed her feet to the feed room. Work had always been the best panacea for emotional upset, so now Cerby turned her attention to the late haying regimen 'with a will,' effectively blocking out the evening's turn of events. (Flagellating herself mentally for all her silly expectations wouldn't put the horses to bed!). Once she had picked out her tools, she went into the tack room to check the official Feed Schedule Board to see if there were any mounts with special diet requirements. With satisfaction she noted Alaerton's stable regimen had not changed much over the years - Mrs. H had obviously seen to that.

She determined that only one horse, Merriweather, was to get a pre-emptive bran mash as he'd had a serious colon impaction recently and it was to be supposed, this would keep his 'miles' of intestines in working order and prevent a recurrence. She hoped she wouldn't have to go back up to the Inn and ask what was required; she certainly didn't want to see or talk to anybody just now, particularly the 'I'. Anyway, did she not use to make mashes for Cyrius as a prophylactic treat every Sunday, years ago?

What were those ingredients now?

It was coming back to her. She put on the kettle, (*mashes are best served warm* she reminded herself) and passing on to the bran bin, poured a couple of cans full into a feed bucket. She julienned some carrots from the fresh food bin and added in a cup of corn oil and a touch of molasses. *No sweet feed,* she chided herself as she passed that bin - *too 'heating.'* With the addition of some of the boiling water, she stirred the whole into a 'mash.' She espied a barrel of apples and decided to chop and add one or two of those too for good measure. She'd get this out to Merriweather first in stall *#8* and then start checking all hay nets to be sure they were full and top up where necessary, making sure also the water pails were also full for the night and reasonably clean of debris; (all of them would be cleaned first thing before breakfast and filled with fresh water.) A quick look at the salt and mineral licks' status would complete the job in each stall.

She turned the wheelbarrow toward *#8*, having put in the pail of mash along with a couple of square flaked bales of hay for Merriweather. A big Bay, he eyed her warily as she opened his stall door but immediately he espied the mash pail, she had to fight him off and push him back - leaning hard into his chest with all her weight. She'd barely got the pail emptied into his feed box when he was scoffing down the treat to ecstatic swaying and energetic grunts. She had to back out quickly herself before he stepped on her and broke some toes in his enthusiasm.

Merriweather's hay net being full she went out to do the next stall inspection, figuring she would make her way from that point around the *Quad*, ending back at stall #7. It was only then she noticed the lights in the courtyard were off, and none of the metal encased lights in the stalls were on either. Only the faint bare-bulbed tack room light was on; she had turned that switch herself. She recalled the main lighting switch board would be in there as well. Well, she'd do a few more stalls on this side and then go back to the tack room and turn on the outside lights for the night, unless a fuse had gone. If that were the case, she would *have to* ask for help up at the Inn. No rush however on that score; her eyes had become somewhat accustomed to the dark which had descended quickly.

She heaved up the wheelbarrow and proceeded to check stalls #9 through #12, and from what she could see and by fumbling around in these stalls, those horses were set for food and water.

In maneuvering her way out of stall #12 however, levering the wheelbarrow as she walked backward towards #13 in the corner, she suddenly tripped over something, falling heavily backward on what felt like a sack of feed. One wrist landed hard on the tarmac. Her anger at the resulting shooting pain and someone else's laziness in leaving a feed sack where anyone might stumble into it, merged into dismay within seconds as she realized the other hand she was trying to use to upright herself, had slid into a sticky mire of some sort.

This better not be a pile of horse shit! she thought crossly, already damning the students whose task it was to sweep and clean the courtyard thoroughly before supper. Sulkily, she held the offending limb far out to the side away from her clothing, her nose crinkling in disgust at the thought of what she had landed in. *Probably ruined my shirt.* When however, she had to put this same hand down and behind again on the ground to push off and up, in descending shock waves she immediately realized this was *NOT* a 75 kg bag of grain she had come to rest upon!

Swiftly, in a totally ungainly manner - trying not to lean back or pushing off using her injured wrist - she rolled off to the side and rose from her knees, turning and stumbling back unsteadily a few feet once she was upright again. Movement ceased at that point, and rooted to the spot, she had a clearer picture of what lay before her. Even in the dark, she couldn't be mistaken. It was a body alright! Absolutely no movement of any kind. Her first thought: *Oh no, not again! Bloody hell! Monte and Mitch will kill me!*

Still standing immobilized with fear and dread, Cerby took a full minute to get her bearings and breathing under control again, recalling Doctor Wentworth's recent incitation to 'Masterly Inactivity.' Aping the flight-animals she tended however, she spun on her heel doing a quick 360 - degree scan of the Quad, weakly calling out: "Is anybody here?"

As soon as she had uttered the cry, she regretted drawing attention to herself in case there actually *had* been someone lurking about. *You idiot!* She railed at herself.

As there was no response however, and no nervous movements within the stalls to indicate anything was out of order (the horses would have picked up on it) she concluded she was well and truly alone, and that any violence must have occurred at some earlier point.

On impulse as a Good Samaritan, she forced herself to approach the body in the remote event CPR was required, for instinctively she was already quite certain that nothing could be done to revive this poor soul. On bended knee, she ascertained that this was true. There were no sounds of any kind and as she laid her hand tentatively on the person's back, no regular rise and fall of breath. On top of that, it had been her right wrist as she fell backward, that had come down in what could be determined now to be a pool of blood. Her fingers moving gingerly up the back towards the body's head, encountering

81

a wound at the base, hair sticky and matted from the trauma. Cerby just managed to stop herself from wiping her hand on her breeches as she reactively jumped up.

There would have to be a phone in the tack room connected to the Main House she reasoned; she should call in the emergency...And she *would* do that, but her curiosity was already bubbling to the surface after the initial shock. This after all was not the first instance of its kind that had occurred to Cerby. She'd dealt with dead bodies before.

The question is, as she looked around for corroboration - *was this an accident?* Perhaps the man (for this much was easily clarified) had stepped on a rake, fallen, hit his head; or maybe he'd been kicked by a horse and stumbled into the yard. All sorts of scenarios were already propagating in her fertile imagination. One thing that Cerby *couldn't* shake however, was an attendant feeling of malignancy.

Though the dark night had descended in earnest, there was a three-quarter moon in a cloudless sky shedding a feeble light on the scene. Her eyes being acclimated to the dimness, some details were immediately apparent.

From where she stood it was easy to see the outward details: a middle-aged man, blue collar sort, dressed in non-descript denim shirt and pants, quilted vest and mucky 'Wellies.' He was lying flat on his face, nose first and hard against the tarmac, half in, half out of the dark glistening pool of blood. There was a clout of dirty straw and manure matted into his own greying hair, just above the ugly wound and largish indent on the backside of his head. Not far from one out-flung hand was a torch whose crystal had been smashed in the fall.

Carefully balanced on tip toes, the one shocking fact that came to light as soon as she began to move slowly, mechanically in a wide circle around the corpse, was that it now seemed obvious he had been hit from behind by a large mucking out spade that itself lay strewn just to the left of his feet. She was extremely careful not to disturb anything that might matter later to the police: she surely had at least learned that from past experience!

Hmmm. Pockets? No, I'd have to turn him over first. That would be too gross…

She cast a last look around at what would soon be called a crime scene. The only thing to flash white in the night was a small piece of paper blown up by the breeze against the stall door of #13. Even in such a circumstance, her training kicked in. She picked it up with the unconscious motivation of an educated groomsman, knowing sometimes even the smallest piece of detritus could make a horse 'shy.' She jammed the refuse into her own pocket and instantly forgot about it. There was obviously a much bigger mess to contend with here. Leaving her own wheelbarrow and tools where they rested, she backed away then and ran for the tack room.

Trying to keep her *inside voice* from becoming an '*outside voice*,' she dialed the Main House extension on Alaerton's own local system, but it surprised even herself who she immediately asked for: "Hello. Mrs. Momfrey? Um… Is Ewan still there, please? Oh, he is? Good. Can you get him for me? Rather urgent. Yes, a problem in the stable (*you could say so!*). Thanks Mrs. Momfrey."

She waited for what seemed an interminable age before Ewan picked up the phone. "Ewan, it's Cerby! Can you come straight away to the Quad? (Unnecessarily she added, as no farm manager would be caught dead without one …) Bring a cell phone. Hurry!"

She hung up, a delayed reaction setting in. Shivering, she hugged herself. In no time however, she heard the sound of heavy gum boots running down the tarmac. It could only be Ewan. She stood in the light of the tack room to greet him, her face wan and resigned.

"What is it? You sounded so strange, Cerby?" Ewan was in decent shape but still a bit out of breath. There was a touch of annoyance in his voice as well. "You didn't call me down here 'urgently' just to have a private chat I hope Cerby, because that wouldn't be cricket in my view."

So, he *had* been aware of her emotional turmoil after all. Or had Bron clued him in? *Men!* Cerby, genuinely peeked (a*lways got to be about them!)* wanted to say haughtily: '*Get over yourself*' but instead, getting back to the business at hand pointed dramatically to the barely distinguishable lump in the far corner of the Quad. "I'd call *that* an EMERGENCY, wouldn't YOU?"

Ewan glanced in the direction she was pointing, the corpse and the murder weapon now totally discernable as Cerby switched on all the interior and exterior lighting. "What…?" Then he recognized the figure and raced over: "Jasper!"

"Jasper? Is that Mrs. H's hired man?" whispered Cerby breathlessly as she quietly sidled up to Ewan who was kneeling down, repeating her test for breath and warmth. "He was dead when I tripped …ah...found him. Did you know him well?"

Ewan stood up, putting his hands in his pockets, staring thoughtfully at the body. "No. He's only been here a month-odd and I've been away a lot lately on the show 'circuit.' It was Mrs. Hill who took him on, on recommendation by someone I think, or maybe not …I don't really know. Damn, this will leave us short!"

Ewan coloured and looked apologetically at Cerby. "Sorry, that sounds pretty cold in the circumstances. Just popped into my head because we've got so much on in the next couple of weeks and it's important we make a success of it. It's bloody hard to find horse-farm labourers these days; they don't get paid much and it's too much work for a lot of them." Casting a glance at the corpse. "Sometimes one has to settle ..."

Cerby remembered the doctor's chagrin at the mention of Jasper's name but bit her tongue.

"Agreed. But could we call the police or something Ewan? We can't just leave him here. And who's going to tell Mrs. H? And the others?" Standing so close to Ewan was awkward now in and of itself, and Cerby herself wanting nothing more than to leave the scene of sudden and violent death.

Ewan at this prompt, slipped effortlessly into his role as the 'I' and exhibited the control and discipline that was second nature to him. He called the police on his cell phone immediately, giving a curt description of the problem and clipped driving instructions. Next, he called Bron at the Main House to ask Mrs. Momfrey to arrange for additional pots of tea, and to take Mrs. Hill into her office and await us there. Then he went into the tack room and took a horse blanket down from a shelf and went back and laid it carefully over Jasper's body. Straightening up, he said slowly: "Cerby, I think you'd best go up to the Inn and be with Mrs. Hill. Advise only those on a *need-to-know* basis what has happened. I'll wait by the body for the police."

Cerby still felt vulnerable herself. *How secure was anyone's safety? And the body wasn't going anywhere; what was the point of guarding it? Surely, he would escort her back up to the Inn?* (Ewan reassured her, confident in and complimentary of her courageous nature.) Shivering but mindful of her own image, Cerby told herself: *It would be to no purpose to acquaint him with the truth on that score.*

"Will you be alright Ewan?" When it was plain by the lack of response and his concentration on the crime scene that he expected her to leave without further ado, she started off, not much liking the 150-yard walk back to the Main House on her own. In the dark and the faint moonbeams, everything took on a sinister cast and although she believed the perpetrator would hardly have hung around after committing the deed, the question remained: w*as it someone here?* Unsettling to say the least.

Stevey and Saffi were first at the kitchen door to greet her, expecting Ewan to come back and let those that witnessed his speedy departure know what the urgent problem had been. They were ready to descend on the Quad if need be, for the horses' or Cerby's sake. Cerdwyn quickly drew them off into a secluded corner of the pantry by the huge old Aga stove and in hushed tones informed them of the circumstances. She put her finger over her lips, 'Shhhhsh!" when both Saffi and Stevey reacted predictably enough.

"What? Here?"

"A murder? Are you joking Cerby? Is this you having us on? This isn't our *Truth or Dare* night; we haven't even scheduled that in yet!"

It took a minute or so to get the 'truth' through to them both and they were eventually able to pick up on Cerby's strained face for verification. "I'm just going to take Mrs. H some tea and we'll wait for Ewan there."

"I think Bron's with her now," offered Stevey.

"Do you think Mrs. Hill would mind if we *all* waited with her?" Concern filled Saf's deep blue eyes.

"I would say *the more the merrier* normally, although in these circumstances..." Cerby hesitated only a fraction: 'But yes Saf; why not? Let's all go in."

Cerby was pleased herself for the company. They marched off to Mrs. Hill's private quarters, intercepting Mrs. Momfrey on the way and relieving her of her burden. Wielding her kidnapped tea tray before them like a crucifix warding off vampires, they entered the private sanctum of Alaerton's owner.

Bron looked up as her three friends came quietly into the room. Ewan had only told her to stay with

Mrs. Hill but given no particulars. She had been bending over a seated Mrs. Hill whose pale face turned now also in their direction, displaying concern and puzzlement. Doctor Wentworth was an unexpected presence, especially wearing a wrathful expression. His hand lay protectively on Mrs. Hill's shoulder.

"What's happened? Is there a problem in the stables? Not fire, is it?" (Always a stable manager's first and worst nightmare). The Doctor seemed to be taking the interrogation lead, warning off any upheaval from affecting Mrs. Hill whose hand angled up over her bosom to pat Dr. Wentworth's, (thankful for the masculine support Cerby guessed.) Saffi, unusually, took the initiative of pouring a cuppa for Mrs. Hill and offering others to those gathered in the room.

Cerby knew no other way to speak than to say things forthrightly: "Mrs. H. I'm afraid there's been an accident. *No, call a spade a spade - the irony of the thought not lost on her in that split second.* I'm afraid it actually looks like murder. (This statement accompanied by gasps from Bron and Mrs. Hill.) It appears that the …ah...victim, unfortunately Mrs. H, is Jasper - your hired man."

"Jasper?" Mrs. Hill's hand pulled out of the Doctor's and dropped to her lap. She seemed not to be taking in first, that it was a murder and second, the murderee." But Jasper had asked for the evening off. Are you quite certain it's him? Murdered?"

Doctor Wentworth looked on with solicitous care at Mrs. H, but Cerby distinctly heard him mutter: 'lazy blighter' under his breath, and on second glance, the practitioner didn't appear to show either much concern or disbelief, only relief?

Cerby nodded emphatically: "It's Jasper alright. Ewan identified him Mrs. H" Then she filled them in on everything from the start of her late haying regimen. It suddenly occurred to her: "Shi...ugar! (An automatic admonition died on Mrs. Hill's lips - nodding approvingly at the 'good catch'. She had never tolerated foul language at the school.) The rest of the horses, they need to have their hay nets and water checked. I 'd only just got started." Cerby half rose from her chair but just then Ewan entered, followed by a capped constable.

Ewan motioned her to sit down. "I've done it already Cerby, while I was waiting for the police to arrive." *There's a true horseman* Cerby thought with vestiges of possessive pride:

'No matter how weary and hungry you are after a long day in the saddle, always tend to your horse's nightly needs before your own.'   - *Code of the West*

"Constable Bayer has asked to talk to you in particular Cerby, and then he'll want to talk to all the residents. Constable, I suggest you use the Common Room for your interviews. Mrs. Hill, I'm very sorry for all the upset. Jasper has been positively identified. Nothing for it, I'm afraid."

Mrs. Hill slumped back despondent in her chair although Cerby was surprised to see a fleeting look of relief, in tune with Doctor Wentworth apparently. She guessed that what had been a working relationship between Mrs. Hill and Jasper, had not been an entirely pleasant one, only forged by circumstance.

Mrs. H doesn't look too, too upset. Nobody does. But who knew him that well? It felt wrong in the circumstances: *'just a hired hand?'*

Seeing her distress, Stevey sidled up to Cerby and whispered: "He'd a bit of a reputation around the barn for being snarly and somewhat uncooperative taking orders from Mrs. Hill. Somebody commented once to me they'd heard: 'he'd *get around to chores when he was damn well good and ready'*. Bit of a ladies' man besides, apparently. Mustn't speak ill of the dead though, " she finished up charitably.

"Bron. Can I see you for a moment?" Ewan whisked her out of the room. An awkward silence descended on the group. Even sipping quietly from their teacups seemed conspicuous in the silence surrounding the circumstances as minutes ticked by.

Bron returned in short order though, with practical instructions. "Constable Bayer. I've set up the Common Room for your interviews. There's a desk, an external landline with cordless telephone and computer access as well if you need it."

"Well, *that's* efficient!" Cerby couldn't keep an acerbic note out of her response, but immediately regretted it when Bron turned on her heel, the Constable in tow. The rest of the group repared to the *Long Room* where all the residents had been asked to congregate. The dining tables had been cleared except for tea trays, all the women nervously sipping and chatting amongst themselves. Doctor Wentworth took proprietorship of Mrs. Hill, consoling her, for there was no doubt such an incident couldn't have come at a worse time, what with Alaerton's fortunes resting on a single throw of the die – the anniversary celebration and associated Midsummer Fête. The *Reunionistas,* occupying all corners of the room, quietly mulled over the implications. Mrs. Hill couldn't help but wince at some of the comments:

'A murder they say!'

'Stabbed to death!'

'Brains blown out?'

'Does this mean the Fête won't go ahead then?'

'This is hardly what one expects at a 25th anniversary reunion, is it?'

Constable Bayer, standing at the front of the Long Room, outlined what he wanted from his audience. In short, he would speak to everyone currently on the premises in turn this evening and get their statements; find out who was missing if any; and he advised nobody was to leave the property until given permission.

'But I've got a hair appointment tomorrow,' one of the women moaned. Shasta Denning politely asked if she could keep a banking commitment in town. Another pleaded: 'I have to go to London for the day to meet with an estate agent. It's only an hour away by train…?'

The chorus was just getting stronger when Constable Bayer raised his hand and advised them all: "First things first ladies. Let's get all these statements over and done. The D.I. will be here in the morning and you can apply to him for Permissions." The Constable congratulated himself for passing that chore off on to the D.I. *Nothing like a flock of well-heeled dollies to have to deal with…*

Cerby's interview with Constable Bayer turned out to be relatively short. She was asked to detail her movements from the minute she left the Wheatsheaf proper. Ewan stood in as Witness to the Police Interviews, a duty the Constable would normally have performed for his Superior, Detective Inspector Wallace, had the Inspector not been away from the vicinity until the morrow. Cerby was a bit embarrassed when it came to recounting her visit to Cyrius first, before the late haying. She saw in Ewan's eyes, as she lowered hers, a quick and sympathetic understanding as to why she had gone *there* after her encounter with him and Bron. This small interaction went a long way in restoring Ewan to his former status in Cerby's estimation.

The remaining events had happened so quickly, there really wasn't that much to tell. The Constable was the one to emphasize the salient points: "And you say the stable lights weren't on?"

Cerby suddenly realized the importance of that - because the last person going up to supper would have turned on both the exterior Quad and KC courtyard lighting as well as the interior stall lights for the *Late Hayer*. "So, it had to have been pre-meditated," she murmured to herself.

"Miss," Constable Bayer waggled a finger and strongly cautioned her; "*you* are not to repeat anything that goes on in this room to anyone. Is that clear!" And of course, Cerby nodded obediently whilst in her head already forming the conversation she was about to have with Saffi and Stevey.

But first, she had been shockingly negligent in communicating with the 'Boys,' (and they with her, when it came to that.) There was an old style pay phone in the hallway outside the *Long Room* and as she was not in the habit of carrying her cell phone with her while working, (or prepared to pay exorbitant roaming charges whilst in England) she made a beeline to it. She listened for the coins to drop one after the other, then cupping her hand around the receiver to mute her voice, called through to the *Highwayman Pub and Lodging* in Alconbury asking to be connected to their room. Thankfully, Monte answered, although by now as it was close to midnight, his voice sounded slightly resentful.

"Cerby, of course it 's you! There's only one person who'd call us this late, and *in this country*. You *have* set your clock to the right time, haven't you? It *has* been a couple of days since we landed, so you can't claim jet lag. Were you just out bingeing with your friends?"

Innocently: "Did I wake you, Monte? Is Mitch up?" She practically ate the phone, whispering more urgently; "I've got something important to tell you."

Mitch, obviously hanging over Monte's shoulder, catching every word and changing gears mercurially as was his wont, cut her off with some enthusiasm of his own. "So do we Old Sock! Honestly, this trip was such a brilliant idea. I've never seen Monte so happy. He's snapping pictures hither and yon of all these lych-gate thingies. We even took the rental and day tripped to Cambridge. That photo nymph is in 7th heaven, and if *he's* delirious, so am I...."

"Mitch! Be quiet for a moment will you. The *Banshee's* been at it again, the...."

"Beg Pardon Cerb, did you say; 'can *she* do it again'? I don't think Monte would like to hear that coming from you, Cerb."

"Mitch! Will you take the worsted wool out of your ears! I said *Banshee. Bannn - shee* dammit!"

Mitch stopped and drew in a long breath, responding sternly: "Cerby. You are *not* trying to suggest... *Please* tell me. Say you are *not* involved in another murder most foul, *pleasssse.*"

Silence at her end of the line rather confirmed than denied the charge. Then in a small voice: "Sorry Mitch; it wasn't my fault."

Monte broke in, voice rough from fatigue and obviously manhandling the receiver. "This is so typical Cerb. It's *always* your fault. Murder follows you around like a 'dementor' for heaven's sake. What is it this time? Contract out on an Olympic rider; local knight errant impaled on his lance?"

Cerby interrupted the criticism and as quickly as possible explained the circumstances. Her friends cooled down somewhat when the event seemed contained to the school and it appeared it wouldn't affect their primary goal now which was researching and photographing some of the quainter structures in the area.

"You know guys, you *might* be a bit more concerned about *my* welfare then your own artistic pursuits. I mean, who knows if the killer is somebody still on the premises?"

"Oh, I hardly think so, *Old Trout.*"

The growl at the other the end of the line was completely ignored.

"It sounds like a pretty straightforward murder to me - maybe gambling debts, or cuckoldry? Something like that, Lass.*"

Lass? "And what may I ask, makes you say that?" asked Cerby, the grinding of teeth almost audible.

"Why, the mere fact the lights were off. Somebody meant to do the deed of course. Not a crime of passion. The perp would have lain in wait, done the deed and is probably long out of the country by now. You mark my words, that's what it will turn out to be. You're all as *safe as houses*."

Cerby found this quick and simple deduction, so in line with her own and apparently the Constable's, irritating but comforting at the same time. When Mitch finished off by saying he and Monte would see if they could make a quick visit out to the stable in the morning, she felt even better.

They said their goodnights but as Monte put down the phone, she could still hear them good naturedly squabbling in the background. Fond as ever she was of the two of them, she sighed heavily. *When was she ever going to find her own soulmate? (*Any thoughts free ranging back to her homeland *on that score*, however, were quickly put out of mind.*)*

A quick glance into the *Long* and Common Rooms showed that the police and all her school mates had departed which meant all the statements must also have been collected to the constabulary's satisfaction. Just about everybody had gone to bed.

No doubt there was a sentry of sorts posted somewhere out on the property.

Cerby made her way slowly upstairs. She was not looking forward to confronting Bron. If it had been awkward before, how awkward would it be now, as 'roomies'? She flushed, thinking of her earlier expectations in reuniting with Ewan, all played out in front of his current squeeze, Bron.

Fortunately, Bron's bed was still made up and the room empty. *Of course! She'd want to be with Ewan tonight if he's been away for a few weeks. Given the same circumstances, so would I. Can't blame her for that.* Although in fact she did.

She disrobed quickly. Finally blanketed up, sheets kicked into submission at the bottom of her bed, the heat of her emotions began to rise again. Pulling the covers up to her chin, she saw herself once again, slim and sassy, not even out of her teens, falling 'head over' for Ewan the dashing Horsemaster and *A.I.* Her first real love. He had proposed, but she had disposed. It had been such an important episode in her life, happening as it did so soon after the death of her parents. But she must have realized intuitively back then, that neither the timing nor Ewan was quite right. She wouldn't have gone back to Vermont otherwise, surely?

Unfortunately, a tally of the *cons* that pulled the lovers apart marched unforgivingly through her brain. Horses were a hobby, not a career for *her*. Homesickness for New England played a part; (her friends, the convenience of living there and yes, decent washrooms). AND, if she was truly honest, not wanting the home and a family *yet* that Ewan a few years older, was already craving. *Perhaps counting sheep would be better?*

Cerby turned on her side, feeling sorry for herself. *What's wrong with me anyway? Why did I never want those things? The few relationships I've had always end badly. Well, that's not entirely true either. Perhaps turn out in the end I suppose, as I subconsciously want if I'm totally truthful.* Still, why weren't there ever any fairy tale endings for her? She deserved one, didn't she? She'd had enough heartache in her life .... Zzzzzzzzzzz.

Chapter Three

Monday

The events of the previous evening did not preclude an early rising. The police had cordoned off a small area of the murder scene in the Quad bound by yellow crime tape. Keeping in mind that the horses still had their routines to be met, morning came too soon again when Kally appeared in the dorm wing 'knocking' everyone up early - Saffi's voice as usual to be heard down the corridor complaining to loud affect.

A bleary-eyed Cerby threw on her denims and stumbled down to the mud room amongst a general crush of other half-awake women to find her Wellies hiding amongst the pile. Once she had shoved her thick-stockinged feet into the footwear, she slipped (literally) quickly across the dewed cobbles of the KC to the old stables and to Cyrius.

Cyrius was already circling in his stall when she arrived. He had a piece of straw embedded in his mane from when he had lain down in the night, but he appeared uncharacteristically nervous and cranky this morning. "Cyrius; boy, you must be hungry," she addressed him softly, leaning in over the locked Dutch door. The laid-back ears pricked forward. He calmed down at this gentle approach and stepped forward in anticipation to greet her.

'Back in a sec,' she tossed over her shoulder instead.

Only a few bales of hay and straw were kept up by the Inn in this small block of stalls. One of the four units at the front, facing the KC, served as a tack/feed room. As the outbuilding had rarely been used during her stay ten years before, therefore ignored by the students at the time, Cerby now found herself looking more closely at the historical structure. Her gaze roved over the old wooden beams, rough stone foundations and lime washed wattle and daub 'plaster' walls. She concluded that in days gone by, this is probably where the ostler lived as well as worked, tending the London coach relay teams. *Well, a horse is back in residence now, and what a beut. The more things change the more they stay the same...*

She soon found an old knife, and dragging out a hay bale, smelled it first to make sure the grasses weren't mouldy. *Smells sweet, probably first or second cut.* She confidently cut the bale bindings so that a couple of the flakes broke forward. *Only the best for my guy! I wonder why Cyrius is the only horse in the mews at present. Hope he's not too lonely.*

She grabbed a wheelbarrow standing on end against the front wall, placing in it the hay, a bale of straw, a pitchfork, and a muck rake. She pushed it down the gravel alley on the far side of the stable, bringing it to rest to one side of Cyrius' stall door. The thought struck her that perhaps Mrs. H had wanted Cyrius close to her, since her office was on this side of the Inn. She certainly liked smoking outside in that particular spot overlooking the flat

50 Acre Field. *Now we've been reunited,* Cerby mused; *I'm going to have to take Mrs. H in hand and help her give up those filthy cigarettes - for both our sakes!*

She had grabbed Cyrius' halter off a rack. Standing hip to his shoulder, both looking forward, she brought down his massive head over her collarbone and slipped it over, smoothing the nose and head band out so it wouldn't rub. Then she took a lead that she had found in the tack room, clipped it to the halter, and led Cyrius outside to a hitching post a few feet from his stall.

"I haven't forgotten," she laughed as the horse danced in anticipation:" Hereee-ss brekkieeee," she announced (à la Ed McMahon) as she tied a stuffed hay net to a higher ring on the post so that he could pull his 'shredded wheat' through the netting. Her charge thoroughly engrossed now in eating and seemingly contented to do so, she wheeled the barrow into the stall to begin mucking out.

Cerby had learned at this very school many years before the importance of mucking out properly, so she didn't really hate the menial work like some of the 'toffs' did. If it was done correctly, it minimized health risks to the horse and therefore expensive vet bills and/or curtailed riding. She had taken the methods used at Alaerton home to Vermont and used them later on leased horses, with the result that her mounts never had any health problems to speak of. Consequently, she was particularly grateful she had had the brains to pay special attention to the lessons on this lowly activity.

First, she went to the durable rubber feed bin and then inspected the *PVC* water bucket. The water bucket in particular was full of mucky strands of hay. She placed them both outside, powdered them with baking soda, scrubbed lightly and swished them under an outside tap until they looked respectably clean again. Before putting them back in place, she also removed severely worn salt and mineral blocks from a standard bier screwed into the wall, reminding herself to replace these later that day with new ones. (Cyrius would need to get his 'licks' in, especially if the weather turned really hot.)

Now the real work commenced, first picking out the manure droppings with a manure rake. Next, she positioned the wheelbarrow just left of centre on the floor. With the pitchfork she began to sort *used* wet straw bedding from the *dry,* scooping up the soaked piles and placing adeptly in the wheelbarrow, with the dryer strands stacked in the middle of the stall. Obviously Cyrius had been well looked after on a continuous basis, as the ammonia smell from urine in the stall was not *so* bad that she couldn't breathe; (it was one of the triggers that really set off her asthma.) Fortunately, there looked to be a large if somewhat antiquated grate over a drain in the floor for that purpose.

"How we doin' out there, Boy," she called to Cyrius. He nickered softly in reply. Laughing, she chided him: 'Don't speak with your mouth full.' Cerby leaned on her pitchfork, gazing out the Dutch door to the field view beyond where beautiful blue salvia and pink clover wove a natural carpet. She could have hugged herself. Just being here with Cyrius - never mind the lowly chores - was one of life's 'shining times' for her. It filled her with immeasurable happiness and gratitude.

She wheeled the full barrow out into the 'yard.' It would be deposited later on the muck heap, some distance from the barn for sanitary reasons. Then she went back into the stall to '*lay the bed.*' The slightly soiled straw would be laid down *economically* against the floor, in this case, sturdy horse defying oak planks from an era gone by, topped by one-inch-thick rubber stall mats. In trying to evenly distribute the *rushes* to the four corners, she noticed a small mound, shards of wood and stone by the far wall. Cyrius m*ust have been kicking the wall,* she thought. *He did seem a bit disturbed this morning. Maybe he got cast?* She immediately laid her tools down and gave Cyrius a quick physical check to make sure he hadn't hurt himself if that was the case.

Satisfied Cyrius was none the worse for wear, and catching sight of the time on her watch, she was reminded Momfrey wouldn't wait breakfast. *Better get a move on.* She finished raking the last of the old 'good' straw into place in the centre of the stall to soak up any new piss. Then she released the strings on the second straw bale and began prying the flakes apart with the pitchfork. Beginning a meticulous circuit around the edges of the stall, she 'banked' up the sides to a foot and a half with clean new straw as a defence against draughts and the rough walls, finishing by fluffing a clean new layer in the middle over the older one. By the time the bed was laid, *she* could have slept there herself, it looked so inviting and comfortable. (The object was always to get a horse to lie down; to take the weight off their disproportionately thin legs and prevent injury.)

"I must say," Saffi drawled, spooking Cerby as her friend silently draped herself over the Dutch door; "you haven't lost your touch Cerb. If you'd care to, I have a groom's position going on the estate..."

Stevey, ever at Saffi's side, both having come from the direction of the Quad, guffawed. "Not bloody likely, eh Cerb!"

Cerby pulled a face. "Maybe in another life, Saf."

Saffi was not offended. "Well come on you lot. There's a piece of lank toast with my name on it."

"And mine," chorused Stevey, followed by a 'me too' from Cerby.

"Let me just put Cyrius in first," Cerby added. "By the way, either of you hear yet who lost that bauble I found?"

With hardly a backward glance, Saf and Stevey shook their heads and made for the mud room. Cerby ran to catch up with them, fight for the boot jack, pull off boots, and pad sock-footed to the *Long Room* and Mrs. Momfrey's weak tea.

Cerby detoured to the Entrance Hall to check to see if there was a response to the note she had pinned on the School Bulletin Board:

Earring found, antique style setting, gold with drop pearl—see Lost and Found

To her surprise, it wasn't there anymore. She assumed then someone must have applied to Mrs.

Momfrey for it. Intercepting the venerable cook's trajectory to the *Long Room,* Cerby assisted her in carrying in the racks of tepid toast that seemed to accompany every meal.

"That's funny," she remarked to her friends as she plopped down beside them on the hard benches. "The memo I put up regarding that earring was taken down, and when I just asked Mrs. Momfrey if somebody claimed the earring, she said 'not to her knowledge.' I quickly checked, and it's gone from the Lost and Found box too?"

Stevey was eating heartily, Saf more delicately.

"Were you expecting a reward, Cerb?" Stevey giggled.

"Hardly," Cerb muttered, mouth full. "'ust hope it went 'ack to the rightful owner."

All ears tuned to the general conversation, the majority of which revolved around how difficult it was going to be to service the pony Smoke in the re-christened 'unlucky 13' corner of the Quad where Jasper's life had been terminated so violently.

Some reedy voice piped up: 'Not to worry; the police are finished with their investigation there. Caution Tape ought to be removed tomorrow.'

Since the police had also given permission for the school to resume its regular equestrian schedules, and Kally had confirmed the riding ability of practically all the former students, she had not hesitated at the morning lesson to set up a row of five jumping poles on the floor in the middle of the arena, spaced to generic length: two 24" cavalettis down one side of the arena and a 3'6" jump down the other.

Cerby had never jumped past 4 foot in her heyday, so a 3.6 jump, after not having done it for a few years, did look a mite intimidating. Nevertheless, she was up for the challenge and quite looked forward to trying it. She could rely on Cyrius, despite his advanced age. His ears had pricked forward the moment he entered the arena and saw the white and red jumping apparatus.

"Ladies. First, we acclimat' you and your mounts. Evervon vill peas' trot down the centre aisle over the poles, make a s'mal circle in the far lef corner and then kom back same vay. We vill all do that twice peas.' Then ve vill line up. You vill trot in single file vonce again don the centre, right turn and tak the two cavelettis. Peas' continue each in the line until I say halt. If there are no problems, you may then trot again don the centre, turn right goink over the two cavelettis, continue with a canter at 'A' into the right corner and tak the bigger jump at 'M,' coming back over the poles and then standink jusst off centre, while the others do their ride. Is that all clear?" Kally took the silence in response for confirmation.

In recent years Cerby had ridden only recreationally, so any previously honed balancing skills were deemed to have abandoned her. She knew she no longer had the musculature of her prime. Even only *slightly* flabbified arms and thighs would provide no advantage for grip or to a centred 'seat.'

However, in going over the poles and cavalettis, remembering to stand up in the stirrups and lift her body forward over the horse's centre of gravity, gave her a false confidence when it came to the larger jump. Coming around the interior corner, gathering speed, she was distracted momentarily by light and movement near the arena door. It crossed her mind that Cyrius might shy on the diagonal away from the 3'6" jump because of the disturbance.

Nevertheless, Cerby leant determinedly forward, looking through Cyrius' ears at the three red and white beams, the standards eight feet apart: *always look where you want to go…* But. In the attempt to squeeze Cyrius' girth with her heels down and out (which proved a bit of a chore given her stiff ankles) instead of a *gathered* canter, he took off like a shot down the length of the arena towards the jump, blowing out his nostrils as he went. The initial unbalance of his haunch thrust caused Cerby to lose a stirrup and control of the reins. All she could do was hold on to his mane, the old countdown useless in the circumstances: '*3- 2- 1*' (normally the length of the horse's 'controlled' strides before a jump). Then they were airborne, flying over, much higher than the jump itself required. The flight seemed interminable. The jolt of landing however, with stirrup gone, put Cerby well up on Cyrius' neck in a precarious position, riding helmet slipping well down and over her eyes.

Confused by her signals (or lack of), Cyrius continued on in a bouncy trot until, as Cerby began to lose her grip and slip further sideways, he suddenly stopped. Cerby held on in an undignified posture for a few seconds - half on, half off the neck and withers but sliding inexorably downwards. Finally surrendering, she fell with a plop on her back in the relatively soft sawdust of the arena floor.

Cyrius had moved aside and now came back, reins dragging, lowering his nose to her face as if to console her for her poor performance. The ungainly landing provoked a round of derisive laughter. Spread-eagled on her back before her mounted audience - humiliation complete - she spat out some sawdust and was just knocking her helmet back so she could see when she inhaled a whiff of citrus, essence of pine wood; reminiscent of Tom Ford's 'Grey Vetiver.' *Impossible!* Sensing a strong hand reaching down to yank her up, she squinted upwards into the light. *That just couldn't be Harry Connick Junior, surely?*

"Thank...*YOU*? **WHAT ARE YOU DOING HERE**?!!"

"Hmm. Is that anyway to greet a Canuck, neighbour?" Aidan smirked, pulling her adroitly to her feet in one fluid motion. He began dusting off her chest *where there was absolutely NO sawdust.*

"I *can* do that, thank you!" said Cerby brusquely, burning from ear to ear, uncomfortably cognizant of her colleagues' twitters...

"Anything hurt?" he asked with mock concern.

"Only the proverbial 'dignity,'" she replied glumly.

"Good!" he replied with a laconic grin. "Then I'll see you for dinner at seven."

"That's *supper*," she corrected weakly, as he bowed theatrically to the mounted contingent and disappeared with a backhanded wave through the arena door in company with a man she didn't recognize.

"Alright ever'body!" Kally shouted to drown out the hoots and twittering, in no way pleased the way the class had ended. "I'll zee you bak 'ere this afternoon for Musak Ride practis.' But *you*," she said sternly to Cerby, "lose boyf'end. Ve 'ave a lot of work to do. Yah!"

Cerby nodded, chastened. Taking Cyrius' reins in one hand and dusting off her rump with the other she found her path barred by Saffi and Stevey, still mounted.

Saffi pointed her crop imperiously at Cerby. "**Spill!**"

Stevey bubbling over: "Whoooo in heck was that? Are you holding out on us Cerb? Looks pretty 'squiffy' to me."

"Is that good or bad," asked Cerby drily, cocking her head and squinting up at the two.

"You tell us," her friends laughed in unison, causing Cerby once again to blush to her toes.

"Well, this *is* an interesting turn of events!" Cerby's tone dripped with sarcasm.

Mitch raised an eyebrow at Monte, who looked away from Cerby's stern gaze. They had arrived at Alaerton as promised, to give her some emotional comfort after the shock of the murder the day before.

"Do I have to ask again? *How* did Aidan know I was here? In England?"

Monte found his mislaid backbone and looked at her unapologetically. "Look Cerb. You weren't answering his calls. He *happened* to look us up, and he is a detective after all, for God's sake…"

Cerby snorted. "Ah yes. He sat you down under a 3000-watt light, flogged and water-boarded you, is that it?"

"If only," muttered Monte. "He's so damned attractive. Being a buff RCMP officer doesn't hurt either."

Mitch protectively intervened for the squirming Monte; (Cerby was known to be surprisingly good at *grilling,* herself.) "We just *might* have told him you were going out of the country. Perhaps also mentioned accidentally the name of the country, the equitation school, and why. (More lamely). He needed a ride out here anyway…"

Cerby stamped her foot and rolled her eyes. "I don't suppose you thought there might have been a reason I wasn't taking his calls?"

Mitch put up one hand. "Enough Cerb. We know you feel something for Aidan even if you can't admit to yourself. Sparks fly off you like, um, a '*sparkler*' whenever you two get together." Mitch glanced over at Monte for confirmation. Monte gave a '*thumbs up*' sign. "You always come up with some reason or other to end a relationship, whenever you're getting too close. THAT'S GOT TO STOP! I say this as your friend Cerb. There's nothing wrong with Aidan and you're not exactly in the prime… Scratch that! I mean, you're not a schoolgirl any…"

"Yikes!" Monte backed away to a safe distance and gave Mitch a 'thumbs down.'

"I don't consider Aidan my last chance Mitch, if that's what you're implying. I'm hardly Methuselah at twenty-eight," Cerby retorted acerbically, striding away in a huff.

"Pretty good shape for Methuselah," Mitch called placatingly after her. "Ummm. Not what I meant at all Cerb. Ooh, for Pete's sake, wait up. We just want you to be happy!" In an aside to Monte: "You've been a BIG help." M&M hurried to catch up with her and make amends.

Fortunately, Cerby cooled down usually as fast as she blew up. In this case, on some level she knew her friends had done this outrageous thing out of love and concern for her. She waved them off in their rented auto after extracting a reluctant promise from them as penance, to chaperone Aidan and herself at dinner that night. Knowing those two now had her back, when she returned to the Inn, she found she could speak to Aidan with some equanimity. She hardly glanced at the tight butt planted firmly on the edge of the desk in the Common Room; the *rest* of Aidan was talking to the man she had briefly seen him with in the arena.

Aidan looked over his shoulder at her approach and slid off the desk. He looked quite fetching Cerby had to admit, in a sage coloured shirt that brought out the green and yellow in his hazel eyes.

Tucked in, it emphasized his trim waist. As usual, he wore dark coloured *comfort cut* jeans, stretched tautly over his four-times-a-week gym-thighs. Aidan reached down from his 6'2" height to give her a kiss, which she neatly deflected to her cheek. His eyes crinkled with silent laughter.

"Ah! This must be *THE* Cerdwyn you spoke of," chuckled the stranger, watching the domestic scene unfold. "I see you are none the worse for your little riding mishap." (*His* eyes twinkled unmercifully.)

Oh, would there be no end to the humiliation...?

"Yes. One and the same. Cerby, meet Jock Wallace - the D.I. on the Jasper Ellison case."

Cerby stepped forward and shook the proffered hand firmly. "Don't believe all you've heard," she quipped unimaginatively. She immediately approved of the rugged Scot however, a little older than Aidan (*in his late 30's?*). A kind, intelligent face, and cultured accent. *No 'Wee Geordie' this one.*

"I'm a policeman, lassie," Jock replied with mock severity; "I base all my findings purely on the evidence presented."

"You know, your name sounds vaguely familiar Jock...Inspector?" Cerby ventured.

Aidan was happy to say anything to keep Cerby from stalking off. "You might remember that Jock *the Scot* was on exchange when we were investigating *The Stones* Biker gangs a year or so back. Jock and I swapped a lot of information on the gang's drug routes through Europe and North America. Couldn't have cracked that case without him, could we Cerb?" He gave her a knowing look.

Cerby remembered now Aidan's silent partner in the RCMP case she'd helped code-name: *'Severance Pay."* She smiled at Jock in acknowledgment of his help there. *Hope he doesn't take it personally that I forgot ...*

"A bit of a plus running into him here." Aid nodded at Jock.

"You mean, on your *pleasure trip* Aidan?" Jock inserted ironically. "Well, two heads are always better than one in a murder case, even if one of them is *unofficial,"* Jock underlining *that* in his glance at both of them.

Cerby managed to look *'innocent until proven guilty.'* "Jock, I do recall now, how much of your work went into that case. I expect we'll run into each other again, less formally. I'm assuming I'm not a suspect, by the way?"

Jock didn't answer although his mustache twitched.

"I've told Jock you're more likely to be murdered yourself by someone who shall remain nameless, then commit it."

"Well, I don't think I deserve *that,"* Cerby said testily, wondering if she was dismissed or not.

Aidan apologized to Jock for the interruption, then steered Cerby over into a corner. He had sighed on learning that the dinner date that evening was to include Cerby's sidekicks, Mitch and Monte, but it was a step in the right direction, nevertheless. He'd take what he could get at this point, knowing better than to rush the advantage in any case.

He informed Cerby that D.I. Wallace was allowing Aidan to shadow him as a professional courtesy while he was visiting, and that the two of them were off immediately to the local Coroner's. He wouldn't see her until later that night in that case.

Cerby suffered Aidan to give her a quick kiss to seal the arrangements. She left him deep in talk with his Inspector friend. As Aidan was putting up at the *Highwayman Pub & Lodging* himself, it was just easier for all parties to meet back there at 7 pm.

It hadn't escaped Cerby either, that having a suitor as her date the following evening at Ewan and Bron's dinner party would go a long way to mitigate any palpable awkwardness *that* event might hold. Aidan *did* have his uses, apparently. Perhaps it was a good thing he'd tracked her down after all.

Mrs. Hill had set up a private little lunch for Cerby and herself at a white filigreed cast iron table under the shade of a Plane tree in the old, enclosed garden. Mrs. Momfrey caught and informed Cerby of the luncheon arrangement as she exited the Common Room. However, in rushing up the stairwell to her bedroom and the WC. to do a quick toilette, Mayfair almost sent Cerby tumbling. The house-helper, vacuuming *down* the staircase backward with no thought of 'traffic,' collided with Cerby at the very top of the first flight of stairs. Cerby lost her balance; *just* escaped falling backwards herself by a wild grab at the banister. *Talk about 'nearly a nasty accident!'*

Cerby flared but the reaction died on her lips when she spied, just peeking through Mayfair's ill-cut straggly hair, the missing earring and its twin dangling from stretched earlobes. *Gosh, those must be heavy.* Although not class-conscious, Cerby felt such finely wrought pieces looked strangely out of place on the cleaning woman.

Mayfair growled at Cerby as if the dangerous stumble had been Cerby's own fault. Despite the lack of apology, Cerby was just about to ply Mayfair for more information on how she came by such exquisite jewelry, when she remembered Mrs. Hill was expecting her. Regretful of not pursuing *this* opportunity, she made a mental note to follow up later.

After a quick splash to the face and wash-up, Cerby changed her denim shirt for a simple capped-sleeve print blouse. Taking the steps two-at-a-time coming down, she soon found herself in the walled garden. Buzzing Mrs. Hill on the cheek, she settled down beside her into a matching iron-worked armchair, laying a damask napkin across her lap.

"Mrs. H," she began slowly, looking around the garden; "tell me truly how you're doing? About Jasper? …" and gesturing towards the ruined plots with a wave of her hand, "... Well… everything?"

After a moment's reflection, Mrs. Hill responded to the sympathy in Cerby's voice. "It hasn't been easy Cerdwyn, you know." She paused again while she marshalled her thoughts. "Did I ever tell you that I am related to the original 18th century owners of the *Wheatsheaf Inn,* several times removed?"

Cerby sucked in her breath: "Wow! Fancy that!!!" she said in astonishment. "No, you never did! Did *you* know Saf is a cousin of Harry and Wills - many times removed?" They both laughed, even though it was true.

Mrs. Hill continued. "My husband bought this place for me on account of *that* history when the Inn came up for sale thirty-five years ago. What a state it was in then!" Her eyes had a faraway look in them. "It took us nearly ten full years, both working at other jobs, to return it to even a fraction of its former 'glory' when it was the Alaerton Manor House, which you may remember it was before it became an Inn. We didn't even open the school until we felt absolutely ready to." She allowed a self-deprecating laugh to escape. "I'm glad Simon isn't alive to see what I've done to the place."

"No! He wouldn't be anything but proud, Mrs. H." There was a catch in Cerby's own voice.

"Well, perhaps," Mrs. Hill grudgingly acceded. "But then, before I knew it, I was a widower. No children of my own. Just a passion for horses and bringing animals and people together." (She patted Cerby's hand fondly).

"Mrs. H, now that we're confessing…I'm not sure (Cerby looked down at her hands, choosing her words equally carefully) if I ever told you how much it, rather, YOU…meant to me when I came here. After my parents died. I know I was a bit hard to communicate with back then."

"Like a clam." Mrs. Hill laughed throatily.

"But it was you Mrs. H. You helped me to cope with the suddenness of it all. You knew that as an only child, I didn't have anyone else to turn to, confide in. (Cerby's eyes suddenly widened). Why, you gave me Cyrius to ride on purpose, didn't you?

115

He was your horse before he was ever mine - I mean, before…"

"Water seeks its own level," Mrs. Hill mused. "He had been an abused animal when I first got him. So much talent locked up in that strong body. He seemed to know immediately that I was hurting after my husband died. He taught *me* a lot. Then others came along that needed a similar kind of healing. I let *'im pick 'em,* so to speak. And then you came to stay that year."

Cerby got off her seat and bent over Mrs. Hill giving her a crushing hug. Tears had sprung to her eyes, and Mrs. Hill's also, who waved her back to her armchair. Mrs. Momfrey had come out, unobtrusively set down the *ploughman's lunch* and stolen off so quietly neither knew she'd even been there until the food presented itself.

"When I was young," continued Mrs. Hill quickly, to break the emotion of the moment; "I could do a lot of the work myself, but the Inn itself is centuries old and it's falling down now - a bit like me I'm afraid. No Cerby, don't pretend it isn't and that I'm not too. I've done my best to keep it going, although the working pupil program fell apart a few years ago. I was still getting some residential pupils but this anniversary reunion event and the money coming in from it was something I *had* to do just to keep us barely in the black this year. If Jasper hadn't shown up out of nowhere and offered to work for just room and board, I certainly couldn't have afforded even one hired hand. As it was, he turned out to be half a hired man. I tried to keep him on a schedule, but he dallied with Mayfair and did chores erratically.

"Ted, Doctor Wentworth, had no use for him whatsoever. Jaspar's lack of commitment made him absolutely furious, though mostly on my account; he knew the stress I was under to get the Centre ready for the events this week. Kally helps out but she only has time to do so much. She takes a cut from the lessons, so they are the priority to her. I don't blame her for that; the woman has to eat! Ewan being back here now (and she glanced at Cerby searchingly) has been a great asset. Having an *FBHS* with his reputation may just be our great salvation."

Cerby reached out and squeezed Mrs. Hill's hand. "Don't worry Mrs. H. Everything will work out." Cerby knew the astronomical amount of work required to run and maintain a successful Equitation Centre but continued optimistically: "I'm sure that Karma will prevail in the end." *If only I could truly believe that....*

She tried diverting Mrs. Hill from such a melancholy topic of conversation. She pointed to the White Rose, budding against the bricks - the symbol of the House of York, and of peace and love. "Mrs. H, you said you would tell me more about the *Wheatsheaf* one day, and now I find you're connected by blood to one of my most favourite romantic spots on earth. Riddle me this? On the paper dining-mat in the *Highwayman* Pub, showing a map and history of the area, there seemed to be some sort of association between the two - the pub and the Inn I mean. Can you explain that?"

Mrs. Hill gave a bitter little laugh. "Yes, the landlord there makes *hay* out of *our* history."

"What do you mean?" asked Cerby, curiosity peaked.

"Do you know the poem *The Highwayman,* by Alfred Noyes?" asked Mrs. Hill.

"One of my top ten, growing up," Cerdwyn enthused, and then with some dramatic license recited:

> '*The moon was a ghostly galleon, tossed upon cloudy seas,*
> *And the Highwayman came riding, riding, up to the old Inn door*'

"Close enough!" Mrs. Hill laughed. "But here, in this case, it was an employee who dared usurp the highwaymen's fame. When this was an Inn in the 1700's, the resident ostler - an unsavoury character named Thomas Haney - was indentured to change and harness the London Mail Coach's relay horses. In that capacity, he had ample opportunity to observe which gentlemen passengers carried weighty money purses, and which ladies were heavily bejewelled.

"The story goes: when he found a likely enough 'mark,' he'd take off like a shot on his own steed whilst the passengers re-loaded (making use of the local short cuts he knew so well) holding up *the very same coach* he had serviced only ten to fifteen miles or so down the road. Since it was said Dick Turpin was also operating in the area, a lot of suspicion and innuendo fell on him, probably rumours encouraged by Haney himself.

"Well disguised; careful to allow enough time between 'stand and delivers;' and savvy enough to vary the locations, Haney got away with it for a couple of years. What finally tipped the constabulary's hand was a stable boy who couldn't help but notice the ostler's absence from the stable on the identical nights as the robberies, although no one could ever testify they'd seen him leave the premises. However, suspicions aroused, the boy kept an eye out. One night he observed Haney, who was nowhere to be found earlier in the evening suddenly re-appear back in the yard, (his foam flecked horse found to be stabled in a lean to in a nearby field). The boy put two and two together and went public. He wanted the ostler's job, you see. Haney made a run for it, confirming his guilt, but was eventually nabbed, taken to Newgate and hanged as robbers were in those days. That's all there is to the story really."

"Wow" Cerby exclaimed. "Are you sure you couldn't make more 'hay' out of that story yourself, Mrs. H? Maybe throw in Dick Turpin or a ghost or two. I bet some good marketing could really work."

"Actually, one of the truer rumours associated with the Inn *had* Dick Turpin hiding out on the premises once or twice, but oh Cerby: it's so wonderful you still have a great imagination and a lot of enthusiasm, but the sad truth is I'm getting too old to come up with new ideas, let alone put them into practise."

"Well, we'll have to try to think of something Mrs. H. In Vermont, everybody's mantra is: '*when I win the lottery*' and of course nobody ever does (not me anyway, that's for sure) but they keep buying tickets anyway. See. It doesn't mean there's not a solution for you out there. You just have to believe in one, that's all."

They finished their dinner with less spirited talk. Cerby could see Mrs. H didn't want to dwell on the subject of Jasper's murder. It wasn't good publicity for Alaerton, and one more problem Mrs. H would have to deal with, although of course she showed remorse for his untimely death. All Cerby got out of Mrs. Hill was that Jasper had shown up one day and self- recommended himself, saying he had worked on a Northern farm for some time. Mrs. Hill was a bit put off by his gruff manner *'but beggars can't be choosers'*, and he did seem to have some knowledge of the work. When Jasper insisted all he wanted was a bit of a change and willing to work for room and board until the spirit moved him to *'ramble a bit', she* accepted his application 'as is.' "Lucky to get anyone in this financial climate," Mrs. Hill sighed.

The conversation drifted into general pleasantries as they discussed the Manor Rose and some of the perennials spottily protruding in the weedy plots by the enclosure walls. Suddenly Mrs. Hill interrupted: "My lord! Look at the time Cerby! You'll be missing your Musical Ride prep. Ought you to get a move on?"

"Holy Horses!" Cerby jumped up from the table. "You're right. Kally will have my *guts for garters* if I'm late. Thanks so much for the lunch, er, *'dinner'* Mrs. H, and for making my visit so memorable in so many ways." She bent down again, hugging Mrs. Hill affectionately. Then she ran off at a gallop in the direction of the stables.

Once again, the riding group was paired off with cardboard numbers on their backs. To her dismay, Cerby found her partner was Shasta Denning, although there was a forced cordiality in Shasta's banal inquiries while they sat mounted, patiently waiting for Kally's instructions. Cerby had decided to let the past remain in the past and responded in kind: "Did you also come over from the States then, for this anniversary 'do'?"

Shasta hesitated before replying: "No, I was visiting my father - divorced for some years. He has a property up North in Yorkshire."

"Oh, yes. He was in films, wasn't he?"

"Yeah, he was working on a movie set there years ago, helping with the screenplay;" (Shasta darted a covert look at Cerby.)

Cerby kicked herself for letting that comment slip. Now she feigned complete innocence, as if she remembered nothing else from that period. She decided on the spot that she wouldn't bother raking up teenaged Shasta's dirty doings. It just wasn't worth it when they had to pull together for the 'Ride', for Mrs. Hill. So, she nodded and added a laden: "Oh, how nice…" to emphasize her lack of interest.

Seemingly satisfied, Shasta added casually: "He was dating my bitchy Stepmother in those days. Fell in love with moody moor-y old Yorkshire too apparently. Anyway, the *Cow* left him in the end."

This unkind reference to her father's wife and Shasta's visible relief when Kally interrupted the chit-chat with her lesson instructions, disturbed Cerby. Remnants of the old Shasta appeared to be surfacing. She suppressed her growing irritation. Fortunately, Shasta turned her horse's rump to Cerby's and distanced herself getting into position, effectively putting an end to conversation.

"Peas walk to *A* in dooble formaatin, and ten accordink to vether you be prime nummer or not, prime nummers to lef' and composite nummers (this had to be explained to the group whose school years were far behind them) to right. 'Primes' vill turn at *B* into centre at *X* passink to lef' of 'Composites' turning at *E* to *X*, continuing both now on different sides of arena to *C* and then valking four-abreast to *X* in centre. Can ve do that? Ja?!"

'Sure.'

'Of course.'

Weaker assents Cerby had never heard. The scenes of the last 'crashes' the day before were clearly on everyone's mind. This lesson however, despite the expectations, actually turned out marginally better with Kally advising all at the dismount that music would be added to the next lesson: "You vill see" she added encouragingly, "the horses vill pick up to the musak."

The Reunionistas looked at each other. 'More speed. Great!' Not necessarily what everyone wanted to hear.

After their short tea break, the mature students gathered in the Common Room. As Alaerton's official BSHI, Ewan would be giving them a lecture on *Bits, Bandaging, and Bedding* - a review for the Horsemaster Test on the day of the fête. Most were of the opinion they needed a year more-like, just to prepare for the written test never mind the riding portion.

When Cerby came in, she could see Bron at the front of the room readying the large chalk board that was used for teaching purposes. Bron seemed positively effervescent now that Ewan had returned. Cerby tried to keep her own feelings in check but somehow, like acid reflux, a tinge of jealousy still threatened to disgorge. *Where are the Tums when you need them?*

Chastising herself for her lack of restraint, she quickly swallowed the bile (without meds) when Ewan came striding into the room. Bron behaved professionally towards him in her role as his assistant and did the introduction portion. Sometimes she would hold up examples of *bits*; (*Snaffles*, *Gag*, *Curb*, *Walking*, *and Show*) whose uses Ewan had already referenced on the chalk board.

Ewan took over aspects of leg bandaging for injury, warmth, protection and emphasized how improper wraps could do a lot of damage if too tight, too bunched up, or uneven. (Cerby, still slightly 'jaundiced,' snorted to herself. She'd never been totally convinced anyway, that wrapping legs wasn't much more than an affectation. *I mean, do*

Wild Mustangs run around the Mesa's with bandages on their legs for Dog's sake?

When he spoke about bedding, Cerby tuned some of this out, believing herself to be educated enough on that score. At last, Bron circulated with some bandaging wraps, and everyone had to practise on their partner's leg. Cerby had no partner once again, so Bron came up to her and indicated her own leg for the purpose.

"Oh, right then Bron. Give us a leg up." The humour wasn't completely lost on Bron and she affected a laugh. If this was some sort of 'make up' on Bron's part, it struck Cerby as immensely funny. Her outburst of laughter soon had Bron smiling, and even Ewan turned to grin at them - apparently relieved by their moment of shared hilarity. Although the ice *had* been broken amongst them, it did nothing to assuage a certain wistfulness on Cerby's part.

The lecture broke up with Ewan issuing a stern warning that the Horsemaster's test would be no rubber stamp version, and that if they needed more information on bits and bandaging especially, to come up to the cottage and ask.

Yeah, I'd like to take you up on the 'bits' part. Cerby however, knew the idea to be too impossible to contemplate seriously. Besides, Bron had reminded her of the dinner party the next night to which Cerby had adeptly inserted a request to bring an additional guest.

Bron's eyes twinkled becomingly: "Oh, would that be the strapping chap who came to your aid in the arena the other day?"

Cerby demurred, feeling a bit badly after all for dragging Aidan into the ménage à trois. In any event it was agreed upon, Bron mentioning Monte and Mitch again as well, knowing they were lodging at the *Highwayman* along with Aidan.

"Just one caveat, Bron. I can't be entirely sure of their schedules, gallivanting as they've been doing all over the countryside." Cerby wasn't even certain she wanted them there now. M&M (her pet nickname for the couple i.e., 'cute enough to eat') had been privy to all her romances. Who knew what might come out of their mouths at any given moment, especially Mitch?

All of that settled however, Bron and she went their separate ways - Bron to the *'I's Cottage* and Cerby to get ready for her dinner with Aidan and the 'Boys' in Alconbury.

"Sorry Mrs. Momfrey; eating out tonight," Cerby exclaimed over her shoulder as she dashed out the front door to wait for the taxi she had called. She almost hesitated upon seeing Mayfair carrying in the dinner trays, those delicately designed earrings still in place. *What? Does she never take them off?* From Cerby's perspective, they were fine enough that they should have been locked up in a bank vault.

Momentum carried her past and out the door without further comment. A taxi waited in the circular drive. It was getting on to twilight, and no murderer having been found as yet, she preferred not to *walk* into Alconbury. Besides, she was wearing her nicest flats; had even opted for a slate-coloured pencil skirt topped by a see-through sheer light grey blouse overtop a matching silk camisole. *It's so nice to be out of breeches and boots for a change* she told herself, the extra effort in no way meant for Mr. Aidan Halifax, one of the RCMP's finest! *Thank you for your 'service,'* the double entendre making her eyes sparkle with remembrance, her mouth curving up in a salacious grin.

The cab sped off toward the *Highwayman* and she arrived punctually. When she mentioned to the landlord her dinner reservation and companions, he directed her out to a lovely patio at the back of the pub - a new addition since her time as a pupil. The flagstone seating area was well lit with old fashioned lighting standards. Flower and herb container tubs lined the perimeter, the lawn sweeping down to the Alconbury brook and pond in which a few ducks and a swan swam. Aidan half arose at her approach. The 'Boys,' who were engaged in some sort of mock argument as usual, remained seated and ignored her.

"Look Mitch, it does so say here on the dining-mat, that Dick Turpin and his horse Black Bess were known to hideout at the *Wheatsheaf* Inn."

Cerby settled into her chair with a laugh.

"Oh, back to *THAT* again, are we? Yes, and George Washington slept there as well." Reversing tact at Monte's crestfallen look; "I know Monte, you'd just love to pump up this next book of yours with local lore, but perhaps I've got an even better tidbit, and with some provenance. Supposedly factual anyway, although you might have to verify it in the municipal archives in Huntingdon.

"This was Turpin's territory alright," she agreed, but then commenced to fill them all in on the tale of Tom Haney, Turpin's contemporary, while the waiter took their dining orders and delivered their drinks.

The Boys were rapt at attention. Monte 's eyes gleamed with enthusiasm. "I think there's plenty of meat here for me to stick my literary chops into."

Mitch punned: "Might have just boarded the 'gravy train,' *by George*."

Monte sat up. "AND, besides the historical angles, given my freelancing foody articles - maybe I can work something of that sort into the book too, along with the lych-gates' designs."

Cerby's first reaction was to pooh-pooh that idea. "Yeah, like those two things really go together: *Lych-gates* and *Lychee* recipes? Lynchings I could see, given the usual sentence handed down to road-rogues for stealing." She chuckled at her own so clever response.

Aidan pinched her.

"Will you STOP doing that Aid! Every time I see you, I end up black and blue. In fact, I seem to be a *pinching* bag for everyone."

"Then stop being so negative," he said good-humouredly; 'and go easy with the puns, punster."

"What, or you'll have me arrested," Cerby countered testily. Privately, she thought she was rather good at punning.

"No, I mean it people," Monte continued, eyes glazed over, seeing the finished product in his

127

mind's eye: "I could tie in a culinary speciality with the locale of the gate: different village, different recipe; throw in some local lore."

Cerby wasn't convinced something similar might already have been 'done' (at least in Europe), but Monte had pulled off crazier ideas and would have easily made a living from writing if he wasn't already wealthy, so she remained silent on the subject. Besides, chastened, she didn't want to be on the receiving end of any more of Aidan's 'painful' rebukes.

After a few minutes more listening to Monte 'spin' the outline for his book, she suddenly sat up erect. "I just had a brilliant thought! I know someone here who loves to cook and might just be the perfect collaborator for you on this project, Monte." Smiling smugly at Aidan, she imparted her knowledge of Saffi's gourmet expertise and suspected she might well jump at the chance to work with Monte's notable experience in the publishing field.

"Cerb; that might just work!"

In response to Monte's enthusiastic eagerness to pursue an entente with Saffi (*'who's a clever girl then, eh'*) Cerby took a big draught of her dark ale, happy to provide a solution for her friend in exchange for his many kindnesses she knew she could never repay.

Aidan immediately pierced her bubble by nibbling hard on the nearest earlobe and murmuring loud enough for Mitch and Monte to hear: "Wonder if there's a Guinness record for clapping yourself **too** many times on the back?*"

After the laughter at her expense died away, Cerby had to face a harder question. It was difficult enough to dismiss Aidan quite so lightly when he insisted on sitting so close to her. *A person could bottle those pheromones.* Cerby tried not to inhale too deeply.

Hoping to divert herself, she turned the patter back to what Aidan and D.I. Wallace had managed to unearth regarding Jasper's untimely demise. Mitch and Monte summoned the waiter for refills once again and expectantly raised their glasses in Aidan's direction also. He caved to the pressure and put his hands up in mock surrender.

"Ok. I can't give you the official details, but even *unofficially* I can tell you there is not much to go on. Jasper has a pretty short bio - we literally don't know much about him."

"Except" cut in Cerby; "that he said himself he was from up North; worked on a farm of some sort there; he'd only been at Alaerton a month or so; *and,* he must have been desperate for the job because he was willing to take just room and board. Oh, and he was rogering Mayfair, the house-girl."

Aidan looked at her half in amusement, half in annoyance. "Yes, they're trying to track his last place of employment," he agreed.

"But don't you think it odd that he'd settle for just *B&B,* when due to lack of job applicants in this area, a farm worker could practically write their own ticket," insisted Cerby? "There must be a reason he came here in the first place."

Mitch cut in: "And whatever it was, logically, has to be tied into his murder."

"Perhaps," Monte added spontaneously, throwing a curve of his own; "he was running away from something, or someone - hiding away in a pretty anonymous location."

Aidan spoke thoughtfully: "Or running *to* someone or something. Mayfair seems to have been a recent fling. On questioning, she reluctantly admitted to the liaison, but Jock and I could tell the amour was more on her side than his. Apparently, they often trysted …"

"Good Lord, Aid. 'Trysted'?" Cerby nearly choked on a mouthful of hops, laughing so hard.

"… in the old stone stable."

"Yecch!" Cerby made a retching sound: "Better not have been anywhere near my Cyrius! When by the way, was their last canoodle?"

"She admitted to a make-up 'quickie' before supper on the day he died. She'd been needed as per her usual routine to help with the serving, so it was the only available time they could get together. That would have been around 4:30 to 5 ish in the afternoon. Said they'd had a major row a day or so before, but he 'd made it up to her with a prezzie - a piece of jewelry or something, so she owed him she said."

"Yeah, I think we saw that argument when we first arrived at the school. I thought the guy had done with the girl; the 'discussion' looked pretty vehement."

"Mayfair swears he was very much alive the last time she saw him on Sunday afternoon." Aidan folded a napkin into an origami crane and put it on top of Cerby's head.

"There's one other angle you're not going to like, Cerby." Aidan wiped his mouth with a large paper napkin. Cerby tilted her head in response, the crane falling onto the table.

"Jock isn't counting out all suspects ... including Mrs. Hill and Doctor Wentworth"

"What!" Cerby's face suffused dangerously.

Aidan raised a hand. "Calm down! He has to look at all the possibilities. You know that the future of Alaerton is hanging by a thread and Mrs. Hill is counting heavily on that festival this weekend. Apparently, some of her run-ins with the laggard Jasper were pretty vocal - a lot of testaments to that fact."

"Mrs. H wouldn't hurt a fly, no matter how obstreperous someone was; whatever the stakes."

"Then there's the good Doctor...."

"What's Jock's crackpot theory there?" Cerby sputtered in anger.

"Well, you probably know he and Mrs. Hill are an item. He's been her knight errant, bawling out Jasper as well on her behalf. Some witnesses in the local pub attest to that affect. He's been retired from the army for many years, but he's still got the heft to have bunged Jasper."

"Except that he's right-handed!"

"What's that got to do with anything," chimed in Monte, both 'The Boys' totally engrossed in the conversation.

"That shovel used to kybosh Jasper - it was flung to the *left*. I noticed it when I discovered the body. Whoever did the deed I'm pretty sure was left-handed, which Doctor Wentworth is not!" Cerby was starting to be frightened for her mentor and her

131

paramour, no matter how logical her defense of them. The way the Doctor looked at Mrs. H, he'd do anything for her she knew.

"Cerb. You never cease to amaze me," Mitch admired.

"Nor me," Aidan sighed.

"Hmm" was the universal response.

Dessert was served before the main course had been completely cleared. Despite demolishing hearty entrées, all being rather hungry, they set to the *sweets* tray on their table with relish.

"Yummy." Cerby chewed on her éclair contently; "Who said *the English can't cook?*"

"The Fren-sh came up with that one, I beliefe Cerb," Monte slurred, referring both to her dessert and the 'saying.' Alcohol was catching up with him and his own mouth was full of decadent chocolate cheesecake.

"Good thing we're not driving, boy-o." Mitch had plunged adventurously into *Blood Pudding* previously for the main course. Now he was spoon-deep in traditional *Trifle*.

There were only muffled sounds from Aidan, last to finish a main course but now equally immersed in a crème brûlée. "This reminds me," Aidan pointed to the remains of a lightly browned deflated 'pudding' on his dinner plate: "the one thing we do know about Jasper - which I am at liberty to tell you anyway - he definitely hails from Yorkshire."

It had turned out to be a lovely evening despite Cerby trying to keep Aidan somewhat at arm's length. He walked her down by the river after the dessert and coffee while 'The Boys' had made themselves scarce on some pretext or other. Cerby was only slightly annoyed with them at this juncture; it was actually comforting to have Aidan's solid presence in the midst of all that had happened recently. In truth, it would not have been hard to succumb to Aidan's subtle request that she stay over at his lodgings: "I have an ensuite," he said *sotto voce*, his five o'clock shadow grazing her cheek, appealing to Cerby's practical obsession for 'Better Johns.' And, if that weren't enough, he also produced from behind his back a good vintage of bubbly, despite the two of them being pretty besotted (in the alcoholic sense at least), already.

Cerby almost caved, but caught herself aptly: "Aidan, I have to get up early tomorrow," she protested.

"Yeah, I suppose," he growled in mock resignation; "so do I, actually. Meeting up with Jock. Guess that means: 'Tis not to be this night then wench, for I trow you prefer mucking out to bedding in, but I *will* take a rain check."

Cerby countered waggishly: "But I wasn't the one offering…"

"You *WILL* be," Aidan leaned in confidently, kissing her hard and purposely on the lips. Cerby swayed a bit, almost falling for his 'friendly persuasion' but found the fortitude to gently push him aside. She was certainly befuddled - the heat; the balmy breeze; the heat; the drinks; the heat; his cologne…. *My, it* was *hot tonight!*

133

"Perhaps," she said, rethinking the merger, not wanting to close the door altogether; "we could have a foretaste."

"*Foreplay* did you say?" Aidan kissed her in earnest then.

Pleasantly suffused and getting into a waiting taxi a little while later, she suddenly turned and reminded her escort of the dinner party the next night.

"Tail-s required?" Reverting to type, he leaned forward insolently.

"Not the only punster here, I see." Cerby pursed her lips, chiding. "No. *Casual,* with a Capital C!"

It was only ten o'clock when she arrived back at the Inn. She found Saffi and Stevey in the Common Room engaged in a betting game of cards. Stevey had a pile of cashews on her side of the table, and Saffi appeared none too happy. They stopped playing however, when Cerby made towards them.

"Well? Any news—about Jasper's murder?" Saffi inquired.

"How's your Fancy Man" asked the other, her mind clearly on the more crucial details.

Cerby kicked off her shoes and threw herself into a comfortable old leather chair by a gas heater. She popped a handful of Stevey's winnings into her mouth. "Not too much really, once we disposed of the ridiculous fantasy that Mrs. H and Dr. Wentworth were suspects." Cerby snorted.

Saffi and Stevey sat up in alarm.

"What rot!" snarled Stevey. "I hope you told your Canadian bloke where to go with *that* theory. And *his* friend, the Inspector Detector!" She snorted derisively.

"Oh, I'm sure they're just exploring all avenues," Saffi quickly came to the Inspector's defence. (Stevey looked at her friend curiously.) "Anyway, I know the best lawyer in London." Saf reached to draw out her cell phone.

"Let's hold that thought for *if -and -when* we need it, Saf. The police have to target everyone I suppose, but the best way to get them off the hook altogether is to find the real murderer."

Saf and Stevey nodded their heads vigorously.

"OK. So; we already knew about the blunt trauma to the head; that was pretty obvious, and Aidan said there was nothing to indicate any other kind of injury. Jasper's a bit of a mystery man one gets the impression; only here a month or two, of no fixed address... Well, not exactly. Apparently, he was from Yorkshire."

"Ah yes," mumbled Stevey, stuffing her own mouth full of nuts: "That accent! Not much of a *Lassie Come Home* type though, I'd wager." She started to choke; Saffi gave her a rather too helpful thump on the back. Stevey coughed and looked daggers at Saffi. "I won them fair and square your hi*&^ness!"

Saffi pointedly ignored her and took a languid puff on a cigarette she was not supposed to be smoking indoors. In watching the smoke spiral up to the ceiling, she muttered absently: "Um... *Whatsits* from Yorkshire, isn't she?"

"Who?" Stevey asked curiously. Cerby waited for Saffi to elaborate.

"Shasta! Well, not herself, but her father has a place there."

"And so do thousands of others," said Stevey, deflating that balloon. "Why even you Saffi, have a cottage up there don't you?"

"Not exactly *mine*," Saffi waved the notion away; "but I do have family up there. Whereabouts did Aidan say that Jasper hails from?"

"Aidan reluctantly admitted to us at dinner that Jasper's last known address information was a ticket bought at the British rail station at Leeds."

"Well, that's definitely in Yorkshire." Saffi stubbed her cigarette out.

"I know Saf. I gather the police are making their usual 'inquiries' up there in the area."

"What 's Shasta's father 's name?"

"Dennis? Denton? Oh, yeah; Denning. Why?"

"Look him up on the internet of course. Wikipedia will probably have a biography of him. Here. Use this computer Bron left for use in Ewan and Dr. Wentworth's classes."

Stevey, the acknowledged computer expert of the group, typed in the browser: "Denning, Disney film,' and 'Yorkshire.' "Stands to reason there might be a connection. Shasta told you that she'd visited her father before coming here for the anniversary, right Cerb?"

"A connection? Not necessarily. I mean just because her father lives in Yorkshire? Nothing nefarious about that."

Within seconds however, the magic of the 'Net' made the connection apparent, for up came a Wiki lead on Paul Denning, mentioning his having one daughter (the women gave each other a significant look) and screenwriting credits on the *Legend of Jack Shepherd (*based on the Daniel Defoe auto-biography of the 18th century Highwayman/Escape artist.) Rated PG, it was un-critically acclaimed.

The bio had Denning currently (as of 5 years before anyway) living in Shipton, Yorkshire at the southwesterly edge of the Yorkshire Dales National Park. Also listed were some of his other fiction and non-fiction publications: the women had never heard of any of them. He appeared to be a hack writer at best. Cerby gave the information another quick scan.

"Still doesn't prove anything though" mocked Stevey. "And we might be looking for things, just because that Shasta is just so plain disagreeable. Everybody you talk to thinks so."

"True. But keep your eyes peeled for anything out of the ordinary anyway." *Nothing about that dipstick is ordinary,* Cerby thought privately. "Whoa! If that clock is right gals, better turn in; another day on the manure heap tomorrow."

Chapter Four

Tuesday

Cerby stirred slightly, still dreaming. All was in darkness except for the faint light filtering through the thin curtains from the night motion-sensor light outside in the Kitchen Courtyard. Her second story bedroom sat just over the mudroom and backed onto the courtyard. She muttered in her REM sleep, having just diagnosed Aidan with *'slipped stifle'* and bandaged him according to Bron's teachings - but a *clip clop, clip clop* softly rebounding off the cobbles in the yard below was invasively intrusive. She dragged herself upright in the bed, eyes still closed. Faint sounds now. She got up feeling drugged, went to the window and threw up the sash *à la* Clement Moore. Swirls of mist dressed the courtyard like a set for a Hammer horror movie.

The ring of horseshoe on cobble sounded eerily closer. Cerby angled her head out the window in the direction of the sound. Suddenly, as if conjured out of the wispy filaments, a black 'ghost' horse emerged out of the fog - the scene, a forgery of an *Alex Colville painting* - running up to the courtyard gate on her right, turning quickly and disappearing again at the other end of the yard into the shadowy night. Cerby said aloud, instinctively turning around; "Did you see that?" but she was alone in the room, forgetting that of course Bron was staying at the *'I's Cottage* now, and her bed was empty.

Cerby strained her ears but couldn't hear anything else. She concluded she must have been sleepwalking or still in an alcoholic haze from her dinner with Aidan. Quickly returned to her warm bed she snuggled in, thinking she had even dreamed raising the double hung window (brought on by all this talk of highwaymen etc. at supper no doubt.) *Shades of Scrooge* was her last thought; *'the culprit must have been the éclair....'*

Insistent banging on her door! "Get up! Get up everbody! Quickly, Hurvey! The horses are loos!" The sharp commanding voice of Kally cut through the walls in the hallway. The urgency was implicit. This was no joke. Yelling out 'Fire' wouldn't have been half as inspiring. Women came to their doorways, nightwear in various states of disarray. "Don't juss stand there, get your clothes on. Horses are loos everwhere."

Two things were apparent to Cerby immediately. *One*, she'd only had about a half an hour of sleep since crawling back in bed, and *Two,* what she thought was a dream was reality - there *were* horses in the courtyard.

One look at the frightened concern on Kally's face as she continued to roust out the students young and old, had Cerby throwing on a white 'tee,' woollen jumper, breeches and socks and bolting down the backstairs to jump into her Wellies like a fireman responding to a five-alarm fire. Despite the seriousness of the affair - horses could be on the roads and running into cars or vice versa - the familiar excitement at any whiff of adventure had her spirits high and adrenalin pumping. *Could this be much better than sighting an apparition or two? Really! I think not!*

Out in the KC, there were now several horses milling around in frightened circles. Shasta could already be seen to have a lead in hand and was cornering Amadeus, the black horse from Cerby's quasi-dream state, trying to calm him enough to slip on a halter and clip the lead on to take him into the closest stall; one of the two empty ones in the Old Stone Stable.

Since the gate that enclosed the Inn stable yard from the tarmac road leading to the Quad was already closed, the only way these horses could have gotten into the Kitchen Courtyard was via the entrance gate at the other end of it and the one leading into the *50 Acre Field* east of the I's cottage. Sure enough, Stevey shouted to Saffi that she had just locked those particular gates. Then the two working in tandem effectively corralled three more horses in a corner of the mews, working to calm them and halter them up with more equipment Shasta brought out from the old stable's tiny tack room. Cerby couldn't fault Shasta in this emergency, grateful for the assistance. The woman seemed to be pulling more than her own weight. Once again Cerby felt credit should be given its due. *Maybe we ARE barking up the wrong tree there,* she thought; *I'll try to be nicer to her in future.*

Sounds were now eddying up their way from the Quad, however. Cerby abruptly left her friends and Shasta where they were, unlatching the gate exiting to the tarmac, (taking meticulous care to close and lock it behind her) and ran in that direction. Bron, hair flying and coming from the direction of the *'I's Cottage* behind her, soon caught up to Cerby. At Cerby's anxious glance, Bron shouted out; "Ewan's already run ahead down to the Quad. He called me from the tack room down there to tell Kally to get help. All the horses have been let loose out of their stalls into the Quad or Big Field."

"What? All of them?"

"Yes. All! And the back gate at the furthest corner of the *50 Acre Field* by the hedgerow road is wide open. Looks to have been smashed in on purpose. Some of the horses may be in Alconbury by now..."

Or Dog forbid, thought Cerby fearfully, *on the A14, or worse, the A1!*

Excitable horses were being rounded up in the *Quad* by the *Reunionistas* (as they were even calling themselves these days after Cerby had christened them such.) It looked like a scene from Wild Bill Cody's Western Show. Some had the skills and were trying to lasso their chargers, while others could only hang on to manes or tails. It was a miracle that no one had been kicked or dragged amongst the milling herd. Bron took charge here, but Kally grabbed Cerby, shoving some halters and leads in her hand, while she herself threw open some feed bins and shovelled oat and alfalfa cubes quickly into a couple of pails.

"Kom' on" she urged Cerby as they closed and latched the gate by the arenas that separated the

Quad from the *50 Acre Field*. Making their way into the mist, Kally admonished: "Stay ver clos," but Cerby didn't have to be told. Kally, at fifteen feet away, was hardly discernable in the thick pea-soup fog.

"Oh, for some infrared binocs," she said softly, following Kally's lead of shaking the cubes in the pail, making as much noise as possible to attract any of the freed ponies.

The ground was rough with grass tuffs and hard to walk on if you couldn't see where you were going. Cerby remembered that a Cross-Country course was laid out in the *50 Acre Field* and included 5-foot deep 12-foot-long reverse jumps. These were deep pits that horse and rider were required to jump *down* into and scramble *up and out* of; it wouldn't do to fall into one of those... potential risk of broken limbs for horse or rescuer.

Sometimes the two women stopped liked statues, listening silently. They could indeed hear the soft thud of hooves on wet turf grass, moving in quiet panic over the sod. Occasionally an eerie nicker carried through the air. But the closer they thought they were coming to a small herd; the herd would take off again like phantoms of the night.

"Kally!" Cerby whispered into the foggy tentacles: "Stand still! Don't be moving about. Just shake your bucket. I'm coming your way." Cerby could tell Kally had taken her advice; she followed the sound of her shaken pail with her ears, determining her now to be about thirty feet to her right. She nearly jumped out of her own skin herself however when *Collie*, a 16- hand Pinto edged up to her backside out of the fog and dug his nose forcefully into her pail for the treats. Regaining her composure and softly reassuring him, she let him munch on the cubes, gently stroking his neck. In short order she was able to throw the halter over his head and buckle it up.

"I've got *Collie*," she yelled triumphantly into the fog, and a response came back: 'I 'av *Marcus*, *Francine*, and *Little Boy*.'

Cerby grunted quietly: "*You* would." But just then, *Caesar* nosed *Collie's* head out of the bucket and Cerby, thinking quickly, looped a lead around his neck so that at least she had hold of him too - if somewhat precariously. "And *Caesar!*"

Kally re-appeared out of the mist, leading two horses in one hand and one in the other, and she took *Collie's* lead temporarily as well so Cerby could fashion a sort of halter out of the lead around Caesar's muzzle and neck.

"We better get these ones back and see who else we're missing."

It was now about 4 a.m. and with the Fen fog still so thick, it was difficult to know what direction they should take to get back to the barn. Fortunately, they heard Ewan calling, and Cerby shouted back: "Ewan, whistle so we can find our way to you." He did, a version of Scotland the Brave, and shortly they were able to hand over their horses to *Reunionistas* who had managed to clear the School Yard.

Cerby hadn't seen Ewan look so grim. "Are there any others out there?"

Bron's serenity had *almost* cracked. It was evident in her quavering voice: "*Lord Jim* and *Sable* are gone." Lord Jim was Ewan's own show horse, a

143

huge expensive beast of 18-hands. Being a dark bay on a dark misty night trotting along a dark road - it didn't bare thinking about...

Ewan gave orders tersely for everyone to check all stall door bolts for security's sake. He was going to take out the school's Rover and check the neighbouring roads. Bron insisted on going with him and took some leads and the bucket treats just in case.

Everybody who had helped reclaim the escapees, hastened to return to the Main House where Mrs. Momfrey, attired in her bath robe, for once had steaming urns of tea and warm toast at the ready.

Bron and Ewan returned after half an hour to get better torches and left again, the strain showing visibly on their faces. Soon the sun would rise and traffic on the roads would increase.

It occurred to Cerby, now that everyone was back at the Inn, that she had not thought of Cyrius in the crisis. She kicked herself for the omission. She motioned to Saffi and Stevey; 'be back in a jiff' and got her stockinged feet into her wet wellies again, then raced across the Kitchen Courtyard, slipping as always on the damp cobblestones. Cyrius *was* in his back stall however, munching on his hay net. But the churned-up bedding on the floor indicated to Cerby that although someone forgot or didn't know enough to let him loose too, he had not been immune to the excitement. Probably the shouting voices and whinnying of other horses had panicked him a bit.

Cerby ran back to the mews' feed room, grabbed a pitchfork, and returned to the stall to fluff the bedding. During her labors, she noted a big square about 3'X3' that had been cut into the centre of one of the four, inch-thick 4'X8' rubber floor mats. *Probably a replacement 'tile'* she told herself in spreading the straw over it. It was situated right beside the old grate and drain so it occurred to her that *that* area of the stall probably got the worst of the piss and muck; she suspected the mats there deteriorated faster accordingly. She made a mental note to check on it later that day and make sure there was no debris stuck underneath deflecting urine away from the drain. Everything else looked in order, and after giving Cyrius a calming pat down, she returned to the *Long Room*.

"Gawd, isn't it cold in the mornings, even in June?" An unknown alumnus greeted her as she came in: "Tea's on, even bacon and eggs, though it's only gone 6 am."

Mrs. Momfrey had outdone herself. The motley crew gathered in the *Long Room*, some with long-sleeved pajama tops still peeking out from underneath jumpers, or the odd curler out of a head scarf, all busily chowing down after the eventful night's exertions.

"Over here Cerb," called Saffi.

Cerby suddenly became very much aware of her hunger pangs. "If I ever have no appetite, better get the undertaker," she quipped as she took her place on the bench.

"This'll warm you up Cerb." Stevey pressed a hot cup of tea into her friend's cold hands.

"YUMmmm; bacon and eggs never tasted so good," she agreed, shovelling some runny sunny-side ups onto lank whole wheat toast. "Where's Bron and Ewan?"

That question was answered when, ten minutes later, Ewan and Bron returned, followed by a motherly Mrs. Hill ensuring there were mugs in their hands full of hot liquid. Ewan stood at the front of the room. His face hadn't lost its grimness.

"Thanks to everyone for your help tonight. What was a bad turn of events could have been a lot worse!" With contained anger he continued; "We lost a horse tonight; (a collective groan escaped). Sable was run into by a truck on the other side of Alconbury, the driver mercifully unhurt! Sable had to be put down."

Ewan took a moment and collected himself amid the strained silence of the room.

"Lord Jim was found in a neighbouring farmer's field. Appears to have a leg injury but won't know about the extent until later in the day. The Vet is coming this morning and will inspect *ALL* the animals. Please be sure when you carry on your grooming today you look for any small cuts, scrapes, injuries as well to advise him of. There will be no morning class; you all look as exhausted as I feel - but there will be a Musical Ride lesson on all horses vetted for the purpose this afternoon. The RSPCA village fête is coming up in a few days and we need to carry on. Thanks again!" He and Bron abruptly turned to exit through the door to the hallway.

"Ewan, wait!" Cerby called out urgently to get his attention, voicing the question all wanted to ask: "What was this all about anyway? Someone said the gate to the *50 Acre Field* was broken open?" Others were prompted to anxiously *second* her query.

"The police have been summoned and will be out shortly." Ewan ran a weary hand over his forehead. Bron squeezed his hand tightly. "There does appear to be some *Show-tack* stolen, (Mrs. Hill sagged visibly at this news) but I'm sure that can be replaced by insurance," he hurriedly explained; (forbearing to mention that new tack has to be 'oil-cured' before use and would they have enough time for that before the event?) "I hope… think …am sure we'll be fine for the weekend fête," he finished on a positive note.

Looking at his watch: "It's now 7 a.m. and we'll start chores around 11 instead today, so no *Elevenses* necessary," turning to Mrs. Momfrey and Mayfair. The cook herded her house-help out to the kitchen to begin the clean up.

Cerby watched Ewan and Bron exit, Ewan's arm draped around Bron's shoulder, pulling her into him. *Joined at the hip* she sighed to herself. *What else can go wrong on this trip?*

It was a sorry looking lot that trudged tiredly upstairs. Cerby pulled off her jumper and reached into the pockets of her tan breeches as per usual, to lay whatever was within on the bureau by the bed. Mostly her pockets were filled with hay and straw chaff, but there was some British change and she also pulled out a scrap of paper. She was about to throw it in the waste can when she remembered its origins; she'd picked it off the school yard tarmac the evening of the murder. It was pretty crinkled and torn. She had to hold it up close to a light to try to read what was on it:

*M t me 7:3   fo..et Hane.. ake..am ...ain ...pton a
k de..g for j.. b..k........fac .*

The ink had run badly in spots. The whole thing was
pretty cryptic at first glance. *Hmm. Hanes'
underwear? Dengue fever?* All too fanciful. Yet,
Haney had sprung to mind almost immediately
since the fellow had been a recent topic of
conversation. *He certainly fits in as far as the
Wheatsheaf goes, but what 's the rest?*

Cerby sounded it out phonetically, slowly then
faster. The first part was simple enough: *Meet me
7:30*, and something to do with *Haney*? *'Ake am
ain'* she finally translated as *take a.m. train*. The rest
was impossible to decipher in her tired state, if it
even had anything to do at all with anything, but her
gut strongly suggested it did, so she placed it
carefully on the night table before sleep overcame
her.

The mid-morning chores were carried out
somberly. Cyrius must have been sensitive to the
activity and events of the morning. When Cerby
rose her hand to pat his neck, he threw his head back
and stepped back anxiously. It took Cerby by
surprise.

"It's me ole boy. Nothing to be frightened of, is
there! Nobody's going to hurt you."

Reacting to the soft tones of her voice he moved
forward again and allowed her to pat his long neck

reassuringly. She kissed his muzzle and asked for one in return. He planted one solidly on her mouth with his lovely lush velvety lips. "Next to Aid, you're the best kisser I know," she laughed. More than that though, she was pleased his nerves had calmed and he was behaving in his old manner without further encouragement.

Not a few tears were shed however, when Sable's stall stood so empty. Anyone pursuing the morning activities in the Quad had to pass by it. First the murder of the hired man, a robbery, and now Sable's not-so-accidental death had created an underlying edginess in everyone's psyche. Cerby felt answers had to be found soon or the *Reunionistas* might all pack up and leave - there would be no Musical Ride, fête fundraiser, or opportunity for Mrs. H to regain some positive advertising and marketable standing. Her luncheon chat with Mrs. H the other day was evidence indeed of the strain her friend was under and underlined the urgent need for capital. In true Mickey Rooney-Judy Garland tradition, the show had to go on: but would it?

Consequently, at *dinner* (held at 1:30 pm for a change), Cerby, Saffi and Stevey met up to discuss Cerby's *find* ('if that was what it was' she had cautioned.) Both Saffi and Stevey studied the scrap of paper.

"First of all, *is* this a legitimate clue?" Cerby questioned, looking each one full in the face. "Can we agree it's connected somehow with Jasper?"

"You found it in the vicinity of the body," Saffi acknowledged; "I don't think we can reject it out of hand. "

"This *time* reference," Cerby pursed her lips. "I'm not sure how or whether this plays into the whole thing. I stumbled on Jasper's body doing *late haying*, between 8 and 9:00 pm, and he was certainly warm when I, ah…fell on him. Someone seems to be referring to the morning of the following day. Are we talking the murderer or someone else? Regardless, if the note was on Jasper, someone may have used it to lure him down to the Quad, and his death."

"Are you going to hand it over to the police?" Stevey asked, being rational enough to be afraid of the consequences.

"I've been thinking about that, and yes, I will turn it over to Aidan at Bron's dinner party tonight," replied Cerby, nodding approvingly as Stevey handled the paper with a table napkin in case of fingerprints; "but not before we check out the handwriting."

Saffi sat up: "You know Cerb, the cursive does look kind of feminine-y. Look at the *loopy* letters"

"Yep, that's what I thought."

"OMG" moaned Stevey sarcastically. "Well, that won't be hard to trace, will it? There's only about thirty or more women here on prem alone, which number doesn't include those accommodated offsite."

Cerby tried to stifle her impatience. "OK. Point taken. But it's a starting place. *They* always say most auto accidents happen within a mile of home (kilometer to you Brits I suppose), so why not murder? What *we* need to do is eliminate all the females already on site. Like the police would do, I'm sure."

"Well why don't we just let the police handle it then?" Stevey reasoned.

"Anyway, who says it's one of us? And who 'We'?" One of Saffi's magnificently plucked eyebrows rose archly.

Cerby had no doubt her band of amateurs could contribute significantly to the professional investigation; (a strong competitive streak had *absolutely* nothing to do with it...) "Stands to reason. We're out in the country and pretty much isolated; I bet the percentages are in favour of a localized perp, murderer, I mean. And look at the murder weapon. The women here are fitter than the average and quite capable of wielding a shovel to that extent."

"So, how are we to check everyone's handwriting then," queried Saffi, now on board. "If we do it overtly, the police will step in and shut us down."

Cerby was silent while she thought. Swinging a leg over the dining table bench, preparing to go and change for the Musical Ride practise, she stood up. "Stevey, you're the brainy computer whiz, and Saf, you're our social/ financial expert. Where would you most likely find signatures? Think! And *YOU* don't need the riding practise; I do. So: I 'm leaving this up to you two to check out."

Both Saffi and Stevey's heads snapped up and shouted at her retreating back: "You're leaving us...?"

"Who made you Queen?"

"What colossal cheek!!"

Cerby without breaking stride looked back and smirked. Saffi and Stevey looked at each other in annoyance and then rose (literally) to the challenge.

151

U

"What did she mean by that last crack, anyway?" Stevey asked, still slightly miffed.

Saffi drawled: "Oh, I got the message alright. I can check any of Mrs. Hill's records and contracts for signatures, and you can check the Guest Book out in the Hall, and if need be, maybe the computer might be some help with tips on handwriting analysis."

As Cerby had left the original scrap of paper with them after all - '*don't lose this on pain of death*' - they went to Mrs. Hill's office and photocopied it, so each had a copy, placing the original in a plastic baggy that Mrs. Momfrey gave them.

"If you find anything interesting, come and get me," called Saffi to Stevey as the latter left to hunt down the Guest Book that all Reunionistas were invited to sign on arrival, (and because of the anniversary, virtually everyone had.)

Saffi asked Mrs. Hill if she minded her pawing through any receipts and/or contracts, if it might help move the murder case along. Mrs. Hill, though dubious of the elegant Saffi's ability to find anything concrete, nevertheless agreed and left Saffi to it once she had shown her where to find the filing in the crowded office space she had once shared with her husband.

"You'll put everything back the way it was though, won't you Saffira?" Mrs. Hill looked sternly over her reading glasses at Saffi, then sailed out of the office.

Not entirely sure that's possible, Saffi sighed as she looked at the cluttered prospect before her. *Well, might just as well jump in at the deep end.* She began to burrow into the untidy filing cabinet drawers, fingering through some tabs and drawing out particular files, refiling, and repeating the process in the desk drawers.

For her part, it took Stevey some time searching for the Guest Book which had originally stood on a lectern by the grand staircase in the vestibule. As she searched every where she could think of, pestering Mrs. Momfrey to distraction on possible locations, (the redoubtable Mrs. M denying that she or Mayfair might have moved it during one of their cleaning blitzes), Stevey began to have serious qualms about its disappearance.

She plopped her short sturdy frame into a leather chair in the Common Room, playing the game: *'If I were a Guest Book, where would I be?'* Whilst cogitating on that mystery, eyes scanning the general layout of the space, she happened to remark a tier of bookshelves that lined one wall of the oak panelled room.

She had never thought about it before but guessed that this had once been a private library. Some people bought books as décor accessories, but here she noticed there was some sort of order in the way the books were lined up - all the books categorized by subject being aligned by descending spine height. Most were old, spines threadbare, with a general film of dust overlaying everything. The something that had jarred her scan was a misalignment on a shelf, second from the top.

She pulled herself out of the sunken seat and walked over in that direction, idly looking at a few books on her way. When she got to the point of attraction, she pulled over a worn old step stool (there for the purpose) and climbed on to the top step. Having almost an eye level view now, she whooped with glee. There, out of most people's sight and reach, nestled amongst a bunch of out-of-date veterinary books, (and *not* according to spine size) was the thin, dustless, and rather newer-bound Guest Book.

Quite the little mystery, Stevey pondered. *No real explanation why or how the Guest Book had migrated from the front hall to this room and landed so inconspicuously on the husbandry shelf. Like Poe's 'Purloined Letter' - hidden in plain sight?* Stevey's hair spikes tingled....

She stood on tip toe and carefully angled the book out (always conscious like Saffi, of the possibility of incriminating fingerprints though painfully aware there could be 'tons' on the volume.) Then she went back to her chair and placing the book on her lap, opened it up. Using a pencil to flip the pages, she set down her photocopy of Cerby's 'scrap' to align with signatures past and present and began scanning for similarities.

In the meantime, since the murder had taken place so recently, Saffi decided to look at the reservation receipts for the anniversary reunion but finding most of these had been *online chargex affairs* with no cursive signatures, she then tackled the *Ride at Your Own Risk* waiver forms that everyone had had to sign personally on arrival. She pulled out a big file of these and as the waivers went back years and in no discernable order, she first had to categorize by same. 'Ay yi yi. Mrs. Hill, Mrs. Hill,' she murmured, shaking her head.

Once the *re-org* had been accomplished, she took the current year's worth and then like Stevey, aligned her photocopy of the 'loopy letters,' intent on matching a waiver signature.

As Saffi was rising from the desk in Mrs. Hill's office sometime later, unkinking her back by stretching her arms overhead, Stevey burst through the door.

"Think I've got one!" The elfin eyes sparkled; "What about you? Any luck?"

Saffi answered grimly: "With so few letters it's a bit hard, and of course the sequence of letters isn't usually the same…"

Stevey interrupted impatiently. "One or two of the 'comments' beside the signatures," she opened the Guest Book, "looked plausible but then other letters didn't seem to match. Still, I managed…"

Not to be outdone, Saffi looked down on Stevey from a willowy good five inches additional height, a small triumphant smile on her face. "I think I found our source, and a link perhaps besides. We ought to compare. You first!"

Rather than a verbal reply, Stevey plopped the Guest Book on the desk Saffi had been using, shoved it toward her, opening it at the page and signature besides which she deliberately set her copy. Saffi breathed in deeply, and similarly, set her Waiver sheet beside Stevey's evidence.

There was silence, finally broken by: "So what does this mean then - exactly?" Stevey's head mimicking a red-crested woodpecker's, tilted to look inquiringly at her friend.

It means," said Saffi resolutely; "I have a telephone call to make!"

Cerby had given excuses to Kally regarding Saffi and Stevey's absence from the Musical Ride rehearsal. As there were spares for the Ride anyway, and Kally knew Saffi and Stevey to be two of the most accomplished riders there in any event, she was only minorly put out, especially when Cerby assured her they would be available for the next practise.

The fête was only days away. After the excitement of the morning (on top of the recent murder) a certain malaise pervaded the practise performance. Kally tried to motivate her charges; who in turn tried to spur on their chargers; who essentially were having none of it. Horses being sensitive creatures, they were all picking up on the latent fear of their riders i.e., they were straining at their bits even at a walk; aiming a kick at the horse behind or trying to bite the horse in front; ears back to show their displeasure. Even the addition of music to the workout had done little to calm either horse or rider.

Finally, Kally called a halt and brought everyone into the centre of the arena. Her own version of a *St Crispin's Day* speech to rally the troops, *did* actually inspire the equestrians to insist on their mounts' cooperation. It was instilled in everybody the importance of rising above their own concerns, reminding them that the fundraiser was for the RSPCA and Alaerton itself. There wasn't a rider there whose time at the school hadn't been special, with Mrs. Hill a den-mother par excellence. The former students didn't need any further prompting.

Cerby on the other hand, momentarily distracted by her social engagement that evening and wondering what her absent friends were up to, performed at a level less than to be expected. Kally directed a lot of 'loud' instruction her way, embarrassing Cerby into paying more attention.

It didn't help either that *that Shasta woman*, who was paired with another alumni on this occasion and taking the outside position, seemed to focus somewhere else and lose control every time she and Cerby crossed paths at the bottom of the arena. Edging over and bumping into Cyrius' rump, Shasta forced him out of the Ride alignment, causing Kally to heap even more verbal abuse on Cerby's riding skills.

"You are messink up the line Cerby. Keep your right leg pressink in and heel out. Push! Avay from the boards I said! Sit up (when Cyrius made unexpected side steps). Kom on Cerby, rein 'im in! You, Shasta. Vatch where you are go'ink."

Connecting with Cerby's over-the-shoulder glare, Shasta acted out and mouthed an exaggerated apology during the bi-pass. As they came in close contact once again however, only Cerby could see beneath the peak of Shasta's helmet, her gloating, infuriating smirk.

This was turning out to be the longest and hardest practise yet...

Back at the Inn, after the post -practise cooling-down walkies for participating horses, Cerby retrieved a message from Monte and Mitch on the hallway telephone stand: *'Dinner at Eight; won't be late'* indicating they were back from their rambles and *would* be coming to Bron and Ewan's small dinner party at the *'I's Cottage*. Saved her the trouble of calling them to find out their plans. Saffi and Stevey, who had been invited also, had made their excuses to Bron that afternoon which Bron had already relayed to Cerby, indicating they had left the school grounds and would be stuck in Huntingdon for the rest of the afternoon.

Cerby had returned to her bedroom, ambivalent about being on Aidan's arm for the night, still percolating over the row that had been partially responsible for her trip to England in the first place. Hopefully, those mixed emotions would quell any nostalgic pain arising from seeing Bron and Ewan together and similarly keep her feelings for Aidan at bay. The old crush-ache on Ewan was fading fast though, now that Cerby was constantly remonstrating with herself for being such a colossal fool. With any luck, she could sensibly put both men behind her for the night.

She threw down helmet, riding gloves and jacket onto her bed in some annoyance at going into the 'lion's den' that evening without (emotional) backup. Stevey and Saffi were nowhere on the premises and had in fact, left a further personal and cryptic message for her with Mrs. Hill that they were *still* in Huntingdon 'on a mission', despite the hour having gone five o'clock.

"Probably clothes shopping," Mrs. Hill had translated good-naturedly. "Am I to expect any further messages? I quite like being secretary for you girls," she chuckled.

Cerby was not likewise amused, however. She had hoped to have something concrete for Aidan regarding the paper clue when he showed for the dinner party that night - an example of her prowess as a natural private eye, perhaps inspire his admiration. It would then make spurning him further all that more delicious. Like the inimitable Darcy's, *'once having lost my good opinion'* she intended to make her's manifest. Even the kisses and 'dry rub' exchanged the night before would only make his punishment the sweeter.

"Aidan. I *said* *Big* *C*-casual. *English*-casual, not *Farmer Brown* casual!"

"My sweet, you're determined to be annoyed with me tonight I see."

His passive aggressive response aggravated Cerby even more. *He's so... so.... bloody sure of himself. Who does he think he is anyway?*

"What I meant to say Aidan," she replied archly, the two of them having rapped on the door simultaneously, now standing at the threshold of the *'T's* Cottage side by side like soldiers: "a dinner party even at an equestrian centre in England, means the men are to wear slacks and appropriate shirt, jacket, and tie - *not* jeans (*tight fitting Tony Hillfigure's regardless*) - and a denim shirt (*open-necked 'Polo', or not*)."

The lecture was cut short by the door being thrown open to reveal an equally denim-outfitted Ewan and Bron. Cerby, overdressed by far in skirt, flowery blouse, and stockings, closed her mouth with a snap, refusing to look at Aidan whose wide grin she could *feel* boring into her back as she passed over the threshold first.

There was the usual gridlock manifested in the vestibule: the men shaking hands and an exchange of banter, while Cerby presented Bron with a bottle of Vin Santo and Biscotti; (hostess accoutrements she had asked Aidan to pick up in Alconbury before taxied out to Alaerton.) Soon enough however, she and Aidan were settled with wine glass in hand on the comfortable chinoiserie sofa in front of the fireplace in the main parlour.

Cerby looked around at the neat centre-hall designed cottage, and couldn't suppress the thought, *this might have been mine once upon a time.* She grudgingly had to admit though, as she got up for a closer look, that Bron was a wiz in the home decorating department, *as well as everything else apparently.* Harrumph. Aidan came up behind her and seeing Cerby's sulky expression, pinched her butt meaningfully in passing.

"Oh, ah! Lovely Feng Shui Bron. Great flow. Did you sew the curtains too?"

Aidan managed another pinch on his return from the hors d'oeuvre table.

"I mean, honestly, everything matches so beautifully. Are you sure you didn't hire Kathy Ireland to do all this," Cerby tittered inanely.

"Awk-ward" Aidan whispered in her ear, as he filled her glass. "Drink up!" he ordered. Feeling also the need to 'fill the space' with a compliment aimed at both Ewan and Bron, he made a show of looking approvingly around the room. "I think you've both (a nod to Ewan's DIY furniture projects) done wonders with this house. If *I'm* ever looking for a decorator, I know who to call."

"I'll drink to that," Cerby said, mustering more enthusiasm with each subsequent sip. She really couldn't deny the talents of either of her old friends.

After another glass of wine, even she had to forfeit to the knowledge that Ewan and Bron fit together like a 'horse and carriage.' *Why fight it? AND,* in a bit of an alcoholic haze, she couldn't help but compare the lanky Ewan to the buff Aidan - chatting now like old friends - finding the former now lacking any attraction after all and the latter gaining points.

Just as the appetisers were making the second round, there was a knock at the door, and as it wasn't latched, Monte and Mitch poked their heads in.

"Come in. Come in," welcomed Ewan, wine glass offerings in each hand, motioning them into the sitting room in hospitable fashion. Both Monte and Mitch pulled up short however, glaring pointedly at Cerby, who coloured and turned her head away as if she hadn't noticed.

"But *you* said," Mitch launched at her: "that this was to be *casual* casual. We *know* what that means!"

It would have been impossible to disregard her Gay friends' sartorial splendour. Monte and Mitch complimented each other in a veritable *Brian Gluckstein* exhibition of browns, grays, and beiges, more appropriate for a soiree in the States, than a country *casual* dinner crowd in England.

"Just a matter of interpretation boys," Aidan jumped to Cerby's defence, knowing flattery would turn the tide. "I only wish the *'Heir and his spare'* could pop in and see you now. Shame really."

"Yes, well wouldn't that have been something…for the princes," Mitch conceded, his flushed face resuming its normal colour. Monte, always behind him, had already laughed off this latest *CL faux pas*.

At dinner, Bron and Ewan sat at either ends of the table; Cerby and Aidan placed on one side and Monte and Mitch on the other. Whether by design or not, Cerby was next to Bron and Aidan next to Ewan. Bron had prepared a lovely repast of chicken, deviled quails' eggs, vegetables, and salad with homemade bread.

When could she possibly have had time to do all this? Cerby sniffed, taking a few more draughts of her wine and another deviled egg 'to go with.' She didn't refuse second helpings of the main course when offered it, either.

Aidan was asking questions about the equitation centre, people, and the surrounding area, letting Ewan respond with obvious enjoyment. Although he looked and sounded like any interested guest, Cerby knew he was listening intently for a reason. Aidan's mind wouldn't be straying far from the crime 'at hand', cherry-picking information wherever he could find it. Ewan was a natural resource.

Eventually Ewan directed a suggestion to Bron. "We should all take a walk to the village after dinner; we can lead the way," which prompted a sharper response from Cerby than she had meant to utter: "I *DO* know the way, Ewan!"

As everyone there interpreted this as a reference to the romance between Cerby and Ewan and their 'Bridge of Sighs' assignations, the statement's dampening effect resulted in constrained silence. Bron dropped her head to concentrate on eating and Ewan stiffly settled back in his dining chair. Aidan, who was not ignorant of Cerby's former liaison with Ewan, *vis-a-vis* Mitch and Monte, was quick to respond likewise. A frown of displeasure creased his forehead as he looked her in the eye and pinched her thigh under the table - *hard* this time.

'Ow!' she wailed, looking at him in surprise. (*Why did he always resort to that?*) Mitch in turn adeptly broke the *sangfroid* by hastily commenting on an oil picture hanging over the fireplace.

163

"Is that a real Landseer, or '*school of*'?" he inquired, flourishing his white dinner napkin in such a way as to unwittingly invite comparison to Hugh Laurie's rendition of an 18th-century *Blackadder* fop. There was a moment of silence, then everyone broke into loud laughter (leaving Mitch in the dark) until Monte, guffawing the loudest, imitated him with *his* napkin, flourishing it even more outrageously*: "*Oh, '*school of,*' dear boy, '*school of*' Obviously*!"* setting off another round of hilarity.

Mitch, unoffended, was only too happy to be both the centre of attention and have had a small hand in restoring the peace.

Cerby did have *buyer's remorse,* however. Whether it was the wine or not, the negativity she felt for Bron especially was beginning to pall and she felt it was degrading to her, Cerby, to carry on that way. She had left England of her own free will. Ewan had not really pursued her to the ends of the earth at the time, more intent on his career it would appear. And ten years *had* passed after all. So, with these thoughts circulating in her head, when clearing of the table began, she deftly removed some of the empty plates and followed Bron into the kitchen.

Bron was studiously loading up the dishwasher. After a silence of a minute or two, Cerby handed her some rinsed Wedgewood: "Bron, can I talk to you for a moment?"

Bron's back stiffened slightly, expecting a verbal blow.

"Bron. I have to apologize - to both you and Ewan. I've been a bit beastly, haven't I?" Cerby was determined to eat crow. Taking hold of Bron's shoulders and turning her round so they could face each other, she said in her direct way. "Honestly, I don't know what I was thinking of? Well, I do actually. I guess my memories were locked in the past and I expected the same circumstances to exist in the present. And yet we've all grown older, moved on, haven't we?

"I just wanted to say, can't *we* go back though to like it was, you and I, all those years ago. We had such good times, and I don't want my stupid temperament to spoil it for us going forward, now that we've all found each other again."

Bron's face suffused with an inner relief. "I'd like that Cerby. That's why I spent those first couple of days in our old room with you. But I soon saw the lay of the land, and I couldn't walk around on eggshells forever. I didn't want to hurt you, but the breakup was so awfully long ago."

"Never mind that now Bron. Don't you remember Stevey, you, Saffi and I: '*One for all, and all for one*,' the one exception being dance partners at the Alconbury disco. Christened ourselves the '*Cavaliers*.' What a hoot when I look back on it now."

Both women grew misty at the shared memory. Cerby grew serious again.

"I mean it Bron. I'm always a bit slow - ask anyone - but I can see you and Ewan belong together. Believe me; I'm happy for you, both of you. Really and truly, cross my little ole *royalist* heart!"

Bron opened her arms with a beatific expression, and they sealed their reconciliation with a heartfelt hug.

When they returned to the couch in front of the fire though, it was obvious that the males of the party - all cowering on the *bar* side of the room - had been waiting for World War III to erupt in the kitchen. The men looked like a herd of deer caught in the headlights, unsure how to handle the women's emotional state when they reappeared. But Bron and Cerby having a good laugh at the tableau *they* now encountered, raised a glass to each other in a demonstrably, comradely way; the tension in the room correspondingly mercuried down four points. The real fun began.

Later that night Aidan walked Cerby the short seventy-five yards back to the Inn. "There was no need Aidan to mark me black and blue at dinner. Women *can* settle their own differences without getting into pitched battle, you know. We do have brains."

"Fortunately for *man*kind," Aidan drawled.

"Laugh all you want, Mr. RCMP Inspector. I had something for you tonight, but now you'll just have to wait until tomorrow." Cerby's tone was punishing, thinking of the paper scrap she'd left in Saf and Stevey's care.

Aidan however had a different interpretation. He grabbed her impulsively and pushed her up roughly against the stone wall of the mews, the scent of his Tom Ford cologne washing over her like a tidal wave. *Was it that or the wine, making her lightheaded and tipsy?*

"And I have something for *you...*" he whispered hoarsely.

He pressed in hard against her, his thighs intertwining with hers, hands slowly inching higher up the sides of her breasts. His clean, male scent was almost more overwhelming in its purity than the cologne.

A small moan escaped Cerby as he nuzzled her neck, his lips zoning in on hers in a long suffocating kiss. Cerby was sinking fast into a hormonal whirlpool. The random thought however, that Mrs. H might be somewhere in the vicinity having a smoke, chastened her immediately and way more effectively than a bucket of cold water. At that moment also, a sprinkle of cool rain began to fall.

"Ahh. Umm. It's a bit too damp tonight..." she dropped her head and exhaled deeply.

"Is it now?" Aidan continued to grope her rump possessively, kneading her nether cheeks suggestively, pressing even closer against her soft compliant body.

Blushing, Cerby gently tried pushing him back. "No. I meant I think it might storm and it's getting cool. Anyway, don't you have a mystery to solve?" she said pointedly, trying to redirect his thoughts, (*and hers*).

"You certainly know how to take the wind out of a guy's ...*sails*, Cerby." Aidan's ironic look spoke volumes. "I take it, you're trying to ditch me for the night." He dropped his hold reluctantly and allowed her to smooth her clothing. He managed one more kiss even so.

How come I'm the one drowning and breathless but he's the one who 'blinked first'?

He bid her a not altogether *happy* goodnight, however. "This is getting to be a habit Cerb. Just remember though, habits like rules were meant to be broken!" He took her hand, turned it over and raised it to his lips, looking determinedly into her eyes. Then he trailed butterfly kisses softly up her arm until she hastily reclaimed it. Taking that as the final rebuke of the evening, he shoved a hand in his pocket as if looking for something. Remembering himself, he took a step back. With a mocking salute that was half 'bow,' he turned and walked off purposely in the direction of the Quad 's parking lot where Cerby knew Monte and Mitch would have waited in their rental vehicle to take him back to the *Highwayman* with them.

It was with some relief from the intensity of the moment that Cerby softly treaded up the back stairs and retreated to her bedroom. She had been more tempted than she cared to admit in letting Aidan breach her defences. *Did **he** know that though*? She was hoping she hadn't carried his *'lesson'* too far. It *was* becoming ever harder to sustain her own 'old' righteous anger; to ward off his advancements. Worse, she wasn't sure she wanted to….

Chapter Five

Wednesday

Another telephone message inscribed on a sticky note stuck to her bedroom door awaited Cerby that evening, indicating that Saffi and Stevey were staying overnight in Huntingdon at 'The George' and did not know when they would return.

Cerby's irritation with her friends increased exponentially. There had been a murder, a robbery (of sorts) and a fête coming up shortly on which, to some degree, Mrs. H's future depended. What were they thinking, shopping or pubbing at this crucial time?

She did not relish making further excuses for their absence to Kally as well. Regardless of their superior riding skills, they needed to sync up with the Musical Ride. Also, she would have to do their morning muck outs for them and that meant getting an earlier start than normal before breakfast. *Blast!* So, after a fitful sleep, in which Aidan figured prominently, she woke up in a foul humour. She had never enjoyed rising with the dawn but even so, Cerby had already calculated on doing the *MIA's* mounts first - Annabelle and Malachi - and Cyrius last. As she worked about in the first two stalls, she dwelt on the post -dinner conversation in the *T's Cottage*, and in particular, Aidan's response to

Ewan's queries on both the murder investigation and the break-in:

> *"Unofficially, because as you know I'm just visiting," (throwing a meaningful glance Cerby's way), my understanding is that they feel both incidents are connected —not separate crimes."*
>
> *Ewan frowned. "What makes them think that? Though I am rather glad if the police have winnowed down the perpetrators from two to one; one's bad enough of course."*
>
> *"I don't think we can be too blasé yet. It may be only one mastermind, but how many are involved? I shouldn't really say also, but it may give you a modicum of peace to know that the tack purportedly stolen was recovered in a culvert not far along from the 50 Acre Field's back fence. Hope you haven't purchased any new stock? (Ewan shook his head; Bron and Cerby looked at each other in amazement). That would indicate the robber wasn't really after that merchandise."*
>
> *Ewan took a sip of his drink, stretching out his long legs to the fire, wriggling his toes in the warmth. "So, what you're saying is, all that commotion, letting the horses out etc. was created to screen something else."*
>
> *Aidan nodded, appreciative of Ewan's quick deduction. "Got it in one Ewan. A Red Herring in fact."*
>
> *"But what was the blighter trying to accomplish?"*

"If we knew that, we'd have Jasper's murderer too most likely." Silence reigned for a moment. "Can anyone think of anything that was out of the ordinary last night - I mean besides 20 horses milling around at 2 in the morning along with 30 people in their jammies?"

Cerby convulsed in laughter. It did seem an odd question and conjured a visual that everyone in the room seemed to connect with at the same time. Hosts and guests were in 'stitches' likewise. After the laughter had subsided, Cerby settled back into the corner of the sofa, balancing her glass of the 'Vin' on her knee and chewing on an almond biscotti somewhat tentatively. After a minute or two, she leaned into the circle of friends.

"I don't know if this has any significance, but after we had recaptured all the horses – except poor Sable and Lord Jim –I had forgotten about Cyrius, so I went to check on him. He was still in his stall, although he looked pretty disturbed by all the goings on. But here's the thing: he was the only one who hadn't escaped or been let out."

Bron cut in: "Yes, but he's at the back of the old stables, and most likely, whoever tampered with the other stalls didn't realize he was back there. Remember that episode with Brandy?"

Cerby shuddered and explained for the benefit of the others: "Brandy was a pony that arrived at the Centre ten years ago when Bron and I were students. He was housed

171

back there in the stall next to Cyrius' by the horse carters. The awful thing was, that as the old stables weren't being used at the time, he was pretty much forgotten."

Bron motioned with her goblet to Cerby: "It was you who fortunately discovered him, and you who asked one of the A.I.'s whether he was to be mucked out or moved to another stall, not knowing his circumstances."

Cerby nodded: "Then all hell broke out, with blame rocketing back and forth amongst the A.I.'s and the 'I 'at the time, Shane Motters. Remember Ewan, you took some courses under him. Well, Brandy, the poor little chap, hadn't been fed or watered for two and a half WHOLE days, the epitome of horse negligence! After the recriminations though, people fussed over him like he was Dr. Manette rescued from the Bastille. The up-side was he became everybody's pet and after that abuse received more than his fair share of treats and care from then on."

"So," Mitch interjected, trying to get the discussion back on track; "if the stolen tack isn't an issue, this criminal isn't somebody who holds a grudge against Mrs. Hill and/ or the upcoming fête events this weekend, right?"

"Fancy you turning all Sherlock Holmesy?" Monte admiringly raised a glass to his lover.

*Aidan agreed in principle. "I don't **think** someone would commit murder just to forestall a Musical Ride -unless one of the riders was really, really, really **bad**." He* *chuckled, delivering his comment straight-faced to a mighty indignant Cerby. Aidan hurried on; "Though that's just the kind of brainstorming that goes on at headquarters. And we can't absolutely rule out the fête event as being at least some part of the puzzle."*

*Cerby sensibly decided not to spar with Aidan any further. "The fête could either be a part of the solution, or a solution to part of the problem?" Golly. How trite. What **was** she saying? She must stop drinking!*

"Wow, that's profound! Good try Cerb, but no cigar. We don't actually seem to be any further along in discovering why the murder? Or the break-in when it comes to that?" Monte patted Mitch's knee fondly, expecting a response from that quarter, but got nothing other than sour agreement.

Aidan continued: "Jock...er... D.I. Wallace is up to his eyeballs in other cases. He's trying to give our case as much attention as it deserves but..." Aidan broke off. The un-spoken word implicit, indicating that this might end up a cold case given the lack of men and resources to handle everything currently on the Detective Inspector's plate. He knew too well about the scarcity of police resources and cutbacks, whatever the side of The Pond one was on. "I suspect," Aidan spoke confidentially; "if it were not for the fact Jock and I are Bro's-In-Law and worked together in the past, this case may well have slipped to the bottom of the pile."

Now he sat back, draping his arm along the sofa and tapping Cerby's shoulder absently, which Cerby shrugged off in annoyance. "Jock's line of inquiry seems to be concentrating more on the murder victim himself i.e., newish to the area; who did he know here if anybody; where did he come from; what are his connections? Unfortunately, there were no prints on the murder weapon of any kind, but not unusual at a stable where practically everyone wears work or riding gloves."

Cerby had wondered again if she should interject at this point and advise the group of the Cavaliers' own line of inquiry but decided until there was really something concrete to say, she would back off. Besides which, she and her cohorts had held back what might be an important bit of information. She could imagine how Jock and Aidan would react to that! No, best to sit on it for a while. She graced Aidan with a beatific smile instead. She was unaware that Aidan was asking himself as he cocked his head in her direction: What's Cerby up to? Feigning ignorance himself, he smiled back innocently too ...

As Cerby ran over the scenario and this dialogue in her head, she gathered her tools together and placed them in the wheelbarrow to make her way up the tarmac road to Cyrius' stall.

If the police think it's not about Mrs. H's financial status or the fête, what IS the connection with

*Jasper? We know he's from Yorkshire, but what was he doing here, a long way away from his home base? There's plenty of horse farms in between, and (no disrespect to Mrs. H) better off for employment purposes. He had to be here for a reason. He **offered** to work for just room and board: pretty unusual in this day and age unless he was a closet millionaire. Wish I knew what the girls have discovered, if anything?*

She shook her head, as if trying to clear some mental cobwebs. *Geez - I better hurry and finish the mucking out. S*he'd completely forgotten that this was the morning of the practise Horsemaster's test. And, later on in the afternoon, another tortuous Musical Ride.

She deposited the tools of her trade outside Cyrius' stall door. Cyrius was complacent today. "Well buddy of mine, coming up to our last practises soon." Cerby gave his lowered muzzle a quick kiss and a firm pat on the neck. "We'll show them, don't you worry. Be back after the test and lunch, m' boy, to clean your stall and tack you up."

She swatted fruitlessly at some buzzing *bluebottles,* writing a '*note to self*' that Cyrius might later require a fly mask and a drop or two of saline solution on the eye lid to combat any lurking conjunctivitis. "Keep cool!" she added, running off in the direction of the arena, the remark addressed as much to herself as to Cyrius.

Cerby had changed from her denims to riding breeches and an informal T-shirt. The Horsemaster's pre-test would be casual Ewan had said, a two-parter: one on tack and the other on horse ridership with the real 'exam' taking place it had been decided, on the day of the fête sometime after the Musical Ride. It would be part of the public entertainment, and although more of a light-hearted gymkhana for the riders themselves, it was hoped that such events would garner interest in the equitation classes offered at Alaerton.

Cerby entered the arena on foot. Along the one end, the letters MCH leaped out at her inconsequentially along the boards, but mats had been laid down in front of these upon which were various bits, harness equipment, veterinary applications, types of saddlery, spurs etc. These items were all numbered, and contestants were handed an entry sheet with a list of corresponding numbers. In this timed event, they had to go down the line and print the name and use of the item presented, check off some multiple-choice questions, then give their list to Ewan at the end.

At *H*, the end of the line for the written test, a sort of relay was set up. There were two teams and six horses. Each contestant had to ride three different horses but did not have the choice of their mount. The relay routine was as follows:

> Walk from *C* to *A*, turn left to *F* and trot through *B* to *X*, canter, turning at *E*.
> Jump over a 36" jump between *E* and *K*.
> Commence sitting trot at *A* back to *C*.

This seems simple enough, but rider and mount get used to each other's quirks over time, and in this case, the equestrians were not allowed to ride their own horse at all, making the test that much tougher in order to showcase true riding skill. Ewan would point out the horse, and the Rider had to adjust stirrups, jump on its back, and execute the routine, three times on three different horses. AND, it was a timed event also.

Cerby could not believe it when the very first horse she was pointed to was actually a small white cob pony (Smoke by name) hardly ten hands high and usually ridden by children. Sitting on Smoke with feet barely off the ground seemed utterly unfair to both horse and rider. She had much consternation in taking him over the three-foot fence.

What were they thinking??!!! Coming up to it, she had no confidence at all that he would not balk and throw *her* **OVER** the fence instead of clearing it, but much to her extreme surprise, he took the jump with ease. Unfortunate it was for Smoke however, that with her lack of confidence, Cerby leant too far back, then boomeranged forward and back again on landing, giving Smoke a nasty sock in the jaw with the *bit*.

She cursed herself, feeling very badly for Smoke and about her performance. However, returning to *C*, and getting into the competitive nature of the relay, she did well on her next two mounts - Annabelle the feisty and barely controllable thoroughbred, and Miracle, a huge lumbering Belgian mix who threatened to split her crotch just sitting astride him.

It was like taking an Indian elephant over the jump, but Miracle landed solidly, nevertheless. Ewan 's praise 'Well done Cerby' made her blush but followed by his 'Could do better' comment on her returned written exam made her realize she had some studying up to do on the tack portion of the test—maybe Bron would help her. She'd have no hesitation now in asking, and she still had a couple of days to brush up.

The test was enjoyed by everyone; the more so as there was no 'public' pressure involved in this one, but the competition would go up a notch on the day of the fête. There would be prizes awarded. Cerby could see that in the *50 Acre Field* some smaller marquees were already being put up in advance of the RSPCA/anniversary celebration. Their festive colours were lifting her spirits. It was hard to recall that a murder had *actually* taken place not even a week ago.

Lunch was an anxious affair for Cerby however, as there was still no sign of Saffi and Stevey although Mrs. H relayed to her that the last time she'd heard from them, she was informed they had some 'tasty' information to reveal to everyone – whatever that meant?

Cerby was mostly concerned however, with Mrs. H's appearance. In speaking with her it was clear the timing of the fête, (and all the organization *that* entailed) following as it *did* hard on the heels of an unsolved murder and pseudo-robbery, had taken its toll. If it wasn't for Ewan and Bron stepping in to be intermediaries with the local participants; calming any fears of adverse publicity; and going the extra mile to accommodate sponsors, the whole event might well have had to be cancelled.

No wonder Doc Wentworth felt the need to stay close by as a support for Mrs. H in the midst of these trials. Cerby herself was intent on the show going on: if Mrs. H had to sell up, any horses that couldn't be found new homes would end up as most horses do, on *'slaughterhorse row'*. Cerby had already sworn and was determined, in the worst-case scenario, that no matter what it cost her (if Mrs. H would allow it) she would transport Cyrius back to Vermont to a friend's farm, letting him live out his retirement pastured there and in her care.

Saffi's left hand whisked away strands of hair whipping into her eyes as they sped along the A-I. The cream silk scarf around her neck was half out the window.

"Are we almost there?" Mitch's plaintiff voice squeaked from the back seat. "And, do you have to drive like a *Formula Oner?* We'd like to get there in one piece, not pieces!"

"I thought I told you to *'go'* before we left," laughed Saffi, ignoring the fear in Mitch's voice.

Stevey, sitting beside Saffi in the front passenger seat was immersed in the map, which also flapped about almost uncontrollably in the wind generated by the rolled down window on her side. "Saf, if you take the next ramp off, we can take the secondary route on to Shipton. There. There's the sign. Pull off here!"

"Holy cow, the speed limit is 30 km on this cloverleaf Saffi, not freaking *80 mph*!" Monte inserted his head between the front seats. So far, he had managed to keep *his* concerns under wraps. "This is *our* rental car you know. We've got to return it in one piece; no dents, bangs or rollovers."

Saffi retorted: "I'll have you know I didn't just jump and racehorses, I was junior Mini Minor Cross-Country Relay driver in my late teens. I've got the trophies to prove it. Anyway, we're not far now. How long did we predict it would take Stevey?"

"Um, about three and a quarter. I'd say maybe another 20 minutes."

"Excellent. We've made very good time then. It will be nice to see my cousin in any event. What's the name of the pub we're meeting him at again?"

"The Lame Duck."

"Sounds *very* promising," Mitch snorted.

"Oh look, look! A lych-gate! Stop Saffi; stop here!"

"Not now Monte. Maybe on the way back. Let's do what we came for first. Despite leaving at dawn, it's after 9, and we don't want to be too late getting back if we can help it. We'll make this short. We might just make it back for the Musical Ride practise."

Monte sighed in disappointment. That meant more speeding. "Ok, but if there's any good light at all, I *do* want to take a picture of the one we just passed on the way back."

After *dinner* as promised, Cerby returned to Cyrius' stall. As the Musical Ride practise would be starting in about half an hour, she meant to do the stall first and then give Cyrius a good groom before she tacked him up. She hung her second-best hacking jacket off a nail on the outside wall, then positioned the wheelbarrow against the inside wall for when it was required.

"Move over. Atta boy." Inside the stall, she pushed Cyrius lightly on the shoulder with only two fingers, and he side-stepped to the far wall where his hay net invited a munch. With Cyrius thus engaged, Cerby commenced to remove wet and dirty straw from the corners of the stall as per her routine, working into the centre.

After a few minutes thus engaged, her pitchfork got stuck. *What the 'hey'?* In removing the soiled straw atop, she perceived that the smaller 'tile' horse mat she'd noted the other day by the centre drain, was lipped up along one edge. The rubber mats in this stall were thicker than the normal half inch and correspondingly heavier. Cerby cursed. She'd have to lever it up a bit in order to shimmy it over and lie it down flat again if Cyrius wasn't to catch his hoof or ankle on it - then she would have to relay the bedding. She sighed. She had not been expecting to do the extra work, and the temperature outside was climbing. Now she'd be that much more tired out, dirty, and *mucho* sweaty before they even started the 'Ride' practise. A quick shower beforehand would be quite out of the question

She reached for the pitchfork and successfully began to pry the heavy, awkward mat up until she could raise it on end and brace herself against the uppermost edge. She put both gloved hands on each of the topmost corners with the intent to jiggle the bottom end properly back into place, then lower it flat again. But, when she got it half raised, piss dripping off the underside of it to her disgust, she was surprised to see embedded in the floor a wooden square with an old iron ring laid flat into it.

Curiosity peeked, and sure that Cyrius was contentedly snacking, she let the rubber rectangle fall sideways (Cyrius moving another step over and away at the sound.)

The shallow hole revealed, proved rather mucky about the edges so she couldn't really get down on her knees. She bent over awkwardly and grasped the ring with one hand, then two, but couldn't pull the door up. On closer inspection and with trial and error, she discovered a clever device in the lock mechanism and instead pulled the ring further up toward her and turned *it* a couple of revolutions. She could hear it grudgingly 'give.' Now she pulled again with some effort and the trap door came up half-way.

Making note of the fact that the opening lay close to the 'proper' drain in the floor of the stall, she presumed the pit so revealed had something to do with a high- water table and 'sumping', although she couldn't recall ever hearing about flooding on this higher part of the property or expected that it would ever take place. Perhaps it had once long ago served as some kind of well, as it *was* bricked on the sides and the floor. The rather small dimensions - 5'X5'X 5' - would appear to discount that theory also though.

Bent over and entirely engrossed in the puzzle over its use, she failed to notice a startled Cyrius' head rear up sharply, or the heavy steel bucket that glanced smartly off the side of her own skull as she moved backward to pull the trap door all the way up. The door fell outward on its hinges as her body was propelled into and bounced off the side of the wheelbarrow. She collapsed onto straw, stunned, putting her hand in shocked amazement to her head and feeling the stickiness of blood running down her scalp.

She thought somehow in her muddled state that Cyrius must have kicked her but shaking off drowsiness and slowly staggering out of trampling range, she grabbed the rough whitewashed wall and pulled herself up, queasy with the effort.

"*YOU* stupid bitch!" a quiet but shrill voice menaced from behind her. "Seems we *were* fated to cross paths after all these years - surprise, surprise!"

Cerby's eyes were clearing although her assailant was out of focus and she herself appeared to be swaying…to the music? *Oi, the music! Someone had turned on the music in the arena for the Musical Ride already. Loud, noisy, brass band music. And she was late. Practically everyone else would be there, either riding or watching the rehearsal.*

"Shasta," she mumbled blearily; "What *are* you on about? hat's going on? Is Cyrius okay?"

"Don't play dumb with me!"

For the first time, Cerby realized with another shock, Shasta was holding a handgun and it was pointed directly at her. The cold and steely weapon matched only by its possessor's visage.

Was she hallucinating? That bang on the head...

"Too bad your stupid little friends aren't here although I guess they did have just enough brains between them to make a connection."

"Connection?? Not *playing* dumb Shasta - I *am* dumb. Haven't a clue what you're talking about?"

Shasta sniggered. "Well, you got that right; the dumb part at least. I saw them in Huntingdon yesterday. Followed them into the Library Archives there. Sure enough, I heard them asking for anything relating to Thomas Haney. You don't think I know?"

"Know **what** for Pete's sake?" *(The effort of raising her voice made her nauseous).* Cerby rubbed her sore head as if that would make the pain disappear.

"You're standing right over Haney's vault; where he hid the goods."

"Are you talking about the Highwayman? From two and a half centuries ago!" asked Cerby, only semi- alert but incredulous, nevertheless.

Shasta sneered in reply. "Well, you're too late to the party obviously, bitch."

"Too?"

"**Stop repeating everything I say:** a question for a question!"

Shasta waved the gun hysterically and Cerby suddenly experienced real fear. This was actually happening. Something else clicked.

"Jasper got here before you, is that it? That antique earring, I found... Holy Cow? Were you the one that took the notice down? But Mayfair found and took it out of the Lost and Found box; she was wearing both. Wait. How did Jaspar know about it; the stash I mean?"

Keep her talking, ask questions. Oh why did this stall have to be so far removed from the people traffic in the Quad?

Cerby felt her deodorant would in no way be able to cope with sweat glands working prodigiously overtime. She followed Shasta's movements with religious fervor, now that she fully comprehended the extreme danger she was in.

Shasta moved slowly out of the doorway to the inside of the stall door. Never veering from facing her hostage, she reached up to unhook the top portion of the Dutch door in order to close it from the inside.

"No one's usually around here at this hour of the day, but why invite inspection, eh?"

Cerby felt a pang at the disappearance of daylight as the shut door plunged the stall momentarily into darkness. She felt woozy, but there was no mistaking the sound of Shasta's boots moving in the stall or Cyrius' body moving away from her. Slowly her heavy eyes got used to the dim interior and she faced her opponent.

Shasta's voice was condescending as she paced like a caged tiger: "Jasper worked at my father's farm in Yorkshire. (*Cerby could tell by the distinctly derogatory emphasis on the word 'Father' there was no love lost there.*) My father was just sooooo proud of the research he had done for that Disney screenplay - the reason he'd dumped me off here at Alaerton in the first place, that time years ago. I offered then, to help him do his research on highwaymen of the period, but he told me I was just a kid. I was seventeen for crying out loud, old enough!"

Her voice descended into self-pity: "Didn't want to be bothered with me; thought I'd be happier orphaned off amongst you lot while he worked and traipsed around England having a jolly old junket by himself. I discovered eventually - years later in fact - that he came across the Haney story in the Huntingdon archives, just like your interfering friends!"

*What **was** she on about? This must have something to do with Saf and Stevey's disappearance. Cerby groaned. She had a bad feeling.*

"But, unlike Jasper and myself…"

*Keep talking Shasta… **Somebody,** please come!*

"…he never took it to its logical conclusion. That's good old *Dad* for ya. Couldn't see the forest for the trees. He was much more interested in that other one, Jack Shepherd. Harrumph! (Shasta's voice assumed a superior tone. Her lip curled in a most unbecoming way).

"In the history books, Haney was caught and hung but there was never ever any mention of his loot being found. Probably his contemporaries just assumed he'd spent it all on drink and women. (Snickering nastily.) Thanks to that bitch of a Step-mother, who wanted me to 'bond' with my father (*harsh laugh*) when I came for summer visits in later years (and to keep me out of her own hair) I was encouraged to read his library of research. There wasn't anything else to do on that Godforsaken moor anyway: spotty TV; too far from town; nobody my own age. So that got me interested; not in history (her chuckle sounded demented) but the question of where Haney had hidden his stuff since he went to the grave - at least it said so in some of the legal documents of the time my Dad had photocopied: '*without contrition or offering up information.*'

"If my sainted father had bothered to take a page from literally, his own copious notes: (in fact, his *Fact Journals* - Shasta laughed hilariously at her pun), there were plenty of references to rumours about Haney's greed and hidden treasure. Dad might have actually written something worthwhile. It was never mentioned in the Jack Shepherd movie-script version either. Haney was barely a footnote in that drivel. Hah!" Shasta crowed with satisfaction, her own cleverness a salve to old wounds.

"Surely your own Da was able to tell fact from fiction though! *Geez. Talk about major abandonment issues here! Try speaking rationally.* It' s just a pit now Shasta; there's nothing there as you can see."

"Of course not, idiot! You already said. That's because," Shasta's voice rose venomously, "that stupid Jasper found it! *I* enlisted *HIM;* can you believe it? (She forgot and pointed the loaded gun at herself in annoyed exclamation). He was a nobody on my father's farm. I thought I might need an inside person when I RSVP'd for this reunion. (How timely was that event, eh?) I had to convince him of the enterprise first, (wasted some prime sex on the wanker in the process) and then *pretend* we'd go 60/40 if we found the loot.

Cerby winced. *That meant Shasta never intended Jasper to outlive his usefulness. So, what did that say for her own chances?*

"We were supposed to be looking every possible place for it, but it was *me* who said it would have had to have been stashed in the oldest parts of the property, either the Inn or the other original outbuildings. Since Haney was just an ostler - (snidely) how often would someone like that, in the stinking horse trade, ever have been allowed up at the Main House - it had to be here in the original stables somewhere."

"Very logical," Cerby said, feeling dizzy but only too aware that four walls *do* a prison make. *How long had they been in here already? Surely somebody's missing me?*

Shasta grinned and nodded at the compliment. "Jasper was acting suspiciously. He couldn't look me in the eye at the best of times. I knew he'd been carrying on with that 'ho', Mayfair. I followed him to the KC stables here on Saturday, the day you people all descended on Alaerton like a swarm of bees for the anniversary reunion. Buggers!

"He told me about working up Cyrius' stall; how he had found the trap door but insisted there wasn't anything there when I cornered him on it. The cocky bastard showed me the pit himself; (he must have thought I was born yesterday!) There sure wasn't any loot when I looked myself, but I didn't believe him for a second. He was such a pitiful liar. I let him leave the stall expecting to tail him."

Cerby's mind leaped ahead: "So, you were having a second look 'round the Mews and in Cyrius' stall the night the horses all got loose, creating a cover for your search. You were the one to steal the tack too that night, before all that commotion! To make it look like a robbery," Cerby guessed.

Shasta's eyes narrowed to slits. "Wouldn't you know it; you found the mate to that damn earring set practically the second you arrived here. I saw the post-it on the bulletin board; must have been right after you put it there. I tore it down - didn't want anyone else clued in, although Mayfair must have already seen the note too, as when I checked the Lost and Found the earring was already gone. *Trinkets for Tricks* I guess in Jasper's case. In my own, validation of my theory he'd bunged the lot. Fortunately, (Shasta sneered at Cerby) you have no eye for antiques."

I beg to differ, Cerby muttered under her breath.

Shasta shot her a dark look but continued: "But it confirmed for me that bauble had to have come from the pit he showed me originally because that's the vicinity where you found it."

Shasta's voice had trailed off, paranoia and suspicion written all over her face. "I figured that Jasper might have moved the loot to a hiding place somewhere other than this stall or the old stables. He wasn't very bright, but after a pretty thorough search that night of the roundup, I couldn't find anything here." She waved the gun expansively to indicate the old stables.

Cerby wasn't sure if it'd be a good idea or not to interrupt the flow of verbal diarrhea but decided anything that could buy more time... "What happened Sunday night, in the Quad?"

"Oh, that! (Shasta's tone blew off the murder as if it was of little consequence.) Yeah. I'd been following the old coot around on his work rounds for a while. He seemed to spend an inordinate amount of energy raking the arena on the FasTrac, but then he always was a lazy sod - liked nothing better than parking his butt on a tractor."

"The night I found him...?" egged on Cerby.

"I lured him down to the Quad with a note. Told him we had to talk. Since there wasn't any loot, I was giving him the boot; that he should forget the whole Haney thing and take the first train out of Dodge back to Yorkshire. Maybe ask my Dad for his old job back like I'd suggested - I'd put in a word."

Cerby's eyes widened in a muted 'Aha!' moment as she recalled the faint but fateful scribbles.

"'He didn't need to stay on' I said. (I just wanted the slug gone). But he didn't seem too inclined to take the hint. *'He liked it here'* he said, *'thought he'd stay.'* What a chump! That clinched it for me, though I let him think he 'd convinced me there was no point in me staying here either. (He wouldn't have gone though, would he, if he still had the loot somewhere on the property. I'd never believe that frowsy Mayfair was his main attraction.)

"I gave him one more chance." She waved the gun ominously. "Unfortunately, he clung to the fiction there wasn't any treasure. What can I say? He was stupid enough to turn his back on me - to walk away. The shovel was rather handy."

Shasta laughed unsympathetically. "So now, I can't let poor Jasper die in vain, can I? Somebody has to profit, and it should be me since it was my idea and research in the first place. So close I can smell it! (She stopped abruptly; her eyes blinked.) "But this is all *TMI* isn't it? Obviously," there was an unsettling tone of determination in her voice; "I can't leave you around to tell the tale either."

Well, that pretty much dots the 'I's. Please DOG, whatever happens, if Saf and Stevey are still out there, let them come to the same conclusion.

The notes of the Musical Ride in the arena were louder, even at a distance, and starting to crescendo. Cerby's senses had returned just in time to realize this was not a particularly suitable time to recover them. *Crazy Shasta* (as Cerby had now dubbed her) had raised her gun and was moving it to the beat of the climbing notes, only marginally aware of an increasing anxiety in Cyrius who was beginning to move his powerful body with alarm back and forth, ears flattened and eyes rolling - showing all of a horse's sensitivity to the distress and tension within the stall.

Just as Shasta lowered her arm and gun to eye level, pulling back on the trigger in time to the music's '*fortissimo*,' Cyrius reared and plunged forward towards her knocking Cerby off her feet into the wall. To Cerby's horror, she heard a popping sound and saw simultaneously a bright red stain spread outward and down Cyrius' pure white neck. He swayed, buckled to his knees, and fell over with a thud.

Uttering a piercing cry, Cerby fell to her own knees, cradling his head as the light dimmed

191

gradually from his bright eyes and the heavy head lolled. "I'm here," she said softly, uselessly, oblivious to her own danger; quietly stroking his broad neck.

At the same time as a foiled Shasta, in her corner, elevated her arm to take direct aim again, someone kicked in the Dutch door. The intruder was immediately brought to ground by a glancing whack to the side of the head by the business-end butt of her gun. Shasta remained in control and stood, waving the pistol between the man sprawled unceremoniously in the dirty straw and the kneeling Cerby.

Though he'd been felled in a similar fashion to his girlfriend, due to a harder head (*as Cerby was wont to comment on*) Aidan was only momentarily stunned. He rolled quickly on his side to take in the scene: Cerby's bloody and tear-streaked face hugging her horse as if she could breathe life back into him, and the barrel of a hefty pistol aimed at his own head. The woman holding it was clearly quite mad.

Once again, after taking a quick look out the doorway to be sure there was nobody else in hearing range, Shasta closed the stall doors, top and bottom, as well as she could given the damage Aidan had inflicted when kicking them open. Cogitating on her next move: "I'll take your cell phone."

Not a lucky guess. It was visibly clipped into a holster on Aidan's belt. Aidan removed it with two fingers and threw it at her feet, wishing fervently he wasn't out of uniform with no weapon of his own.

Same request of Cerby, who mumbled dispiritedly: 'Don't have one. Check my jacket.' To Aidan: "Is that how you knew I was here?"

Hands raised and cupping the back of his head at Shasta's command, he nodded imperceptibly, and added out of the side of his mouth. "That, and your scream.

"Stop talking! Get in!" Shasta urged, indicating the open pit at her feet with her pistol.

Aidan rolled over onto his knees. *If I stand, she'll be intimidated, and who knows what she'll do?* He noticed the hole in the floor for the first time. "You can't be serious! Look how small it is. It won't hold two people. We'll suffocate in there. C'mon. Be sensible. If you stop now, and give me the gun…"

"You've seen way, way too many *American* cop shows. They all end happily ever after," Shasta spit out. "I'm bi-continental. The Brits do it up right here. They have *THE* most eccentric criminals in the world. And can you believe it, my *father* never thought I would amount to anything." (*Shrill laugh*) In real life, the police are only reactive; the villain quite often walks away. Now. *Do* me a favour!!!"

The revolver pointed authoritatively to the pit. There was no reasoning with her that was obvious. The glint in her eye was eerily reflective of the one off the metal gun.

"I'll return the *favour,*" muttered a 9 mm-chastened Aidan, "if I ever get the chance."

Shasta smirked in her infuriating way. "Don't believe you will, however. *I- SAID- GET- IN!*"

Aidan dragged Cerby up and away from Cyrius. Her eyes were dazed, and he could feel her staggering weight leaning heavily into him. *Concussion* was his immediate thought.

"Get down: get in there," hissed Shasta again.

Aidan dropped into the hole first. With his height and body mass there was scarcely any room for Cerby, but he pulled her awkwardly down and in, putting his hand protectively over her head as the heavy oak door dropped summarily down and into place over them. Their last glimpse of Shasta had been of a woman intent on business. They could hear the dreadful grinding sound of the rusty ring locked in place.

For long seconds muffled sounds reached them from above. Cerby surmised Shasta was trying to tug out the rubber mat that disguised the trap door from underneath Cyrius' dead body. Once levered into place, except for the question of Cyrius, there would be no evidence either she or Aidan had ever been in the stall.

She knew if their roles had been reversed, she would have done exactly what Shasta was actually doing, raking up the straw over the floor mats and removing Cerby's jacket from its post outside the stall. Cerby thought despondently of Ewan's lecture on stable management: *thick rubber stall mats are not only a prevention for injury but also uncommonly useful for sound control.* Nobody could hear them even if they cried their lungs out!

When Cerby had mastered her initial terror, she declared despondently: "The damn Butler did it."

"What?"

"Well, you know how usually there are so many suspects in a case that you find it hard to choose among them?"

"Umm...sort of. Where are we going with this?" Aidan squirmed a bit, trying to get comfortable. He was squatting and his thighs were beginning to burn.

"Just that it had to be the one person nobody liked in the first place. It's been so... so damn linear," she said with real disappointment.

"Interesting. Good old Occam's Razor." Aidan pushed fruitlessly on the roof of their small prison, soon subsiding back into his former position. "The simplest solution is usually THE one."

"I suppose. You know what *I* mean though," Cerby continued (talking kept the bile down): "In old detective novels, you always suspected the Butler right off. I should have realized Shasta had something to do with all this. She was bullying me from the start and for no reason I could pinpoint other than a small indiscretion from the past on her part, that I didn't even know if she remembered - which she apparently did by the way."

"Don't beat yourself up Cerby. In fact, most crimes are pretty 'linear' as you call it, in the end, because most are impulsive not pre-meditated."

"If I could twist into position and kick myself right now, I would," she sighed. "She's the stereotypical nutcase. How did I not see it? Always bumping me into the boards in the arena, getting me in trouble. It seemed to be a private joke with her?"

She shifted her own position slightly in a direction she thought faced him. It was darker than dark. "I suppose this probably isn't the right time to tell you either, but I found a scrap of paper the night I fell over Jasper. It had some writing on it. Shasta referred to it herself. She wrote it."

Aidan's voice flared in anger. She could feel it course through the body opposite, arcing through his knees tight up against hers. "Cerby, why didn't you hand that over to Jock, a constable, or at least give it to me. It might have had fingerprints. We might have been able to place her at the scene. And we might not be here now!"

Cerby's voice wavered and got defensive in return. "I just picked it up automatically that night. As students we were always trained to pick up litter anywhere on the property. I forgot about it until I was emptying out my pockets a day or so later. And then I gave it to Saffi and Stevey…" Cerby came to an abrupt stop.

"You WHAT?"

"The last I saw of them; they were going to look around and see if they could find any matching script anywhere."

"Cerby! This isn't a game. What were you thinking, dragging your friends into a dangerous situation like this? Look at us. How do you know what's happened to them?" Aidan regretted saying that almost immediately.

"I know. I can't stop thinking about it." Cerby's voice quavered as her own fears redoubled. "I haven't seen them since yesterday." She proceeded to tell Aidan everything that had passed between Shasta and herself before he came on the scene.

Aidan could hear the misery in her voice. "Cerb," he said in a gentler, more conciliatory tone; "Shasta…,"

"'*Crazy Shasta,* '" Cerby corrected.

"…Crazy Shasta then, okay? She'll be too busy trying to find the stuff Jasper copped from her; so, unless your friends got so much in her way as to prevent her from doing that, they're probably safe for now. From what you've told me, she may have seen them in Huntingdon but split when it was obvious they too were on the 'Haney trail'. She'd want to get *there* first."

It was what Cerby needed to hear, but she said in a defeated tone. "It's not like I solve crimes, is it? I just get involved in them somehow; they happen, and I'm sucked in."

This touched Aidan, but he burst out laughing all the same: "Let's just say you have an interesting way of contributing."

If Cerby thought Aidan wasn't being entirely sensitive to her feelings in the moment, she was however extremely relieved he was no longer angry at her or her interference. Both subsided into silence and their own thoughts. The dark was practically impenetrable.

After a few minutes, both starting to cramp up, they tried moving about within their confined space.

"Ouch Aidan. Something's jutting into my butt."

"Are you suggesting my love, that we do the 'Doggie'?"

"Aid: I do NOT believe your one-track mind! *Like we'd have the room anyway*... "Seriously!" Despite a throbbing headache, Cerby's survival instincts were definitely on the rise.

"I wouldn't need to keep 'thrusting' my *suit* if you'd make an honest man of me Cerb."

That hung in the air between them for a long minute. (All Aidan had ever suggested was living together.)

The spark of humour quickly dissipated however as the knowledge of their dire situation continued to press hard upon them in the dark confines of their tiny prison. Aidan broke the bleakness by suggesting some action. "We can't sit on our haunches forever. Let's try to get more comfortable, and then we can think."

"Aid!"

"Not that kind of comfortable Cerby. Besides, I like my women conscious.'

For a couple of minutes, it was a bit like the children's game, *Twister*. Cerby couldn't help but giggle at the absurdity. With eyes becoming marginally accustomed to the dark, both tried moving arms and legs around each other in wrestler-like fashion, the activity finally culminating in as much of a comfortable positioning as two people in a small dark pit could attain.

Aidan sat with his legs semi- drawn up and Cerby was nestled in on his lap, facing the same way. Her hands rested on his soft washed-cambric thighs. Although the back of her head was in his face (she could feel him pulling some of her hairs away from his nose and mouth) in her mind's eye she could picture the frontal version: his light gray Ralph Lauren shirt slightly open at the collar with a curl or two of chest hair just peeking out. She sniffed pathetically. *When they find our dead bodies, he'll be the one on the best dressed list or awarded the title, 'Sexiest Man (once) Alive' but I'll only be fodder for Joan River's Fashion Police, never mind worms.*

Tired and drowsy from their exertions and the fouling air, she leaned back against his torso, attempting a lighter sauciness: "Don't you dare say anything about lap dancing …"

It was a brave sally, but soon Aidan could literally *feel* her emotions start to give way, the slight constrictions on his chest a telltale sign as she cried silently for their tomb and her lost Cyrius. He wrapped his arms around her, hugging her tightly. "Don't give up just yet Cerb."

"But if anyone even thinks to look here, it won't be for a long time – do you recall the Brandy story?"

"Shush now!" he said confidently; "I've been thinking. 'Member how I said I would give up smoking." (The *foul habit* had been an obstacle at first to their relationship.)

"Yeh-essss."

"Well, another of my sins: I lied!"

"WHAT?" Resignedly; "*Now* you tell me."

"Not as bad as all that Cerb. I'm on that program, the one where you gradually cut down to a couple a week."

"And are you there yet?" she asked testily, as if it still mattered.

Aidan was grateful for the trace of skepticism in her voice. "Almost."

"Hmm."

"The important thing is, I have (accompanied with a small flourish), voilà - a lighter," and a small flame burst forth in front of them as Aidan held his lighter aloft.

"Yes, but the flame will eat up our precious oxygen."

"I'm *not* about to burn it continuously; I just want to see what our situation is."

"Okay" said Cerby, somewhat doubtfully. "I suppose there is no point in me screaming."

"None at all: that *WILL* eat up our precious oxygen."

"Aid, you're always so *absolute* about everything; that really ticks me off if you hadn't guessed."

Aidan ignored the barb, too busy trying to flick his BIC again without burning himself. At last, a glow. "A virtual *flare* we've got here." He moved the small light down first one wall, and then the other. For a couple of centuries, the mortar had lasted well, but it was definitely crumbling in spots. "In fact…"

"Aid. Do you smell that odor?"

"What smell?"

"It stinks like urine."

"Well, it 's not me; more likely to shit my pants in times of stress when it comes to that."

"No. I'm not liking this Aid. I react badly to ammonia - gets my Asthma going."

Aidan *had* noticed she was already taking shorter breaths and swallowing more than usual.

"I don't have my rescue puffer; it was in my jacket. (He could detect real concern in her voice.) You don't know this stall, (pausing to suppress a coughing fit, then continued) but there was quite a big urine drain beside this pit. As old as the original stables I think."

"Really?" Cerby could feel Aidan tighten in excitement as he sat up straighter. Any information was *good* information. The pit and the drain appeared to be separate entities in the present, but in the past ...? "Ok, which way are we oriented?"

"I've completely lost my sense of direction Aid, what with us trying to get comfortable in the dark. I'm a *Wrong Way Corrigan* anyway, you'll recall."

Aidan reached out awkwardly, bringing the BIC lighter into his other hand, and moved it slowly along the near walls, inspecting them carefully. "I feel a bit like Lord Carnarvon," he mused aloud.

We're definitely cursed that's for sure, Cerby thought resignedly.

After a minute or so: "By Jove, I think I may have something."

Now it was Cerby's turn to anticipate: "What?"

"There *IS* considerable damp and green algae on this side of the pit, and none on the other: urine seepage *I'll wager.*"

"You and your Briti-sisms Aid - taking lessons from Mitch?"

Something in her fading tone made him shake her. "Keep awake Cerb! I can't keep beating on you and try to get us out of here, too."

Sleepily she responded: "I'm fine, I'm fine."

You're not though, are you? he thought, with a growing desperation. He dug in his pant pocket.

"Here's my trusty Swiss Army penknife. Let's give this a try." *Thank God Crazy Shasta in her haste hadn't asked him to empty his pockets.*

He started to dig away at the damp mortar and was relieved to see it crumbling rather quickly away. Before too long, he had made one brick fall in. "Here put this between your legs."

"Oh Aid." (Weak laugh).

"No, I mean this stuff. There's nowhere else to put the debris."

"Ah! Talk about the *Great Escap*...."

"More like the *Cask of Amontillado.* Cerby! Damn it! Wake up I said!" He gave her a shake. With little response from that quarter... *I hate to do this, especially without your permission.* He placed his hands over both breasts and tweaked her nipples, (which he knew to have some of the most sensitive nerve endings in the human body) **hard!** Which brought her wide awake with a correspondingly automatic elbowing in the region of his groin. A chorus of:

"Ow, Ouch!"

"Ow! Crap!!"

"Damn, why'd you do that?"

"Why'd *YOU do that?"*

"Sorry."

"Sorry, don't cut it," Aidan shifted his privates away, protectively.

At least Cerby was awake. Aidan resumed stabbing fiercely at the brick face with his small tool. Every now and again, he would turn the lighter off, to rest and conserve oxygen, but he *was* making good headway and the hole was producing a bit of light and even more importantly, a bit of fresh air.

How long had it been; an hour? Two? Hard to tell.
To keep Cerby engaged he said: "Think about this
Tom Heinous character for a moment."

"Thomas Haney," Cerby corrected.

"Whatever. If this was his den for hiding his
stolen goods, he must have bricked it for a reason. I
mean, you could just dig a hole in dirt and bury the
stuff when it comes to that. And why these
dimensions?"

"People were smaller in those days - poor
nutrition," Cerby reasoned. "He could have gotten
in here himself: like a Monk's hole to hide in if
necessary."

"Exactly, but a lot of Monk's holes had an
alternative escape exit, and even if subsequent
generations decided to brick it all up for some
reason … (More grunting and wrestling of
foundation stones) Hallelujah! There's *'light in the
piazza'*!"

Aidan angled his head into the opening and turned
his gaze upward at the small-diametered, six-foot-
high bricked pipe drain. "I can see up through the
drain on this side so, if we have to yell, we'll be
heard eventually but best of all," *and here he hauled
himself to sit upright again, giving her an
enthusiastic hug,*" there does seem to be an old
horizontal tunnel opening. Bet that's how the
S.O.B. went a-marauding undetected. Come on
Cerb; spelunking we will go."

He gradually widened the hole in the wall to
squeezable dimensions. He was genuinely afraid
now for Cerby's physical state. It might well be a
considerable time yet before Cyrius was discovered

or they could call for help 'up' the drain - they had to get moving now!

Aidan pushed forward the fuzzy-brained, catarrhic Cerby. Once she was off him, propped up on her knees against the opposing wall, he pulled himself on to his own to squat before the hole he had made in the pit wall. He stretched out his arm and flashed the lighter. The tunnel once again flamed into view, still shored up through the years with wood, brick and field stones, and except for a few roots here and there, looking more like a reasonably pristine sewer of the Victorian era. The trajectory pointed due North-west, but no end was in sight.

"Here's hoping there's been no cave-ins in the last couple of centuries."

"Or have any now" Cerby shuddered.

"You first, Watson." *I'll have to push her to keep her going.*

"No. I insist, you first!" *I can hold onto him if I start to fall back. And there might be spiders...*

"Alright then," Aidan conceded; "but keep up; it's a small tunnel and I can't reach around my back to haul you along manually if you start falling behind."

"Don't worry about me!" Cerby said, with more courage than she felt.

It turned out to be a close fit, especially for Aidan who tried to push fallen brick and earth out of the way as he went to make it easier for Cerby. And he did worry. He could hear her cough and her hoarse breathing as they made slow careful progress for about twenty minutes. Just when he could feel her lagging behind: "Cerb, there's some kind of a wooden slat wall in front of me. Stay where you are. I'm going to try something."

Cerby tried to do even better by wriggling backwards although exhausted to the core.

Like Mark Spitz making a lap turn in a swimming pool, Aidan managed somehow to get his feet that were behind him into position in front of him. Bracing himself in 'bridge' position, he gave a mighty kick; then another, and another - hard enough that old rotten boards and plaster caved in on the other side. He managed to haul himself out of the tunnel, feet first, and then crawled back in headfirst to help pull Cerby along and out.

"What the...?" Standing on his cellar stairs, sandwich in hand, responding to the noise in his basement, Ewan Ogilvy looked on in shocked surprise.

"Ewan," a dirty, overly fragrant Aidan ordered; "Quick; call 911 or whatever your emerg equivalent is over here. Cerby's been concussed! She's pretty sick. Oh, and sorry about the damage."

The two men, supporting Cerby on either side, drew her upstairs aiming to place her on the sofa in the parlour. While Ewan gently prepared to place a throw over Cerby - *'No, over the couch Ewan: my clothes, so dirty. Bron will kill me!'* - Aidan was immediately on the landline phone to D. I. Wallace, apprising him of the necessary details and requesting backup. He then seconded a cell phone from Ewan, and calling to Ewan his directive, "Look after her, will you!" dashed out to search for Shasta.

That Bedlam candidate isn't going to get away with this thought Cerby as she snuggled her head into a soft pillow and groaned with the slight effort. Her head ached fearfully, chest tight as a drum from the effects of asthma, but Ewan had prepared - what else? - a strong hot cup of sweet tea which actually, with his help, she was grateful to sip. (She censored herself from berating Mrs. Momfrey's usual weak tea offerings in comparison; being injured and dehydrated, she'd have gladly drunk a gallon or two, no complaints!)

But the horror of what they'd been through, and the death of poor Cyrius: "He saved me Ewan. She was going to kill me, and he threw himself at her. He knew. I swear he knew," forced the tears to splash down her cheeks uncontrolled. Ewan tenderly took her hand, pressed it gently, and drew her protectively into a hug against his chest.

Such was the sentimental tableau that greeted a defensive Bron on walking through the front door into the parlour. The *com* in 'passion' wasn't immediately evident...

If it hadn't been for the blood on Cerby's face, and her dirty boots standing by the fire, Bron might have misconstrued the scene far longer than the first impression. No one on the property yet knew what had occurred - she herself was just walking home from putting her horse away in the Quad after the Musical Ride practise. Though she had caught a momentary glimpse of Aidan in the distance, climbing over the fence of the *50 Acre Field* and making for the gate on the far side like a berserk runaway, she had not connected that with anything untoward. Her cool inquiring glance to Ewan had him rise to his feet and take her aside into the kitchen.

"Did Cerby take a fall?" Bron's first surmise put to Ewan.

Ewan sighed. "If only. Worse than that…" and he sketched for her what Aidan had told him of their ordeal. Bron's hand flew up to her mouth in real shock and genuine consternation. "I can't believe it, Ewan—none of it."

"All true I'm afraid. Look. I'm going down to Cyrius' stall and close it off for the police. She needs her puffer. I'll see if I can find her jacket. Is Dr. Wentworth about? Perhaps you can call Mrs. Hill? She'll have to be told the latest; rather you did that then me. Then I'll help Aidan search the premises if I can. You best stay with Cerby; we've called for medics." He planted an intense kiss on Bron's forehead. Turning around in the doorway he added: "They said to try to keep her awake." Then he left at the run.

Bron went back to sit with Cerby whose heavy bagged eyes were closed. She shook her friend gently.

"I'm just resting my eyes Bron," Cerby responded wearily; "My Da used to say *that* all the time when he had been napping, but *I'm* awake. I wish I *could* sleep Bron. I just can't believe it all happened; it's such a nightmare!"

Bron said some soothing words and went to get a basin of warm water to rinse off Cerby's head wound and clean her face. She had considerable veterinary experience but, in this case, knew the cleansing activity would be comforting and refreshing for her human patient, if nothing else.

When Bron began her ministrations, she found a rather large gash and major bruising on the right side of Cerby's head. "In my clinical opinion," mocking herself slightly while her gently probing fingers demonstrated the professionalism: "this is quite deep Cerb; it'll need some stitches I'm afraid. You were very lucky. An inch or so down - that soft spot on the temple, here (she gently touched the skin in question) - we might not be having this conversation."

Cerby laughed weakly. "Lucky, is it? Good ole Bron. D'ya think I got some sense knocked into me at last?"

"Would that were possible," Bron smiled good humouredly.

"Well, at least I'm in good hands."

"The best!" Agreed Bron.

"No false modesty there," Cerby experienced a momentary chill, causing her to wince inwardly. Hadn't she said the same thing to Saf not so very long ago? Though grateful that Bron and she were back on 'old friend' footing, she was consumed with worry, where were her other mates? The spectre of Shasta hovered.

"I'll just be a moment Cerby. I need to call the main house and tell them what's happened." Cerby groaned with the foreknowledge of how Mrs. Hill would take the news - *all* of it.

Mrs. Hill flung the front door of *'I' Cottage* open and marched over to Cerby's side, with Doctor Wentworth in tow. 'Fortunately, he was just visiting,' Mrs. Hill answered Bron's raised eyebrow. She looked past her own distress with great compassion on the battered aspect presented: "And, oh my Darling Cerby, how *IS* our patient?"

She bent kindly over Cerby, smoothing a loose strand of the victim's sticky, curly hair away off her forehead, revealing the ugly gash and puckered yellow and purple bruises above the temple. Alaerton's owner drew in a ragged breath at the sight.

Mrs. Hill's warmth and concern opened the floodgates again. "I'm so sorry Mrs. H. He saved my life. Cyrius; *your* pet."

Mrs. Hill bent down and kissed Cerby on her hot cheek. "My dear, he did what he had to do - for you! I couldn't be prouder." And she hugged Cerby awkwardly, so as not to move or hurt Cerby's head. Bron put an arm around both, and all three had a good cry.

Dr. Wentworth gave them their moment, then gently pried them all apart. "I *do* need to inspect the patient, you know."

"Emergency unit has been called already as well Doctor, and they should be here any minute."

"Very good, Bron;(the doctor much appreciative of her cool efficiency.) Now Cerby. If you can sit up for a minute and let me have a look, I promise to *do no harm.*"

Cerby looked up at that and laughed, even though it hurt to do so, finding the phrase entirely ironic - a reminder of his lectures. "Sure Dr. Wentworth," but trying to reassure them: "I just get a bit dizzy, that's all." She struggled into a sitting position.

"I'd be surprised if you weren't! Still, you've fallen off a lot in the past…"

"Not *a lot* Doc!" Cerby protested with some vehemence.

Doctor Wentworth chuckled, turning her head skillfully this way and that; "…so I know you've got a pretty hard noggin."

Whilst Dr. Wentworth continued to attend to his patient's examination (Mrs. Hill looking on supportively), Bron left them alone for a bit and rustled up some light soup and sandwiches in the kitchen. Mrs. Hill and the Doctor accepted the offer graciously, but Cerby declined, feeling still somewhat nauseous. And then they all waited for word.

It wasn't that long in coming. Both Aidan and Ewan blew in together through the French doors on the garden side of the cottage. Aidan's look was thunderous, and Ewan's was full of concern. "She's bloody nowhere to be found!"

The Emergency crew entered via the front door almost simultaneously, loaded down with all their paraphernalia. Cerby winced, looking up beseechingly at the concerned group around her. "Look! Couldn't I just stay here? Doctor Wentworth says it 's just a mild concussion and I'll be fine in twenty-four hours or so."

"Or SO!" emphasized Aidan, standing protectively beside the divan she reclined on.

"That's not exactly what I said Cerby. Must be the knock on the head." Doctor Wentworth had assumed his 'no-nonsense' demeanor. "I want you to go to the hospital to get thoroughly checked out –all the bells and whistles; if they confirm my diagnosis, I'm sure you can come back but you'll still have to take it easy for a day or two even so."

Finding no support from her friends, Cerby gave in and allowed herself to be strapped unceremoniously onto a stretcher and removed in embarrassed silence. Ewan draped her jacket over her, (Aidan had found it thrown carelessly behind some bins by the escaping Shasta.) She immediately found her Puffer in the inside pocket and inhaled twice. As they were carrying her out and sliding her gurney into the ambulance (a small crowd having gathered by this time in front of the *'I's cottage*) she cricked her neck and called out to Mrs. Hill standing in the doorway: "Mrs. H! Promise! Don't move Cyrius until I come back! Please Mrs. H, I have to say good-bye…" and the doors closed upon her.

Cerby's friends trouped back to the parlour, deflated by the events that had occurred. Aidan ran a hand through his hair and pivoted uncertainly on his heels, the only outward indication of his own emotional strain. Mrs. Hill reached out and tapped him on the arm with motherly affection, then sat down pensively on the couch Cerby had vacated. She absent-mindedly folded the blanket Cerby had lain on and passed it to Bron (it would require a good cleaning.)

Ewan leaned in toward Aidan, saying quietly: "Look; if you want to follow her to the hospital, I can handle everything here for now."

"I'd like nothing better Ewan, but duty calls. She's out of danger for the time being. Jock Wallace is on his way and wants a full report. We've got to catch this woman Ewan - she's insane. This myth, this obsession about the Tom Haney treasure; I don't think she'll give up looking for it despite the fact she knows that we know, and I would say that makes her twice as dangerous."

Ewan paced in front of the fireplace. "We've got the fête on Friday, Bank Holiday as you know Aid. In essence, only one day left to try to flush her out or we should really cancel." He became aware that Aidan was studying him.

"Now, hold on Aid. If you're thinking what I think you're thinking? We can't put people at risk. Why, just look at Cerby for heaven's sake; how knocked up she was. Oops, poor choice of words (on seeing Aidan's momentary grin) but I can't allow anyone else on the property to be in jeopardy. You see that Aidan, don't you?"

"I get where you're coming from Ewan! But the fact is, while Shasta Denning is running loose, we're all in jeopardy. Nobody knows that better than me. She's a sick, sick broad, and I want her locked away for a VERY long time. But if the police don't find her by tomorrow, we have to assume two things: *one,* she's already a long way away from here or *two,* (and more likely) she's coming back - those OCD issues driving her. I say carry on with the festival, fête whatever you call it. No, hear me out Ewan. We can have a contingent of undercover, plain clothes police officers on site. It's our best chance of getting this loony put away for keeps, if she shows, so she can't harm anyone else.

"And the Shasta rationale aside, this fête is huge PR for Alaerton and possibly some financial stability for Mrs. Hill. Cerby would literally have our scalps if we were the ones to kybosh the whole thing. I don't fancy having to deal with a berserk Cerby too, do you?" He put up the sign of the evil eye with arms outstretched in front of him, though his laugh was the antithesis of terror-stricken.

Aidan dropped the facetiousness and scanned in turn everyone still in the room for agreement. Mrs. Hill standing by Doctor Wentworth, looked frazzled and uncertain; the Doctor himself looking grim but ready for battle. Bron looked to Ewan. In his unofficial capacity, Aidan didn't really have the right to force anyone (owner or managers) to accept his proposition.

For a long moment Ewan stared down into the fire he had lit to warm Cerby, his arm draped along the mantelpiece, one hand playing with a knick-knack. "I don't like it, (Aidan grunted impatiently) but I

213

think you're probably right. She may go to ground for a time..."

Aidan smiled at the fox hunting imagery.

"... and pop up again just when we no longer have police protection - and then what?"

Aidan knew Jock Wallace would back him up on this plan. He clapped Ewan on the back for coming to the same conclusion. Now that they were embarked on a plan of action, a little optimism wouldn't go amiss. So: with a cheeriness and mocking intonation that even so rang a bit hollow under the circumstances, he rallied the room with as stirring a British rendition as he could muster:

'RELEASE THE HOUNDS, B'GOD!'

Chapter Six

Thursday

Nothing and no one turned up to further the case the next day. Police had temporarily cordoned off Cyrius' stall. Staff and students connected with the Inn went about their duties with a heightened sense of inquietude. The last Musical Ride practise took place with a subdued group of Reunionistas wishing they were anywhere else but knowing their 'holiday' would soon be at an end and they could leave Alaerton to its fate. The anniversary celebrations so far were nothing like anybody had ever anticipated.

Ewan and Bron were more security conscious than ever, making sure there was enough police protection in shifts both day and night and constantly checking on their charges, both equine and human.

The Doctor, concerned for his good friend Mrs. Hill *and in case of any future developments*, was staying near-to-hand on the premises at her invitation. Unknown to anyone, he carried an old service revolver in his pocket 'just in case.'

Mitch and Monte had dropped an exhausted Saffi and Stevey back at Alaerton on their way to Alconbury, initially unaware of the dramatic events but just in time to see the ambulance carting Cerby away. They were hailed and brought up to date, as well as sternly instructed by Mrs. Hill not to visit Cerby in hospital so she could rest overnight. The foursome acquiesced with little grace. They had much to tell and could hardly wait until they had the opportunity.

Cerby was forced to stay the night in the Huntingdon Civic Hospital for observation, but truth to tell, she was happy enough to do so after her ordeal. Only Monte and Mitch were in attendance until the end of visiting hours, M&M stubbornly ignoring Mrs. Hill's prior instructions much to Cerby's grateful appreciation. They insisted on administering to Cerby's every whim; (taking their solemn oaths seriously as stand-ins for Aidan who was off partnering with D.I. Wallace on the case). They *had* agreed however, in a pact with Saffi and Stevey, not to fill Cerby in on their own exploits until she was recovered enough and back at Alaerton.

Cerby spent a restless night away from her chums, her fretful sleep populated by dreams of Cyrius, miniscule dungeons, heroes, and villains. Her headache however, was diminishing slowly with medication and isolation from all the disturbing factors responsible for her hospital stay. She had to admit it was far better to be incarcerated in a secure institution with access to a decent mattress, sanitary washroom, and even bad hospital food then be buried alive with Aid in that preposterous Poe- pit at the hands of *Crazy Shasta*.

Aidan called the hospital first thing in the morning and stopped by as soon as he learned about the discharge routines. Cerby lay on her bed in the clean clothes (jeans and a light cotton tee) that Monte and Mitch had brought for her the evening before, waiting for the release papers.

Aidan hesitated at the door. Despite her usual bravado, she looked smaller and more vulnerable lying there. He suffered a twinge of guilt. He had rescued her, but he had not *protected* her in the first place. Immediately he realized how impossible that would have been, but he felt the inadequacy nonetheless, swearing to himself that she would never be endangered again. *This **IS** Cerby you're talking about, right?* His inner voice spoke rhetorically, of course.

Cerby's still-sensitive eyes were closed against the strong sunlight streaming in through the window blinds, but she sensed a benevolent presence in the room. A nuzzling of her cheek and neck and sweet (*suspiciously*) minty breath announced that her own personal security officer had resumed duties. She forced one eye half-open.

"That in no way makes up for the anti–climax I've endured," she scoffed, not looking at him directly and with affected nonchalance.

"Maybe, but I feel a climax *'coming'* just the same," he murmured, his eyes softening with desire.

"Not here you don't!" Her eyes wide open now, Cerby's half-smile belied the response. She made no effort to sit up either and remained reclining comfortably.

Aidan disregarded the admonition (as he was meant to) crawling up on the bed. He lay beside her, turning her carefully towards him so as not to jog her still painful head. "Why not *here*?" He enfolded her in a body embrace and began to kiss her; "Or here? Or here…Or…"

"Aidan Halifax. You think everything can be healed by sex. *I* fall off a horse and bruise my tailbone: SEX! *You* have a migraine: '*SEX please!*' *I* stub my toe …"

"SEX! I'm so glad you concur!" Aidan laughed heartily and planted a sloppy kiss that hit Cerby's ear as she turned her head aside, giggling also. She was finally free of any ambivalence towards Aid. *Nearly dying will do that to you…*

"Well Gyp-Tease, if you insist on putting me on hold once again, Jock has arranged for a car to take us back to Alaerton where I have no doubt you will be spoiled rotten for the next day or so."

"I have no objection to being spoiled for *a day,*" Cerby rose and slowly gathered her things; "but I'm damn sure riding in the Musical *Ride* tomorrow. And don't say I'm not well enough, Aid! I came here to help Mrs. H and I'm damn well gonna do it! It won't be the same without Cyrius of course," her voice faltered, then gathered strength; "but I need to do it for Mrs. H *and* for him, if for no other reason."

Aidan knew pressing the point with her at this time would not be in the best interest, but he hoped her friends would talk sense to her. Instead of arguing further however, he took the carryall from her in one hand, put his other arm through hers, and lock step in time with her's: "Come on then, let's blow this joint! Never could stand hospitals."

Arriving back at the *Wheatsheaf's* kitchen door, greeted warmly by Saffi, Stevey, Mrs. Hill, and Mrs. Momfrey dabbing an eye in the background, with even Mayfair striking a sympathetic albeit somewhat morose pose, Cerby's heart gladdened at the sight of them. But, before anything else, she needed to make a kind of peace. She asked them all, including Aidan, if they would wait for her there, that she just wanted to see and be alone with Cyrius for a moment. Mrs. Hill was going to have his body removed and he was to be buried in the *50 Acre Field* immediately after. (It was after all, the warm month of June and before long even Cerby realized, an interment would be imperative.)

She ducked under the yellow police tape and went 'round the back of the old stables, stiffening a bit in apprehension with the recollection of what had happened there. A young constable leaned against a tree, sipping tea from a thermos. He obviously had been warned she would be coming at some point, but he stared piercingly at her for a few seconds just the same before allowing her to proceed and resuming his post.

Peering over the stall door Cerby immediately saw Cyrius' lifeless body. It brought the reality home to her. The initial *rigor* had relaxed however, making the scene look like he was just down for the night on the straw. She went over to him, and numbly taking a cleaning rag she'd found by the stall door, wet it in his water bucket and began washing the blood gently off his neck. She was thankful death had been almost instantaneous, but she could hardly believe that just the other day he had been alive; she had ridden him, been feeding him his treats, apples, and carrots.

Cerby gently laid the big heavy head across her knees, stroking his forehead and muzzle with one hand and with the other, his long neck down to the withers. Holding a private conversation with him, she thanked him for saving her life; wanting him to know that she would have taken him home with her if circumstances had required; that she'd never forget him.

Animals had personalities and souls; Cerby couldn't envisage any afterlife without them. Being finally alone to grieve in full measure, the sobs washed over her like a thunderclap - and then slowly subsided. Her determination to help catch Shasta if at all possible, would be the last homage to him who gave up so much for her.

'I won't say goodbye Cyrius—it's too hard. Never been able to fathom infinity or eternity but I *know* in my heart we'll meet again. I just know it Boy. *And, if there truly **are** parallel dimensions... universes...spiritual realms... you could be gambolling about somewhere on another plane, even now - looking for apples I bet.''*

Assuming that theory was correct, nothing ever died really. It gave her comfort to think so, anyway. Subconsciously she fingered the Celtic *triskele* locket her late parents had given her on her 'sweet sixteenth' which she never took off. The 'rampant' horses on it would now also always remind her of Cyrius.

She got up and somewhat shrunken from her emotional ordeal, went out and closed the stall door gently but firmly behind her. Aidan, despite her instructions, was waiting a little distance off. He hesitated to come forward, but she walked straight up to him, grasping the lapels of his jacket, and buried her face in his chest. He was taken aback initially, unaccustomed to her rare displays of 'need,' arms limp at his sides while a dry sob escaped against him. That was his cue to wrap her in a tight hug, resting his chin gently on her bowed head. There was only one more heartfelt half-sob as he ran his hands up and down her back in a feeble attempt to comfort her.

"Aidan, I'm so afraid. I'll be leaving soon and going back home, but *SHE*'ll still be out there, and my friends will be in danger."

"Even if that were so Cerb," Aidan pushed her back gently, holding her out at arm's length so he could look her directly in the eyes; "Jock and the police here won't let this go. She's a loose cannon, and her own worst enemy. She's made mistakes and will make more. Sooner or later they'll nab her. Now, you go rest and don't even think about this for a while."

"Fat chance," she sniffed.

Instead of the dormitory in the Wheatsheaf, Bron and Ewan had offered Cerby their guest room in the *'I's Cottage*. It was a lovely space and cheerily done up in monochromatic garnet and cream toile, ticking, with French cottage gingham for design balance. So, it was to this room where Cerby repared and held court with her friends.

Bron brought in tea and edibles. Mrs. Hill had hugged Cerby and then left to take care of Cyrius' burial, a mutual ordeal for all of them but a necessary one. She had solicited construction machinery, a Digger, from one of her neighbours who kindly offered to hollow out the grave for Cyrius. The rest sat in chairs around the bed where Cerby, fully clothed, now reclined.

Dr. Wentworth could see recovery was well underway, and with a couple of stern admonishments to rest and stay calm, left to follow and support Mrs. Hill in her solemn duty. There was no disrespect in the group's subtle winks at his enthusiasm for the opportunity.

Aidan retired to the Quad to seek Ewan's help in arranging security for the fête the next day.

As far as anybody knew, M&M - having discharged care of Cerby to Saffi and Stevey - were motoring about, pursuing more images for Monte 's book. Presumably, they were well out of the reach of danger.

Cerby looked Saffi and Stevey sternly in the eye. "Okay, now *YOU two,* spill! Where have you been and what have you been up to? And don't even think of leaving anything out."

"Compared with what you've been through, it hardly bears repeating," Stevey commented with heartfelt regret. "We're so sorry Cerb! If we'd only advised the police what we found out about the handwriting, maybe we could have averted some of this." She waved her hand expansively. Bron and Cerby looked at each other, wondering if that might truly have been the case.

Cerby shook her head, whipping herself for giving a crucial piece of evidence to her mates in the first place. "No. I'm the one to apologize. I should have handed that note over to Aidan, or Jock, or even Mrs. H right away. You two could have been in danger. Maybe Cyrius would still be alive?" She fought back tears at the thought.

Saffi had settled into a wing backed chair, hiding her emotions by fiddling with her gold bangles. She straightened her ascot, part of her riding outfit to be worn later in the dress-rehearsal of the Musical Ride. She coolly dismissed this line of thinking: "Don't be silly Cerb. Somebody was bound to come afoul of Shasta. She's completely insane! If anything, we're lucky she didn't do more harm than she did."

Carrying on with the recitation, Saf went on to explain in more detail, her's and Stevey's separate lines of inquiry. "Looking through Mrs. Hill's papers and conducting a search for the Guest Book, we confirmed from a signature via it and a found waiver, that the handwriting on 'your' scrap Cerb, was Shasta's. And when we thought about it, we realized a couple of things. Remember how she was already out in the paddock, ostensibly the first one out there trying to corral the horses the night they all got loose?"

Stevey eagerly chimed in: "It had to be her in hindsight, who let them all out in the first place - to divert everyone's attention from her searching Cyrius' stall. Don't you see? He was the only horse who *wasn't* let out."

"Amazing, you gals. Too right! She admitted it herself when she had me at gunpoint - about the cover-up that night."

"So; Shasta was responsible for Sable's death and injuring Ewan's horse too?" Bron's face was unreadable, but her hands were clenched tightly in her lap. "No, but thanks for asking. Lord Jim's quite okay now, although he won't be jumping for a while yet. Ewan's cautious on that score."

Relieved to hear that Ewan's horse was recovering, Saffi continued: "We *have* turned over the original piece of paper to the police, by the way. I'm sure her fingerprints will be on it, if they even need any more evidence, given what you and Aidan can testify to yourselves."

"Yes, but here's the good part. Oh, *WAIT!* These scones are delicious Bron. You might want to go to work for Saffi in the cookery business. I'll just take another if that's … Alright! I *AM* getting on with it!" Stevey set down her plate with a bang.

"So; we looked up her father Paul Denning on the internet, given that story you told us Cerby about your run in with her years ago, and found he lived in Yorkshire near Shipton. Bit of a coincidence that the last letters 'pton' were on that scrap of paper, and Jasper was from Yorkshire. In mysteries, aren't they always saying: *'there are no coincidences where murders concerned',* at least they do on tele in *Midsomer Murders*."

Stevey choked on another scone and Saffi gave her a wallop on the back. She spluttered and continued. "So, Saf had the brilliant idea of calling her cousin in Yorkshire who - get this - lives in the village one over. She asked him if he knew Paul (Denning, *the father*) and he did, quite well; as so-called 'local writer in residence.' A very social being Denning was by all accounts. Bit of a pub-ster. An open book the family was itself, apparently."

Saffi pulled her cuffs down at her wrists, shrugging her hacking jacket into place and buttoning it up. "First Cerb, your having deciphered 'Haney' for us, we decided we should just take a bus and go into Huntingdon and look into the local archives to see what we could find out on the blighter. We thought we'd be there and back in short order, but actually ended up spending considerable time going through the records - it's all on that awful microfiche; (would you believe they go back to 1550, well before Cromwell was born in this area.)"

Stevey joked: "And talk about dry, dusty work; we had to *crawl* to the nearest pub eventually for food and drink."

"I bet," Cerby said dryly, and then more seriously; "At some point, Shasta saw you. She must have followed you close enough to hear you talking, because she knew *you* knew about Haney. That seems to have spurred her on; that, and me finding the earring. I think she had the nutty notion I knew more than I actually did! Crazy bi - rod!" (Cerby remembered after the fact the lady-like Mrs. H wasn't there to hear and disapprove of any bad language.)

"She's been called worse, I'm sure," Saf agreed. "Getting back to the Huntingdon Library. Who knew there would be so many dusty old ledgers on civic events, including criminal proceedings from the 1700's? Of course, it isn't as easy as just pulling a book from the shelf, fingering a particular chapter. Lord, the writing itself is so hard to decipher, what with all those long calligraphic ʃ's and § 's... But to get to the point (Cerby impatiently giving the 'wind up' signal muttered 'Please do') we finally found information in one volume on the trial of Thomas Haney." Saffi paused and looked around at her

225

captive audience for greater effect. "There was mention of a search that had been made to recover all or part of his stolen goods. Haney was 'uncooperative' which I suppose in that day meant he was silent despite beatings, torture etc. The next pertinent entry said he'd been hanged with no last words. He never did give up his secret."

"How would that be, I wonder," asked Cerby of no one in particular; "to go to your grave with that secret on your chest?" Silence reigned while they all pondered the gruesome end of the ostler, and the question mark he left behind.

"Regardless," Bron leant into the circle of friends as she refreshed the food tray: "Shasta obviously either read or discussed this subject with her father at some point in her life. Paul mightn't have been interested himself (apparently), but *she* believed there was a treasure."

Cerby nodded in affirmation. "Not only believed but obsessed about; you should have heard her!" She shivered slightly in recollection. Bron rested a comforting hand on her shoulder. "I don't suppose she ever told her father about any of her recent theories; she was bent on *proving it* to him instead, I think. She felt he didn't care about her, so she was going to *show* him. All that Freudian stuff about childhood angst being carried into adulthood - think I'm a convert now."

"In the event," Stevey continued on with her partner's account, "we were so tired with our day's efforts, and too late for the rides back at Alaerton, that we decided to stay in Huntingdon for the night. We ran into Monte and Mitch in Huntingdon outside one of the book shops. We went for dinner with them later and over drinks told them what we found out and were intent on doing. They were excited and wanted to come with us as Saffi had called her cousin in Yorkshire and we 'd planned to take a train up there the next day. Since we'd taken the bus into Huntingdon and were car-less (Saffi's was back at the Inn) they volunteered their car and Saffi offered to drive us all. It just seemed logical, if we all wanted to get a really early start in the morning, to stay over at the *Highwayman* and leave at dawn."

"Speaking of the terrible twosome, where are they now?" asked Cerby with concern. She couldn't be unaware that anyone associated with her could be in danger, no matter if it was only a longshot.

"Oh, they've gone off tilting at lych-gates today. They'll be happily up to their wellies in someone else's gardens no doubt. Don't worry Cerb. And wait, we're not finished." Saffi swirled an asparagus spear into a creamy dipping sauce. "Bron, I *must* get this recipe from you! It's absolutely yummy—so flavourful; is that Herbs de Provence?"

Bron nodded, delighted by Saffi's experienced culinary approbation.

Stevey interrupted hurriedly and rescued the conversation from a longer discussion on food prep. "You should have seen the cousin's, Nicholas Carlton's, estate. Beckwickdale. *Only* a slightly smaller version of *Pemberley*." Stevey's dewy eyes shone. "He's an only child; about thirty-five; tall bookish type on the order of Harry Potter; runs the place himself; lovely sky-blue eyes framed by nerdy glasses…"

"Just the facts ma'am, just the facts," laughed Cerby. Her friend was clearly smitten.

"As *I* was saying!" Saffi harrumphed. "My cousin Nick up there in Yorkshire, revealed quite a lot. We met him at the local pub, then followed his directions to the town library and stacks where we pulled out Denning's annotated *Fact Journals and Screenplays*. We all poured over them for about an hour, and then at Nick's previous invitation, nipped back to his estate for a quick spot of tea.

"So; without even being prompted (he seemed somewhat taken with Stevey, God knows why?) my coz gave us the *buzz* on our quarry. He told us all that he knew of the bloke and even referred to some of Paul's *Fact Journals*.

Apparently Paul, in a gesture prompted by ego or magnanimity, had donated a set of those copies to the local library in Shipton which was the branch Nick used. As Nick had heard of Paul and his motion picture status, he'd in the past taken out the material to read, just out of curiosity. He said they weren't up his alley really, but he *had* scanned the script and accompanying research for the Disney movie based on Jack Shepherd, one of the original Highwaymen. Found it geared to the adolescent and was a bit incredulous about notes on the side in the corresponding *Journal* referring to a Thomas Haney and his rumoured treasure. It was crossed out on the script however, and never used in the movie either apparently."

"Yes," said Cerby thoughtfully: "Shasta alluded to that very fact."

"All the locals knew about Paul's unfortunate relationship with his daughter. She was a troubled teen *('Yeah, no kidding!!)* who got into scrapes locally as a kid, and as an adult had quite the reputation for sleaze in the local pubs. Paul was always relieved apparently when her short 'custody' visits were over, and she could be packed off, back to America. So too was his then wife, Shasta's step-mother, who didn't get on with her at all. One could almost feel sorry for Shasta."

"NO! Skank!" It was a word Cerby abhorred, next to the c --- word, but in this case, it fit.

"Alright Cerby: don't get excited, not good for you. Anyway, Nick also knew of Jasper Ellison by reputation - an additional plus for us - as a farm labourer on Paul's property and others in the area when required. A surly and reticent fellow by all accounts, he was not one who appeared to do any job satisfactorily. Nick's estate manager had used him once, coming to the same conclusion as some of the other landowners i.e., wouldn't hire him again. Nick also volunteered that though he couldn't attest to it himself, a rumour had circulated in the neighbouring pubs Ellison was having it off with Shasta, 'that film bloke's daughter."

"Well!" Cerby exhaled. "That establishes the connection between the victim and the 'alleged' killer; they definitely knew each other. That'll be provable in court."

"Does anyone mind if I have some more of these mini-sausages, as Cerby doesn't seem to have much of an appetite. Whattttt?"

There was a lot of shaking of heads as Stevey, chipmunk cheeks bulging, turned an inquiring and then accusatory glance their way. "Research is hungry business," she said, wiping her fingers and mouth unapologetically with a crumpled napkin. Saffi waved for her to continue.

"We wanted to get back for the Musical Ride practise later that afternoon. Talk about Saf *putting the pedal to the metal* - but we were too late for that. We went straight to the arena to apologize to Kally thinking you would be there, Cerb, but when she said we weren't the only ones to miss the rehearsal, that you and Shasta had been absent as well, we were afraid something bad had happened to you. We arrived up at the *KC* just in time to see the ambulance taking you away. Learned about what had happened from Bron and Mrs. Hill. Cerby, we are just soooo thankful you came through all *that!*"

Group Hug!

After which Cerby spoke with some gravity. "As you know everyone, my time here is limited. I'll have to be going back to Vermont in a few days. I don't know what's going to happen with this case, but I expect you three to look out for Mrs. H no matter how long it takes and keep an eye on what's happening. You'll let me know if there is any news whatsoever? Deal?"

"You had to ask? The 'Cavaliers' vow on Cyrius' dead body Cerb! *NO* fear!"

Each woman there nodded solemnly.

Cerby *WAS* spoiled for the rest of the day. Her friends left her to rest up as she was determined to be in the ride the following day. Saffi and Stevey needed to partake in the lesson and rehearsal time they had missed previously, so they hurriedly ran down to the arena to join Kally and the other members of their group. Besides the riding, Bron had her own chores to attend to. Cerby shut her eyes after they'd all departed, still plagued by a dull headache. She drifted off to sleep despite an annoying subconscious thought that kept coming back to that scrap of paper—the last thing that Jasper had had on his person that gave any clue at all to the events that had taken place.

After a few hours, Mrs. Hill came and gently woke her. "Cerby, Dear. We've buried Cyrius and I thought you might want to come with me to see where."

Cerby instantly awake, rolled stiffly off the bed. "Thanks Mrs. H. I would be honoured."

So; the two of them left via the back door of the 'I's Cottage and walked down a grassy path to the Fifty Acre Field. Mrs. Hill pointed to a large oak tree in the distant far corner, and they trod carefully, arm in arm, over the June wildflowers to where a fresh mound of dark earth awaited.

Cerby had been picking the wildflowers as she went, and now had a sizable bouquet which she laid reverently on the centre of the oversized grave. She stepped back and standing side by side with Mrs. Hill, arms around each other's waists, laid her head against hers, both looking forward so neither one could see each other's internal grief. After a few minutes Cerby's sniff ended the silent homage. Mrs. Hill quickly dabbed away some moisture at the side of her eye with a bandana she always wore around her wrist for emergencies.

"We'll put a simple bronze plaque just here," she said, indicating the location with her hand.

"It's a lovely spot," said Cerby looking around. "I bet this oak has been here for a couple of hundred years. He would have seen it from his stall."

"Indubitably. Look at the girth of the trunk and branches," Mrs. Hill conceded.

"Fitting for our boy then! I'll take a picture before I leave Mrs. H. I have others – more recent - of him and short video clips from when I first arrived. I'll have them all downloaded and give you copies." *Thank goodness for the digital age.*

Mrs. Hill only nodded in response. What both of them wouldn't have given to have Cyrius standing there beside them, *in the flesh.* Somehow two-dimensional pictures, although they would be cherished, just wouldn't be the same.

Talk of leaving however, added another sombre note. Mrs. Hill walked away from the tree and struck up one of her long continental cigarettes. "I don't suppose you'd care to extend your visit..." she asked hopefully. "I feel you were robbed a bit with all that has happened."

"I'd love to," Cerby said regretfully, "but me and my friends - er, my friends and I - will need to get back home. But (brightly, for Mrs. Hill's sake) I suspect we'll be back before too long. Monte wants to do more research on his book, and maybe all of us can go on a trip within a trip. I'll suggest that to Bron, Saffi, and Stevey too."

"That would be lovely Dear. A real treat, and something to look forward to, certainly." The slight sadness in Mrs. Hill's tone, made Cerby look in her direction. She impulsively hugged her to her side, and they walked co-joined back to the *'I's Cottage*.

That evening, everyone (including Doctor Wentworth and Mrs. Hill) gathered at Ewan and Bron's for another repast, and no one had to be told about the *casual* aspect. They were all happy to be dining together again, and for other reasons as it turned out.

In the middle of the dinner, Doctor Wentworth raised his glass for a number of toasts: "First" turning towards Aidan and Cerby, "let's toast continued good health to our two friends here who in other circumstances, might not have been with us tonight."

Everyone raised a glass, sincerely echoing the sentiment.

"Next - to our hosts, Bron and Ewan."

More '*hear, hears.*'

"To new friends," motioning to Monte and Mitch, "who know their wine!" (Ripples of laughter.)

"And old friends like Saffira and Stephanie, who went the extra mile—on the A1."

More titters, and clinking of glasses, followed by the shocker.

"I'd also like you all to raise a glass to the future Mrs. Wentworth."

He turned to his right and raised his glass to a seated Mrs. Hill, who smiled in embarrassment to be singled out so. The goblets had stopped midway in the air on the announcement, but then everyone stood up and enthusiastically cheered the elderly couple. Mrs. Hill then rose herself. Doctor Wentworth, usually so formal, planted a resounding kiss on her blushing cheek. Cerby was especially happy for Mrs. H, but it was not the last of the announcements. Mrs. Hill bade everyone sit down, but she remained standing.

"You all know how much I love Alaerton, and how much I have put into it, *but...*" (they all looked a bit apprehensive) "...there comes a time when the old should make way for the young."

Cerby couldn't help but moan: "You're not going to sell up are you Mrs. H, (she shuddered) to developers??!"

"NO m'dear! Certainly not," Mrs. Hill responded emphatically, "but I spoke to Ewan and Bron today, and they are willing to take over the equitation centre and property on a vendor-take-back mortgage. They will run it as their own, and they have such clever ideas, so much energy, that I am positive they will be incredibly happy and prosperous here. I couldn't be more pleased." Mrs. Hill smiled around the table and waivered over Cerby. Cerby knew the burden had become too much, and now it was time to let go. Maybe Cyrius' death had planted the seed.

"*Hear, hear* for Mrs. H, Doctor Wentworth, Ewan and Bron—four of my very favourite people," Cerby clarioned, showing Mrs. H she was entirely of an accord with her decisions. This seemed to matter very much to the older woman, and amid another standing ovation around the table, Mrs. Hill sat down, real happiness evident on her face.

Cerby's own face was alight as well. Aidan was equally affected, so he couldn't help squeezing her hand. "Ouch," yelped Cerby: "you *never* know your own strength, Aid." But her eyes sparkled, denying any ill will and promising resolution of their own relationship's impasse.

Chapter Seven

Friday

"Are you SURE you're up to this?"

Cerby nodded. "Headache's pretty much gone, and sure I'm a bit tired (who wouldn't be after that ordeal) but I'm not going to miss this for the world."

Saffi, Stevey and Cerby were taking a brief walk around the fête area in the *50 Acre Field*. There were at least thirty marquees and tents of various sizes and an equal number of smaller kiosks and tables. The RSPCA was represented locally and nationally as well as various charities in whose support the day's events were occurring. There were also merchants from the surrounding villages, equestrian tack and product salesmen, a smattering of Huntingdon retailers, and even some from as far away as London and Scotland—a pretty good showing all things considered.

"Gates open at 10 am, Musical Ride at 11 and the Horsemaster's Test - Ewan put it back on the schedule to try to recruit new riders - starts at 2:00 pm. Do you think Jasper's murder will keep people away?" Stevey asked, concerned, looking at her watch.

"Hardly!" answered Saffi definitively with her marketing expertise. "*Any* publicity, even the negative variety, is *good p*ublicity." She added, "If anything, it will probably be the main reason for attendance. You wait; all the curiosity seekers will come out of the woodwork in droves."

"I'd like to get my hands on just one," muttered Cerby defiantly.

At quarter to eleven, all the special event riders were lined up in twos in front of the arena entrance. Dressed in formal riding attire (helmet, high-necked jaboted blouse, hacking jacket, breeches, boots and crop) they looked like a creditable troop, despite the lack of uniformity in colour of dress, size of mounts etc. All the riders had insisted on paying a registration fee to be in the event - their contribution to the cause. Many had also collected sponsors for participating, and as quite a few of them were well-heeled to begin with, the final benefit to the RSPCA and Alaerton was expected to be excellent.

Kally walked up and down the double line like a military officer inspecting 'parade,' checking the odd tack, making low comments to some of the riders, but stopping by Cerby, now partnered by Bron.

Kally looked at her searchingly. "You vill be feelink ok today? Annabelle, she is not Cyrius (Cerby's eyes threatened to liquefy) but she will do her best, and you are adequate rider." (High praise indeed from Kally who looked away also with some emotion). The A.I. continued down the line and then the other row of riders until once again standing in front of the troop.

"I vill go in and stand on bleachers. You know the musak, and so do your horses. Vatch your speed vhen it comes to the *passé duble* (a private joke shared by all the riders) and remember: k'ep your posture ereck but relaxed. Vhen you 'ear the 'Introduction,' start komink in arena and don centre *A* to *C*—all stop—and then vhen musak begin, you're on your own. Good luk, everone!"

Cerby was not as confident as she had said, only because she had missed a practise or two, but Bron had said to follow her, and she would. As it happened, when the *Intro* began, it was like a dancer on stage - all comes back, even ten years later.

Once they were in the arena, Cerby looked about and saw that her friends Monte and Mitch were sitting alongside of Aidan, Mrs. H and Ewan in the bleachers. Doctor Wentworth had said he would visit the St. John's Ambulance crew attending the fête, so he was not of their party. He would meet up with them later at the refreshment tent.

The whole event was being professionally filmed by BBC news, with print interviews by Horse and Hound; no one was going to miss a moment of it. Mrs. Hill was doubly pleased as everyone would get video and magazine copies as a memento after the newsy articles had seen 'air' and/or been published. Ewan was sure much of this publicity could be used in future promotional materials.

Cerby sat up a little straighter. She gave Annabelle a pat; took the reins firmly enough to have control but loose enough for Annabelle to manoeuvre; nodded at Bron - and they were off.

The horses picked up at the music and the intricate *Maze* and *Wagon Wheel* went off without a hitch to be followed by two more formations and a cavalry drill. The whole half hour performance went like clockwork, and Cerby, beaming with pride and exertion, sweaty hair plastered to her forehead, doffed her helmet with the rest of the riders at the drill's end to a standing ovation. She saw Aidan stand up on the bleacher adding his *two thumbs up* to those of M&M's, finger-whistling shrilly so she could see *and hear* how proud he was of her too.

Everyone found their way to the 'tea' tent after the horses were put away in their stalls. Those mounts that were to be used later in the afternoon for the Horsemaster's Test, were left hitched with loosened tack so they would be easy to re-tack and lead out again. They were allowed to snack on hay nets between the events.

Cerby and friends had worked up an appetite and joined Mrs. Hill, Doctor Wentworth, Ewan, Aidan, Monte and Mitch for a sit-down cup of tea and sandwiches. It could have been a cricket match: the tea was served in good porcelain under an elegant white marquee, sandwiches on Wedgewood china, and everybody in the V.I.P. area had their own individual wooden folding deck chair. But this was the horsey crowd after all, so wine and champagne were cooling as well at the cash bar (proceeds going of course to the charities).

Ewan bought a *round* to ring in the future changes at Alaerton, with Aidan not to be outdone, buying the round after that. The chatter was light, and only once, when Aidan squeezed Cerby's hand while they sat back together in companionable silence, did

Cerby think of Jasper's murder and Shasta Denning's cruel behaviour toward them.

But now, uncharacteristically, the sun was out and shining. She was bathed in its warmth and a closeness to Aidan that had enfolded her since the events of the last couple of days. She would not bring the subject of Shasta up and spoil everything; this was a day to savour.

Around 1:30 pm, Kally came to roust Ewan to perform his role as the BHS Instructor conducting the Horsemaster's Test in the arena. The public were expected to watch and would be invited to sign up for classes at the Test's conclusion. Bron was extremely hopeful that a truckload of students would be imminent for the July/August Sessions. Cerby turned on her side toward Aidan, reluctant to leave him, it had been so pleasant.

"Are you coming to watch this? Won't say I'll win First, Second or Third, but I think I'll pass at least."

"You're a winner in my book!" Aidan poked her playfully.

"You have to say that, you're my…"

"My…?"

Cerby blushed. "You know."

Aidan pressed his advantage by looking acutely puzzled. "My…? What?"

"Fiancée, okay! You did ask some time ago, before we came over here, before…" Cerby faltered a bit. "I mean, if you're still asking, of course?"

"Hmmm. Well, that depends on the living arrangements, because actually I asked you to *live* with me if I recall." Aidan tried to hide his enjoyment of Cerby's discomfiture.

"Oh. Um. Ok; semantics! Must be the cop in you. Is this better? I accept your… Ah…*Invitation*…To *live* together then once we get home. Of course, *where* will be the question?" Cerby was never going to completely surrender!

"Right then!" Aidan grinned conspiratorially. He knew how hard it would be for Cerby to give up her *Rose Cottage*. He had dual US-Canadian citizenship so a Green Card wouldn't be a problem, and fortunately where Cerby lived was not too far from the border and his job. However, he could see the term *living together* wasn't exactly the romantic turn of events Cerby had expected. "And we'll discuss the 'f'' word when the time and place are more appropriate." His hand reached over the gap between their chairs and entwined a strand of her curly hair in his fingers "Now that I've got you on the hook, I'm not about to let you break the line."

Saffi and Stevey standing nearby, were busy pretending to adjust the chin straps on their helmets, having heard the whole conversation. When Aidan stood up; bent down and hauled Cerby out of the deck chair; swung her arms up and around his neck in one fluid motion; kissed her surprised mouth soundly to seal the deal - Saffi saluted the couple with her crop. "About time too!"

"Yahoo!" Stevey cheered.

There had been a good crowd of locals and others, with some media presence in the morning, but most had enjoyed the day so much, they had stayed for the afternoon events as well. The RSPCA reps were positively euphoric as to the estimated takings for the day, and publicity of the Last Chance Horse Ranch and the local regional Animal Shelter was bound to garner future rewards. So, the Horsemaster's Test, as the last big event on the schedule for the day drew many to the bleachers once again in the Arena. This was a fun event, and a fitting end to a spectacularly successful promotion.

Cerby had done so–so once again in the timed, written portion of the test. No one would be caging any answers off *her c*heck off sheet. As for the riding event following immediately after, she had drawn two new horses, Dunby (a quarter horse Dun with a black stripe down his back); Andy (a rather stocky mixed Cob); and for her last run, the little pony Smoke. (*Egad! Not again.*)

Cerby's attention was centred wholly on what was going on immediately around her at her end of the arena. She was completely *over-the-moon* happy for Mrs. H and her Doctor, Ewan and Bron, and ecstatic that people were loving the event-filled fête. Any old rancour between Aidan and herself could now be said to have been completely put to bed (and would be, if the evening arrangements panned out as planned). Cerby exhaled deeply at the prospect.

The Horsemaster's Test was both instructive and entertaining - a casually competitive Gymkhana event which horses, riders and audience appeared to be enjoying immensely. She took a moment to look again up in the stands, searching for her 'man' and friends, pumped to see they were avidly following her progress. Aidan in particular seemed acutely aware of all that was going on. Well, she preened: *I HAVE already racked up some points in the games' section, and jump-relayed two steeds; only Smoke left.*

Cerby rushed to mount the pony for her last run and jump, having executed a beautiful one-legged flying dismount off Andy. In the corner of her eye, she caught a movement along the walkway in front of the bleacher stands, hauntingly familiar it was in some way. She turned her head just in time to see Aidan stand up in the stands, pointing to a man on the other side of the arena who nodded and raised his cell. She whipped her head around, to see two more - what must be plainclothes policemen - jumping down the tiers of the bleachers.

Swinging her head to the front again, the person she had originally remarked was now in the middle of the *FAQ* end of the arena busily working at something on the audience side of the kickboard wall; totally oblivious to anything else around her. In a flash, Cerby matched the gangly physicality and swagger to the owner - Shasta Denning - despite a disguise. She was sporting a blond wig, sunglasses, and kerchief; obviously dressed casually to blend into the event crowd.

Ewan, unaware of unfolding events, was shouting at Cerby to begin her jumping run: '*You're holding up the line. Go Cerby! Go!*'

Aidan and the police were swimming upstream it looked like, (being held up precious seconds by the crowd milling about at the bottom of the bleachers, leading toddlers, or balancing confections in hand).

They were still stuck at the opposite end of the large arena.

"Kally!" Cerby yelled as loud as she could. When Kally's head snapped up at the frantic call, Cerby raised her fingers to make an *A* and pointed down the arena.

Kally to her credit, made the connection almost the second she saw someone frantically pulling at the boards just behind the '*A*', and the urgency in Cerby's voice confirmed it. She too recognized her former pupil. Pointing out the problem to Ewan, mouthing 'Shasta,' she swung gymnastically over the closest boards herself, pushing her way towards that end of the arena, taking the opposite side to Aidan.

At the same time, this all happening within virtual seconds, Cerby gathered up the little pony Smoke: "C'mon Short Stuff, over the jump and get me to '*A*'". Smoke obliged by sailing over the obstacle jump with the same panache as before and ran a jerky gallop in the direction Cerby pointed. As she came alongside the boards, Cerby slowed Smoke down to a trot and managed to heave herself off, athletically but awkwardly sliding onto and over the boards to the gasp of the crowd.

Was it part of the show?

Shasta couldn't fail to see Cerby drop ungracefully to the ground right beside her. She had the same flinty pistol out of her pocket in a flash and aimed at Cerby. In slow motion, Cerby could see Aidan and some police rushing up the sides but intuitively she knew he would be too late—*I'll never get to live with Aidan after all...*

Just as Shasta raised her arm, a dead smile on her face and a bundle clenched tightly to her chest in her other hand, Kally came around the corner like a long distance hurdle-jumper, leap-frogged over a bystander carrying a hotdog and a drink, and jumped on Shasta's back (who managed to stand her ground despite the impact), pinning Shasta's arms down to her sides.

"Hold her Kally! Hold on!" Cerby dived for the gun, yanking it out of Shasta's fingers, just as a couple of rounds went off harmlessly into the ground.

Shasta fought like a demon. Extricating one arm, using the free one holding the heavy bag as a weapon, she tried to bludgeon her captors.

But don't tangle with an A.I. in great shape! Or, a Cerby Llewelyn fueled by revenge and adrenalin, whose inspired 'embrace' lasted long enough for the police to arrive and take over. Aidan muscled through the staring crowd to find Shasta in full custody.

Cerby, having disarmed and relieved Shasta of her bundle, stood now between Kally and Aidan, recognizing Jock as he ran up in discarding a *flat cap* (his attempt at disguise obviously.) They all watched with relief the snarling, swearing murderess marched away out of the arena between two burly uniformed police constables, followed by a couple of plainclothes officers.

The crowd apparently thought this dramatic episode was all a part of the planned entertainment - a bit like the Wild West shows of old. *Perhaps the cops & robbers' scenario would become an annual event. Sort of a summer-style panto, only with horses. Great for the Grandkiddies!* They clapped and booed enthusiastically as the 'acting' prisoner was led away.

The 'high' experienced by *one* of the leading characters was soon overtaken by shaking limbs: "Can we sit down please for a moment?" After all, Cerby had stared down the barrel of that gun for the second time in a week and lived to tell the tale. Kally asked if she was alright, patted her hand and ran back to Ewan to finish off the 'games'. The whole shocking scenario had taken less than five minutes.

'You're a better man than I am Gunga Din,' Cerby thought, watching Kally resume her place in the Horsemaster's Test as if nothing had just happened. While the show went on to finish up under the professional stewardship of a stoic Ewan, Aidan sat beside Cerby on a lower bleacher, holding her tightly - the comfort working its magic. When her breathing had finally returned to *almost normal,* in a weak voice she said; "I thought I was never going to get to ...I thought I was going to die." Then, after a moment's lapse, her voice rose in annoyance: "Aidan Halifax. You're totally impossible, you know that! What's a girl got to do? Die!"

"Hold on there *Firebrand.* Cerby, you **will** have things your own way, won't you? I suppose however, getting nearly killed twice in a week does count for 'cred' towards the 'f' word." Aidan looked about him sheepishly, and leaning in to Cerby whispered; "But let's not make a fuss and tell anyone about it just yet."

Cerby shook her curly haired head at him in disbelief. Then, in a nervous reaction to what had just *gone down* burst out in loud throaty laughter, just happy to be alive and that no one else had got hurt." Don't ever change," she whispered into his ear.

It was then she noticed the bag on the cement floor by her feet. She bent down and picked it up intending to give it to Aidan to give to Jock who was deep in conversation with some of his cohorts. At eye level however, she noticed a crude hole in the arena's boards, on the bleacher- facing side of the '*A*.' Obviously, this had been Jasper's secret hiding place for whatever was in the bag. Aidan watched her as she shook it. There was a jangling of metal on metal. It was a very old musty linen bag with a tie closing. She struggled with some knots to undo it.

"Aid, she tried to kybosh me with this. See how heavy it is."

"You have a skull made for bopping apparently," Aid laughed. "Do you need some help? Careful."

"Yeah, just hold onto the bottom; there…think I've got it. Ouch, there goes a nail. Stupid knot. Holy Cow!!"

Aidan peered inside the bag as well. "Looks like Thomas Haney's loot is lost no more."

The full compliment of friends met for dinner that night at an upscale restaurant in Huntingdon called appropriately enough: *The Fox's Den*. The women were happy to eschew their riding togs for a chance to dress for dinner; foxy ladies hanging on the arms of a skulk of handsome smartly attired *Reynards*. M&M were hard put to keep the flamboyancy down to a minimum as usual.

There was a lot to celebrate, but it would be a sad parting for some as well. Cerby would be packing up the next morning and Aidan was coming by in his own new rental car, picking her up with a view to carrying her off to London for a few days of *R&R* before flying home to Vermont together. He'd spent the day with his friend, D.I. Wallace, going over the closure of the case against Shasta Denning - now remanded into custody and awaiting formal charges in court. Due to an important prior engagement, Jock reluctantly declined to meet with the group back in Huntingdon for dinner, but his Scottish friend's eyes glittered with enthusiasm when Aidan suggested he come *across The Pond* for a fishing date with them next summer.

Saffi was equally disappointed the D.I. couldn't make it.

Mitch and Monte were staying on in England for another week, touring up to Pitlochry in Scotland and researching lych-gates along the way for Monte's photo book. Nick, Saffi's cousin, had graciously invited them to partake again of some hospitality and accommodation if passing through Yorkshire on the way. He suggested Stevey and Saf might like to tag along?

Saf and Stevey however, had to get back to their own affairs. Stevey couldn't wait to relieve her Mother of the twins. Both women wanted to seriously sit down and combine their resources in a new business venture, a series of *YouTube* videos or podcasts on cooking for the internet: *Jaimie Oliver, watch out!*

Monte and Saffi had also had preliminary conversations about her culinary additions to his book. Stevey couldn't wait to be the 'tester' for both endeavours and lend her graphics and *IT* expertise.

As for Alaerton Equestrian Centre, its future looked bright and secure. Although Cerby had had to hand over Haney's 'treasure' to the police, and there was some dispute as to its true legal ownership (i.e. The National Trust or The British Museum) if nothing else when that was all determined Mrs. Hill would be entitled to at least a 50% finder's fee of the estimated worth of the centuries' old priceless, historic, gold, silver and jewels; perhaps as much as 2 to 3,000,000 £, if not more. Since Mrs. Hill had put any profits she'd made over the years into Alaerton's equestrian centre, this would mean a more secure retirement for herself and the Doctor and an extremely lenient mortgage for Ewan and Bron starting off as the new owners. (They stubbornly refused to accept the property as a gift).

"Mrs. Hill," Mitch suggested, as if he had just thought about it; "you could write a TV or movie script yourself. Why this story has all the basic elements - -murder, intrigue, even treasure. You could make a fortune on top of the fortune you're already getting."

Mrs. Hill threw up her hands in mock horror and Doctor Wentworth spoke for the both of them: "No, I don't think so. Henceforth, our main job is just to relax and enjoy life as it comes, right Rowena!" No disagreement there.

"You know," Monte looked up at the ceiling a tad dreamily and being the author in the group anyway; "for once Mitch, that's not totally insane. You may have something there."

Mitch glowered: "It's *MY* idea"

Soothingly Monte countered: "Quite right, we'll work on it together…"

There would be a trial of course for Shasta Denning. Charged with both the murder of Jasper and attempted murders of Cerby and Aidan, it was still up in the air as to whether Cerby too, or just Aidan, would need to come back to England to testify, as a cornered Shasta run to ground had spit out a full confession in the end. Apparently, she was looking forward to the tabloid publicity of a court appearance—still trying to one-up her father in her perverted sense of that relationship.

Jock Wallace had filled Aidan in on the details so that he could fill in the group over supper. Saffi and Stevey took the lead with their own colourful narrative during the entree.

"Yes, well Cerby might fancy herself an action figure, but we drew some conclusions ourselves you recall. And, that paper you found originally Cerb, *was* really the whole answer all along. Not only did it point the way to Shasta…"

> '*Meet me at 7:30. Forget Haney. Take morning train back to Shipton and ask Denning for your old job back*'

quoted Aidan as per Jock,

"... but also, to where Jasper had hidden the treasure," Saffi continued airily. "We weren't quite sure at the time when we were pouring over that scrap, if there was one or actually two unique styles of handwriting. I think it is apparent now that Jasper wrote on that note Shasta had sent him, a memo to himself for future reference. We thought the *fac* he had written down was either short for, or a misspelling of Fact, as in Paul Denning's Fact Journals which is funny if you consider that that misunderstanding on our part helped put Stevey and I on to the archives and the Haney Treasure in the first place. We never connected it with the hiding place Jasper had found in the arena: behind the '*A* 'at the end of the arena in the *FAQ* line of sight. The 'stick' on Jasper's 'q' was missing, being all *small caps*. Major coincidence, the whole thing."

"Or serendipity," mused Stevey.

Aidan folded his napkin and reached for his wine glass. He summarized: "Shasta admitted that she had not wanted to be too obvious a presence herself. After doing her own research based on her father's movie script notes—the same ones Saffi and Stevey checked out in Shipton, she had started an affair with and fed Jasper some tantalizing information on the Haney treasure. She convinced him eventually to leave her father's employ and seek a position at Alaerton on her dime. He was to have a look around himself and report back to Shasta, and for about a month he did just that. Unfortunately for him, he found the treasure but intended to keep it for himself. Shasta suspected something when his reports 'faltered,' so although originally hesitant, she decided to come down herself for the reunion."

'*Good timing, eh?*' Cerby paraphrased Shasta's comment.

Aidan nodded. "That antique earring that Cerby found and the pair Mayfair wore, twigged Shasta to rightly assuming the jewelry was part of Haney's treasure. Before their final meeting, she withheld from Jasper this presumption, pretending not to have discovered the truth. She confronted him, trying to get him to cough up the rest of the puzzle. Feigning ignorance himself, Jasper gave Shasta what he thought would be just enough to sate her curiosity - Haney's empty monk's hole. He expected *that* would be pin prick enough to burst her bubble, force her to toss up the project and leave. Instead, to Shasta, it proved him a liar and major liability. He had said enough however, to make her think the prize was somewhere still on the premises. She obviously had enough faith in her own powers of deduction to go on without him.

"The earring was Jasper's death warrant. Lured to the Quad by Shasta's note, when he turned away from her that evening, with no remorse (still lacking apparently as she sits in her jail cell), she whacked him with the shovel and then ran back to the Common Room in the Wheatsheaf to establish an alibi.

"We were right in assuming that the fake robbery, in combination with letting the horses loose that night, was a red herring. After the murder you might recall, Shasta had begged permission of the police to go into Huntingdon on some errand or another, but what she really did was rent a car, which was what she used to smash in the gate at the back of the The 50 Acre Field around midnight, the night the horses were turned loose.

She preceded to put some of the better tack in the rental. As she had volunteered to do late haying that night, there really wasn't any reason for anybody else to be down by the Quad. Dumping the stolen tack in a culvert further up the road shortly after, she was able to hide the damaged rental itself in the unused driveway of a derelict shed that she'd scouted previously, about half a mile away.

So; after accomplishing all these things, on returning to Alaerton, Shasta unlatched all the stalls in the Quad. People started to be aware of the horses being loose a couple of hours later, so she made it look like she was first out in the KC, helpfully rounding up horses when in fact, she'd only minutes before finished giving the old stables there the once over, looking for Jasper's hiding place."

"Why was she in Huntingdon the same day we were," Saffi asked?

"Taking back the rental car and paying off the damages she told the agency was due to a fender bender, not her fault."

Cerby nodded her head, thinking back. "So, that was why Cyrius had been so upset the morning after the Midnight Rodeo. All her activity in his stall and the yard the night before would have been annoying and upsetting to him. Horses react to disruption. And also, one morning he had a halter on when I came by his stall –I thought that was strange at the time. She must have put one on to tie him up while she made a preliminary investigation of the stall."

Aidan continued; "Yes, well, when you posted that message on the Inn's bulletin board Cerby, about the other earring in the set found just outside Cyrius' stall, that's when Shasta got really afraid that someone might make a connection or had already. When she fortuitously saw you," he looked directly at Saffi and Stevey; "and then followed you in Huntingdon to the library archives, listening to you two discuss the writing on the paper, that's when the penny dropped. You referred to the '*fac*' clue a couple of times apparently, and to give her credit for her equestrian knowledge, it came to *her* almost right away what that stood for. One of Jasper's main duties was to till the sawdust floor in the arena, so where else would he have ample opportunity to hide the treasure - *de FAQ-to*? (Cerby winced at the bad pun; everyone else laughed appreciatively).

"Problem was, after Shasta kyboshed Cerby and me, (Cerby pointed to Aidan's head, and then knocked the wooden table a couple of times for effect) she was on the run, so how to get to it. That's when she decided to take her chance on the day of the fête, when everybody's attentions would be on the activities. Of course, we know how that ended."

A collective sigh of relief went around the table. Everyone raised their glass companionly to Cerby's final toast (in the manner of one of her father's favourite 1950's TV heroes, *Sergeant Preston of the Yukon*): "Well, King, this case is closed!"

Chapter Eight

Saturday

The next morning, Cerby rolled up all her clothes in the manner of a seasoned traveller, packing her suitcases quickly. She had breakfast with Saffi and Stevey who were departing shortly likewise, with tears on both sides but promises for visits back and forth, which this time all swore on Momfrey's limp toast as 'Cavaliers' to fulfill.

Cerby would certainly return for another visit in regard to Mrs. H's wedding later that Autumn. Saffi had promised to do the catering and Stevey all the invitations, with Ewan and Bron in charge of decorating the Wheatsheaf.

Jock was trying to coordinate Aidan's court appearance with that event in mind - he was determined not to miss the wedding himself especially as Saffi had agreed to be his date for that celebration. (Saffi had also slyly suggested that Nick call Stevey on the subject; he hadn't needed any prompting either...)

After the wedding ceremony, Ewan and Bron would be moving officially into the Main House as the owners, with Mrs. Hill and Doctor Wentworth taking up permanent residence in the *'I's Cottage*, so that Mrs. Hill would never have to leave her beloved Alaerton.

As expected, publicity swirling around the sensational murder elements as well as the entertaining RSPCA sponsored village fête resulted in mass signups for summer and fall students. Preparations were underway for those proposed classes and beyond. Preliminary discussions had already begun in regard to other future public events as well. With profits looming in the future, Ewan and Bron were already discussing improvements to the property. The future of Alaerton Equestrian Centre was secure with a solidarity of purpose.

Cerby's leave taking from Ewan and Bron was affectionate and miles away from the emotions she had entertained on first coming back to her teenage haunt, hardly a week before.

Mrs. H, now even more like a second mother to her, was more difficult to part from. Cerby was suddenly aware how Mrs. H had aged over the years. Though she felt a bit more protective of her in parting, she knew also that in Doctor Wentworth Mrs. H had found the perfect partner for her golden years.

Mrs. Momfrey got a huge bear hug. She would be staying on of course, as Alaerton's venerable cook. (Saffi was determined to get her a fool-proof toaster.)

Mayfair got a good gratuity.

Aidan rolled up in a Morgan sports car (Cerby's favourite) at the prescribed time. The top was fitted down. Aidan looked a total *crumpet*; that is to say she could have eaten him up, he looked so incredibly delicious in a crisp checked honey coloured cotton shirt with rolled up cuffs, cream coloured chinos and jaunty chocolate-coloured racing cap. A sports jacket lay flung across the driver's seat.

Why are male forearms so sexy, she drooled; m*ust be those lovely little golden hairs catching the light."*

Aidan got out of the car, kissed her possessively, and put her bags in the trunk. "Well Madame, your chariot awaits. Glad your suitcases are small. This baby doesn't have much room for a lot of baggage."

"Neither does *this* 'baby'!"

Cerby rested her hands on his chest as he bent to kiss her again. "I just need to do one thing, Aid. Just give me a moment. "She glanced sadly towards the *50 Acre Field*.

Aidan understood. "I'll be waiting. Take as long as you want. We're in no hurry."

Cerby looked at him gratefully and reached up to peck his cheek. "Thanks, Big Guy! Be back in a Jif."

Off she walked over the cobbles in the courtyard, past Cyrius' stall, unable to forbear just glancing in at the lonely empty interior, and on into the *Fifty Acre Field* following the path to the English Oak on the far side. She stood there, head bowed over her friend, conscious of a debt she couldn't repay:

I wished once that you were coming with me Cyrius, although I know now this is your home really. Humans are selfish, I guess. I would have taken you away from all this—not fair of me. And now you'll be here for ever with Mrs. H. Sort of appropriate that a tree, perhaps a seedling in Haney's era, stands as your monument now Boy. Thank you for my life. I'll be back soon enough to see you, but we'll meet again properly someday, I know it. I love you Cyrius.

Cerby kissed her hand and kneeling down, laid it gently on the grave. A tear fell. Mrs. H had promised to plant a sprout of the Royalist's Rose at the mound's head, and there it was, a small shoot bravely growing towards the sunlight. Cerby got up and looked over the mass of clover flowers in the field, doing a 360 that took in the whole property at one fell swoop. Not for the first time she cursed memory's habit of changing things; mental snapshots clouding over as time passed. *You have to always be in the moment, and savour **that,*** she concluded, a shuddering sigh escaping. *But I intend to, from now on.*

Aidan was leaning against the fender of the car and started guiltily when Cerby returned. Her eyes narrowed, and her brows furrowed. "Fee, Fi, Fo, Fum…" She sniffed the air dramatically and pointed a finger accusingly.

"What?" Aidan cried innocently.

Cerby sidled up to him, her short skirt dancing in the breeze. In a very seductive manner, running a polished nail lightly down his cheek, she leaned forward to whisper softly and sultrily in his ear: "If you're flicking your *BIC* Mr. Aidan Halifax, you won't be *dipping your wick* any time soon."

She turned away with a *come-hither* half-smile and saucy flick of the tongue. Adjusting a sun hat in front of the car's bonnet, her sunglasses suddenly (and mysteriously) fell to the ground. She bent over - almost in slow motion - to pick them up and in such a manner that her exposed limbs and pert derriere showed to advantage in the rear and side mirror views.

With this ultimatum so forcefully brought to his attention, Aidan ran around the car's hood and quickly helped to stash Cerby in the passenger seat. Then he got into the driver's side, surreptitiously dropping, then crushing out a cigarette stub with his heel to the ground on the way.

Aidan was as good as his word and surprised Cerby with a self-directed *Murder and Mayhem* London Tour: (*'You call this R&R?'*)

They visited the Tower of London where Cerby angsted over the mysterious disappearance of the Little Princes in 1483, assumed to have been murdered by the Duke of Gloucester, later to be Richard III.

Over tea they debated whether King Richard should be buried at Leicester Cathedral or York Minister having been recently disinterred from underneath a parking lot. Cerby was pretty sure her Da would have had an opinion. They celebrated the fact that it was the Canadian connection - a relative's DNA on Richard's mother's side many generations removed - that provided *grounds* for either option. (Cerby made a mental memo to ask Saf if she was related in any way?)

Cerby was next delighted with a tour of old Newgate prison, but couldn't suppress a sigh for Dick Turpin, listed as: *Highwayman, York, hanged in April 1739* and his mentor of sorts, Jack Sheppard in 1724, the subject of Paul Denning's movie script.

Aidan quickly took the romance out of these 'damn thugs' by referring to her romantic heroes as the *'great unwashed'* - *full of lice and bed bugs, ugh!*

After a quick side trip to Tyburn/Marble Arch, where they shopped and learned the antecedent of the phrase *'pulling your leg,'* they rested their own sore feet at a pub called the Creaky Gallows and ordered 'head on a steak' for lunch. Cerby was NOT impressed to find out that the head part was actually 'head cheese', (meat jelly made with flesh from the head of a calf or pig). Aidan had no qualms however eating hers!

Wandering back along Whitechapel Road debating once again, this time if the Duke of Clarence was really Jack the Ripper, they ended up for dinner at another pub in Pepys Street not far from their Charing Cross hotel, the Clarendon (Aidan had splurged). In the snug, they got to sit under a plaque detailing the hang, draw and quarter death of Major-General Harrison by the restorationists on that very spot in October 1660. They both consumed 'hogs-heads' of wine, extremely happy to be living in *this* century.

Finally, back in their hotel room and contentedly squiffy herself, Cerby came fresh out of the shower, Turkish cotton bathrobe in disarray. Falling on the king-sized bed in joyful abandon, she luxuriated in the fine linens and accommodations.

Aidan had pulled off his sports jacket, throwing it on the bedside chair, then loosened his tie. Watching Cerby revel, but also remembering their close call in Haney's pit, he was once again impressed with her resilience. He sprung on to the bottom of the bed, crawling energetically forward until he hung suspended on all fours over her, pinning Cerby's arms out to the sides with his own, blood heating up his nether regions.

"Had enough of the wages of sin?" he crooned softly, lowering his head, and giving her an *Eskimo kiss* on the nose.

She giggled and tried to shake her head vigorously in the negative.

"What *was* it we were fighting about anyway - before we came over here, to England?" he asked, deftly loosening the sash of her robe with one hand, while she in turn, arms released, had pulled his face closer, winding her hand round and round in his tie. Now, she averted her head to the side in a pout at his query.

"You called Frankie a beast. Don't laugh Aidan. Insult my dogs, insult me. He's been the best pal I've ever had, human or otherwise. Always curled up by my side; follows me everywhere; and when I'm down he makes me laugh. You made fun of *me* by insulting him, and by association Cimba. I don't make fun of that she-wolf of yours, Blissie. In fact, she's all but adopted *me*! And don't go categorizing me as one of those sad ole cat-lady types either, just because I treat Frankie as a soulmate…"

Aidan looked at her incredulously. Sitting back on his haunches (as her hands wandered up to his chest) he tried to pacify her while he *let* her unbutton his shirt: "You certainly are not! A cat lady I mean. AND I would never do that Cerby: make fun of you. I didn't say 'beast' by the way, I said *Feist*. It's a type of mixed terrier breed brought to the States in the 1800's - a common enough farm and squirrel hunting dog in those days. Even Abraham Lincoln had one I read."

"Ah" an appeased Cerby said thoughtfully; "so that's what Frankie is? Never knew his heritage but people pointed out the mix of Jack Russell, Chihuahua, and Italian Greyhound parts to me. Squirrels were his favorite play alright, but never prey: too fast for even those long legs of his."

Aidan stoppered her mouth with a long seductive kiss. *(God knows between us we've got enough of the critturs, although where we'll put 'em all...?)* "I *like* your dogs Cerb... (he drew a finger tantalizingly down her cheek, neck and between her breasts in a slow erotic zig zag) ...but I *LOVE* their mistress." With one hand planted firmly under her back, he drew her up tenderly but purposely, repositioning her underneath him.

She looked up expectantly, gazing deeply into the green swells of his hazel eyes, allowing the titillating sensations to take precedence. Shortly thereafter: "Oooooooh," she moaned faintly; "Who's a *feisty* boy then?"

"Woof! Sargent Preston at your *'service,'* Ma'am. A Mount-ee always gets his woman."

"Villain," was the sultry response....

GLOSSARY

DSLR Camera: Digital single lens reflex (SLR)
cf tuathal déithe: A Welsh druid invocation to the Gods
dinner: British word interchangeable for lunch as is 'supper' for North American 'dinner'
John Byng: 5th Viscount Torrington, Author of The Torrington Diaries. Published 1935-38 New York, H. Holt
Bomb-proofed: Trained, unflappable horse
Levade, Capriole : Dressage terms, equine Dance movements
Mister: Formal Title for Doctors in Britain. Cerby defers to the international title 'Doctor'
Snuggery: Private alcove in a portion of a pub bar
'Corie': *Coronation Street*- Long running British Soap Opera
Blimpie: Fictional Burger Chain in England
Shandy: Blonde ale and lemonade or ginger-ale
Chub: Non-edible bottom feeding brook fish
WC: Water Closet/Loo/Restroom/Washroom.
A.I.: British Horse Society Assistant Instructor
The 'I': British Horse Society's BHSI (top level stable management and instruction.) Considered an International Horse Expert. Often just abbreviated to the authorative title, The 'I'

Elevenses: Late morning tea break

Northern Dancer: Famous Canadian bred American Triple Crown Winner 1964. At only 15.2 h he is revered in Canada as *The Little Horse That Could* and internationally as one of the best racing sires.

FBHS: FELLOW of the British Horse Society

Ploughman's Lunch: Usually soup, bread, cheese, fruit, and ale

Cast: Horse's legs so close to the wall on lie down that it cannot reposition itself to get up, requiring manual help

16.5 h: Horse height is measured in *Hands*. To compare, ponies are often referred to as under 14 hands. Average height example, the Quarter Horse, approximately 15.2 h. Anything above 16 h. is getting 'tall'

BOOTS: British Pharmacy chain.

AGA: Popular British Brand of gas oven/stove.

Flying Changes: Horses changing from one correct 'lead' to another with great fluidity, keeping the pace in a canter or gallop.

Lassie Come-Home: Tearjerker dog story by Eric Knight.

Slipped Stifle: Common- knee joint injury in horses and other four-legged pets

Alex Coleville: Canadian Painter- *Horse and Train, 1954.*

St. Crispin's Day Speech: Shakespeare's Henry V, Scene iii 18–67.
Brian Gluckstein: International Interior Designer.
Blackadder: BBC 1980's pseudohistorical sitcom.
TMI : Vernacular- 'Too much information'.
Triskele: Celtic Symbol: Spirit, Mind, Body/ Past, Present, Future.
Sgt. Preston of the Yukon: North American 1950's radio/TV series - an RCMP Mountie and his dog King resolve their 'cases' always with: 'Well King, there's another case closed!' and King barks.
Pulling your leg: Easing suffering on the Gibbet by a friend the felon, to shorten the suffering.

About the Author

Charlotte H Broadfoot writes the Alaerton Alumni Mysteries under the *nom de plume*: Charlotte Helion. She writes short stories under her own name. She likes to divide each year quite simply by two: six months of winter writing and six months of beachifying, trekking, and vengefully weeding invasives from her garden palette. For more information on written works and interests (blog/crafts/recipes) see her eclectic website:

https://1windlass1.wixsite.com/beachcombersbookery

Coming Soon

From

The Beachcombers Bookery

Charlotte Helion's

The Alaerton Alumni Mysteries:

Celtic Knots

Cerby Llewelyn and the 'Cavaliers' reunite for
a wedding, only to find themselves involved in
another bizarre adventure that richochets from
the New World to the Olde World. Join them
won't you, as murder and intrigue leads them
on a secret and dangerous hunt into the wilds
of Scotland and Wales.
Will Cerby be able to lay the past to rest once
and for all? Does the future of Great Britain
hang in the balance? Can love ever be far
behind? *WAIT FOR IT...*